THE MARY-ALICE FILES
BOOKS 1-4

MARY-ALICE MOVES IN | BAYOU BUSYBODY | THE VANISHING VICTIM | ALOHA, Y'ALL

FRANKIE BOW

J&R FAN FICTION

CONTENTS

MARY-ALICE MOVES IN   1

BAYOU BUSYBODY   63

THE VANISHING VICTIM   141

ALOHA, Y'ALL   243

RECIPES   329

MARY-ALICE MOVES IN

CHAPTER 1

Mary-Alice Arceneaux parked her Oldsmobile 88 in front of Harriet's Books, shut off the engine, and peered into the rearview mirror. She checked her teeth, reapplied her coral lipstick, and reached to open the glove box for her travel brush.

Mary-Alice wanted to look her best for the official start of her new life in Sinful, Louisiana. She had made up her mind that she would not rebuild in Mudbug. Mary-Alice wanted to forget about the fire and all of the other unpleasantness, and it was hard to do that with her neighbors whispering behind her back. Fortunately, her house had been fully insured. And the Sinful real estate market was such that Mary-Alice could afford to buy anywhere she liked.

As the glove compartment popped open something slid out and landed with a *thunk* on the floor mat. Mary-Alice undid her seat belt and reached over to pick it up.

It looked like a black pane of glass with rounded edges. About the size of a book, but much thinner, and surprisingly heavy. Mary-Alice was pretty sure she knew what it was. Beulah Monroe in her crafting group had something like it.

She turned the key in the ignition to restart the air conditioner, pulled out her phone, and called Mudbug Auto Body.

"I just picked up my car this morning," Mary-Alice explained to the receptionist. She had to shout over the sound of the air blasting from the vents. "1999 Oldsmobile 88, Dark Caribe Metallic. You fixed the front end and replaced the bumper. Such a lovely job, and you left the car so clean. Thank you. Oh dear, I'm rambling. I called to tell you that someone in your shop left a computer tablet in the glove box. You know what I'm talking about? The kind you can read books and watch movies on."

The receptionist put Mary-Alice on hold, and after a long time came back on the line to tell her that nothing was missing from the shop. The tablet must have been in the glove box when the car was towed in.

It had to be Caden's, then. The thought cast a shadow over Mary-Alice's bright mood. She took a deep breath and punched in the number for her grandson's lawyer.

The man didn't even let her finish her first sentence.

"Mary-Alice, the item you describe is not Caden's."

"But Audy, he's the only other person who drove my car. I've already called the body shop, and they told me it doesn't belong to anyone there."

Mary-Alice heard the man take a deep breath. She imagined Audy puffing himself like an old bullfrog, something Mary-Alice noticed he did when he wanted to seem large and important.

"Now see here, Mary-Alice. Your grandson, that is to say, my client, has no knowledge of any device that may have been found in your glove box."

Mary-Alice hadn't mentioned the glove box.

"I see. You're telling me it's not Caden's. May I keep it, then?"

"I can't answer that."

"Well, it certainly isn't mine. Shall I bring it to the police?"

4

Mary-Alice pulled the phone away from her ear as the lawyer had what sounded like a choking fit.

"No. No, no, no. There's no need to do that, Mary-Alice," the man sputtered when he had recovered. "I can't tell you what to do, of course, and this is not to be construed as legal advice. But if I were in your place, I would take it to an electronics recycling drop-off where it can be disposed of properly,"

"But Audy, you haven't even asked Caden. What if he needs...I see. Well, thank you for your time."

As she pressed the disconnect button, she realized what was going on. The tablet most likely did belong to her grandson. But his lawyer didn't want to risk unearthing any more incriminating evidence.

Maybe if she hadn't sent Caden to computer camp when he was a boy...no, he would have simply found some other way to get himself in trouble. Caden had Joe Arceneaux's blood in his veins. There was no getting around it.

Heartsick as she was over her grandson, Mary-Alice knew there was no point in dwelling on unpleasant things. She locked the tablet back in the glove box, switched off the engine a second time, and went into Harriet's.

The bookstore's interior smelled of scented candles and old paper. The early afternoon sun slanted through the large front windows and lit up the sun-faded hardcovers on display. Mary-Alice took her time browsing and eventually picked out a mystery, two steampunk novels, and one romance, *Passion's Promise*. Something about the author photo appealed to her. Perhaps buying all of these books wasn't the most frugal thing to do, but now that Mary-Alice had decided to move to Sinful for good, she wanted to be a good neighbor. She had seen her favorite bookstore in Mudbug close, a year to the day after the big chain store moved in. Then, not five years after that, the chain store itself had shut down.

Mary-Alice paused, scooped up a few more books, and

finally tottered over to the counter carrying as many books as she could hold. As the woman at the counter was ringing her up, Mary-Alice got a good look at the author photo on the back of *Passion's Promise*. Gertie Hebert. Was it the same Gertie she knew? The one who had stopped by with her two friends that terrible night, and saved her and Celia from the fire? The picture looked vaguely like the same woman she had met, only a couple of decades younger, and wearing a scandalously low-cut blouse with sharply-padded shoulders.

"Excuse me," Mary-Alice said, "but is this Gertie Hebert the same Gertie who lives here in Sinful?"

CHAPTER 2

Mary-Alice smiled as she hefted the bag of books onto the driver's seat, and buckled the passenger-side seat belt over the bag so the car wouldn't beep at her. Joe would have scolded her for her extravagance and reminded her that she could get all the books she wanted at the library. But she had been a wise steward of her modest bookkeeper's salary, and later, of Joe's life insurance money. She could buy all the books she wanted. In hardcover, if she pleased, and she did.

It had been lovely chatting with Harriet, the bookstore owner. Harriet had confirmed that yes, Gertie Hebert was a Sinful native. Mary-Alice knew a real, published author! Sinful was much more sophisticated than she had assumed.

The conversation had taken an awkward turn when Harriet eagerly shared the latest news about Celia Arceneaux's cousin's grandson going to prison. Mary-Alice informed Harriet in the gentlest possible way that she herself was that very cousin, and that recent events involving her grandson had indeed been quite trying. Harriet quickly made amends by doling out fresh tidbits of Sinful gossip: a rumor (unsubstantiated) that Francine's Diner was looking into a gluten-free banana pudding

7

recipe; the lawsuit old Mister Gaudet took out against his neighbor, who had painted her house Pepto-Bismol pink (he claimed the color gave him fits); and the arrival of a new youth minister at the Baptist church, the handsome young Pastor Chad.

Mary-Alice bore no ill will against Harriet for her initial tactlessness. Instead, she felt buoyant with a sense of fresh possibilities. Her new life in Sinful was beginning in the pleasantest possible way, with agreeable conversation and a bag of brand-new books to read.

As she fastened her own seatbelt, Mary-Alice's attention wandered to the glove box. She felt her curiosity rising. She wasn't due to meet Cousin Celia for another hour yet.

She glanced up and saw Harriet through the window. Harriet smiled and gave her a little wave. Mary-Alice waved back and started the car. It wouldn't do to sit in the car in front of the bookshop; Harriet might suspect that Mary-Alice was up to something. She pulled out and drove a few yards down the road and into the dirt lot of what looked like an abandoned taxidermist's shop. Avoiding eye contact with the stuffed deer head hanging in the front, she pulled out the tablet and examined it. Then she ran her finger around the outer edge until she found a button to press. The pane of glass lit up, a black background covered with a grid of colorful symbols. One of the icons on the screen got her attention: A single eye, with a yellow iris and a pinpoint black pupil. She hesitated, then touched the eye.

She was surprised that the device had started up with no password. Her grandson had been fiercely protective of his computer privacy. All to the good, as she had walked in on him one time when he was online, and seen something on his computer screen that was better forgotten.

The screen went black and for a few seconds, nothing happened. Mary-Alice was about to give up and put the device back in the glove box when she heard a shuffling noise coming from the device.

She stared at the black screen. There was no visual, only intermittent scraping sounds. Then, instantly the image flared to life, and Mary-Alice saw a bare room. The camera was swinging wildly, but Mary-Alice made out white walls, against one of which stood a rectangular beige object. Then a low, bare table, a shot of nubby brown industrial carpet, and a close-up of the beige rectangle which turned out to be a file cabinet.

The screen blinked out and went dark. A loud metallic bang was followed by a woman's voice uttering some very angry and impolite words.

Mary-Alice powered the tablet down and slipped it back into the glove compartment. She had never been fond of those avant-garde films. She preferred movies where the plot was clear and the cameraman had a steady hand. Like Fried Green Tomatoes, or even Steel Magnolias.

Mary-Alice started her car and headed over to Celia's house.

CHAPTER 3

Mary-Alice tapped on Celia's front door. There was no answer, so she tried the knob and let herself in. As soon as she was inside, she heard Celia talking on the phone. Celia's voice was loud and clear, a good thing for a mayor-elect who had frequent occasion to speak in public. It was not ideal for privacy, however. Mary-Alice placed her bags by the front door and took the gift basket of jams and jellies into the kitchen. As little as Mary-Alice wished to eavesdrop, she couldn't help that Celia's voice rang out through the house.

"No, Beatrice," Celia was saying, "It has nothing to do with freedom of speech. It was just plain disrespectful. In fact, I should sue them for slander. Oh, is that a fact. Well, I'll tell you what Pastor Don said. 'Here in Sinful, we don't deprive someone of their right to vote just because they've passed on.' And you should have heard Pastor Chad laugh! Like jackals, Beatrice, jackals, both of them!"

Mary-Alice knew Celia's conversation wasn't meant for her ears, but she couldn't exactly help hearing, could she? She placed the basket of jams and jellies on the counter next to the fridge, where it was visible but not in anyone's way, and busied herself tidying Celia's cluttered kitchen.

"Listen, Beatrice, Marie's hands aren't clean either, I'll guarantee you that. Anyway, I did a little digging, and I think there's more to this Pastor Chad than meets the eye—oh, Mary-Alice is here. I'll call you back later."

Celia appeared in the kitchen, her demeanor transformed from righteous wrath to benevolent condescension.

"Mary-Alice, dear. Right on time. How lovely."

The women exchanged a hug.

"I knocked," Mary-Alice said. "But there wasn't any answer, so I let myself in."

"No need to apologize. Is this all for me?"

"Yes, I remember how you liked biscuits with tallow honey."

"And you had them put in pepper jam and rose petal jelly too. So unique of you, Mary-Alice. Are those your things by the door?"

Celia picked up Mary-Alice's handbag and led the way to the spare room, leaving Mary-Alice to lug her big valise, overnight case, and lavender Harriet's bag full of her new hardcover books.

"I trust you'll be comfortable here." Celia placed Mary-Alice's handbag on the nightstand next to the single bed. Mary-Alice dumped her burden next to the tiny wardrobe. She could worry about putting her things away later.

"So nice of you to let me stay," Mary-Alice said. "I promise I'll find a place of my own and be out of your hair in two shakes."

Celia gazed thoughtfully through the small window to the slightly overgrown yard.

"I suppose by all rights I shouldn't even be speaking to you, Mary-Alice, after what your grandson did to me, but I'm willing to let bygones be bygones for the sake of family."

"I'm so happy to be here in Sinful," Mary-Alice said. "I feel

11

like things are looking up already. Let me help you set up for supper."

Mary-Alice set two places at the table, taking care to fold the paper napkins nicely. Celia popped a frozen lasagna into the microwave. Mary-Alice knew that Celia's phone conversation was none of her business, but she was dying to know what was going on.

Mary-Alice had been relentlessly curious ever since she was a girl. Her mother would tell her it wasn't ladylike to go poking her freckled nose into other folks' business. According to Mary-Alice's mother, there were few sins worse than being unladylike.

"I stopped by Harriet's on the way over," Mary-Alice remarked in an offhanded way. "Lovely little shop. Bought a book or two."

"We do have a library, dear. Although I suppose it's your money, and you should be able to spend it however you please."

"I had a nice chat with Harriet when I was there. She told me the Baptists got a new youth pastor. Did you know?"

"Oh, that's old news," Celia scoffed. "Pastor Chad. Piece of eye-candy they brought in to try to get the kids interested in going to church. Good luck to them, they'll need it. The kids are more interested in tearing around the bayou in their loud motorboats. Still, you can't blame Pastor Don for trying. His congregation's dying off. You look around the Baptist Church on a Sunday morning and it's like Heaven's waiting room."

"Have you met this Pastor Chad?" Mary-Alice wondered what Celia had meant by "more to him than meets the eye."

"Yes, and I wasn't terribly impressed. Although I'm sure he's trying his best, bless his heart."

Which meant that Celia hated Pastor Chad with a burning passion.

Sinful may have been orders of magnitude smaller than Mudbug, but so far it was promising to be every bit as interesting.

CHAPTER 4

The following morning, Mary-Alice treated Celia to breakfast at Francine's Diner. Sinful appeared to have only the one restaurant, but it was a good one. The aroma was savory and wholesome, the employees were sweet as pie, and the food was heavenly.

A harried but good-natured waitress seated Mary-Alice and Celia. Celia concentrated on her menu, but Mary-Alice spotted two familiar faces across the room. She smiled and waved. The two white-haired women waved back, as did the middle-aged man sitting with them. Mary-Alice noticed that the man wore a clerical collar with his chambray shirt.

"Celia, look! It's Ida Belle and Gertie."

Celia continued to study her menu.

"Is that Pastor Chad with them?" Mary-Alice persisted.

Celia snorted. "I see them. And no, Pastor Chad is much younger and better-looking. That's Pastor Don."

"Aren't you going to say hello?"

"I'm not going to holler across the restaurant, Mary-Alice. Have you decided what you'll have?"

As soon as Celia and Mary-Alice set down their menus, the

high-strung waitress came over to refill their tea glasses and take their order (waffles with blueberries and cream for Mary-Alice, chicken-fried steak and eggs for Celia). This time, Mary-Alice was able to read the young woman's name tag.

"Thank you, Ally," Mary-Alice called out as the waitress hurried off. "Celia, everyone here seems so nice. I really think I'm going to like Sinful."

"Lucky for you, you're related to the new mayor," Celia declared. "Not every newcomer in town has such an advantage."

"I know you're very busy and I don't want to take too much of your day, but you said you could start me off house-hunting?"

"I said I might be able to. Now, how much of a payout are you getting on your Mudbug house?"

Mary-Alice told Celia the number that the insurance agent had told her. Celia briefly choked on her tea, but recovered quickly.

"Mary-Alice, this is your lucky day. I have just the place for you. It belongs to a very respectable lady who is a member of our group. She wants to sell and move in with her mother. I happen to have the information right here." Celia pulled a file folder out of her bag and set it on the table. Mary-Alice opened the folder and tried not to look disappointed.

"And with your cash in hand from the insurance," Celia continued, "you won't have to worry about all that nonsense with the mortgage companies."

"It's so kind of you to be thinking of me," Mary-Alice gently closed the folder. "You said the seller is a member of your group? Which 'group' is this?"

"Why, the God's Wives, of course."

"Oh, yes. Your ladies' group."

"In fact, Mary-Alice, if you play your cards right, I might be able to get you in. No guarantees, of course."

Mary-Alice didn't want to quibble with Celia, but privately she thought it irreverent and a little presumptuous for Celia and her friends to call themselves "God's Wives." A name like the Sinful Ladies' Society—like on the little bottles of cough syrup in Celia's medicine cabinet-- would have been in better taste.

As they were finishing their breakfasts, Celia's cell phone buzzed. She glanced at the screen and announced to Mary-Alice (without apology) that she would have to leave for an emergency GWs meeting.

"I trust you can amuse yourself," Celia said as she stood and collected her handbag. "I'll text you later."

After Celia left, Mary-Alice paid the tab and then went over to say hello to Gertie and Ida Belle. She was tempted to thank the two ladies for rescuing her and Celia from the burning house, but she refrained. She didn't want to bring up all of that unpleasantness in front of the man with the clerical collar. Instead, she said hello and introduced herself. Gertie, in turn, introduced Mary-Alice to Pastor Don.

"He's having a bad day," Gertie added. "I hope you have some good news for us, Mary-Alice."

"Well, in fact, I do."

"Come on, then. Join us."

Pastor Don gloomily scooted over to make room for Mary-Alice.

"It's good for me, anyway. After losing my house in Mudbug, I decided to move to Sinful." With a twinkle, she added, "And what a nice surprise it was to find out that I'll be neighbors with a famous author!"

"Really?" Ida Belle asked. "Who?"

Gertie dealt her a punch in the arm. "Me, Ida Belle. She's talking about me."

"I bought *Passion's Promise* at the book shop yesterday, Gertie, and I'm very much looking forward to reading it. Why, I didn't even realize it was you at first."

"No kidding," Ida Belle said. "That photo you got on the back is about a hundred years old."

"Don't exaggerate, Ida Belle. It's from the nineties."

"Is it? Well, that explains the barbershop quartet in the background."

Pastor Don cleared his throat and took a gulp of coffee.

"Will you be staying with Celia, Mary-Alice?" he asked.

"Only temporarily. Celia's already picked out a house for me to buy."

"Not Simone Favreau's old place?" Pastor Don regarded her with concern.

"Why yes, that's the one. Why do you ask?"

CHAPTER 5

Mary-Alice hurried over to the General Store that afternoon to meet Celia. She was glad she'd stopped to chat with Gertie and Ida Belle and, of course, Pastor Don. It always paid to be neighborly, Mary-Alice thought. She didn't look forward to telling Celia what she'd heard that morning, but there was no way to avoid it.

Mary-Alice fidgeted as Celia perused the offerings in the candy aisle and finally made her selection. She started eating candy out of the bag before they were even out the door. Celia didn't offer her any. As soon as they were outside, Mary-Alice let the dam burst:

"Celia, it's the most extraordinary thing. I happened to meet Pastor Don this morning, and you'll never guess—"

"It looks like you've picked an exciting time to come to Sinful," Celia interrupted her. "I heard some interesting news at my meeting."

Mary-Alice was relieved to put off the confrontation just a little longer.

The two women started walking down the row of shops on the bayou side of the street. It was the hottest part of the afternoon, and Mary-Alice felt like she was being steamed like a basket of shrimp. She thought it would be pleasant to go home and sit in front of the fan, but not until she'd said what she had to say. And anyway, Celia had insisted on taking her on a walking tour of Sinful.

"Old Mister Gaudet," Celia said. "Have you met him?"

Mary-Alice shook her head.

"Lucky for you. Horrible man. Eulalie Bertrand painted her house a lovely shade of rose, and now Mister Gaudet, he lives across the street, you see, anyway, he's suing her, can you imagine? He claims that she's ruined his view and that looking at her house gives him seizures."

"That's terrible." Mary-Alice was torn, and secretly sympathized with both parties. People should be able to paint their houses any color they liked. On the other hand, no one should be forced to look at a pink house all day if they didn't want to.

"Anyway, I told Eulalie, don't you worry about it for another second. I'll see to Beauregard Gaudet. No one messes with the mayor's friends. Now, what were you going to tell me about Pastor Don?"

Mary-Alice hadn't expected Celia to hand the conversational reins over to her so abruptly.

"Pastor Don? Well, he has lovely manners, for a Baptist. And he was so helpful!"

"Helpful in what way, exactly?"

"Well, you see, that house you were telling me about, the one your friend Simone is selling? It seems the church handyman has a second cousin who's a home inspector, maybe it was a second cousin by marriage—"

"Get to the point, Mary-Alice."

"Oh. Sorry, Celia. Well, Pastor Don told me that he, the cousin, told him that house has been on and off the market for a year now, but no lender will approve a mortgage because it's full of those Formosan termites. He said it was so bad, the cabinets were falling right off the kitchen walls."

"Oh, what nonsense," Celia harrumphed. "Don't listen to him. Even if there are termites, I'm sure you could afford to knock down the whole thing and rebuild it if you wanted. You certainly have enough money to do whatever you want. Not like poor Simone, not that I'm saying you need to feel responsible for her, but ever since her husband passed…well, that's all I'm going to say about it for now. But you'd be passing up a good deal, Mary-Alice."

The two women were headed up the street to where the Baptist and the Catholic churches faced each other across the road. Mary-Alice thought of West Side Story. She envisioned the Baptist ladies facing off against Celia and her friends, both sides snapping their fingers and menacing each other with jazz hands.

"Celia," Mary-Alice asked, "is that crime scene tape?" As they neared the church Mary-Alice saw an X of yellow tape across the front door and another ribbon of tape around the circumference of the building.

Just then a young deputy sheriff popped out from the side of the building, still unrolling the yellow tape.

"Deputy Breaux," Celia barked, "what are you doing?"

The young man jumped.

"Why, just marking the scene."

"You're being wasteful. You're not wrapping a birthday present, Deputy Breaux. Now you go back and wind that tape right back onto the roll."

"Okay, Celia, I mean, Your Honor."

"Honestly, if your mother weren't one of my dearest—wait a minute. Is this a crime scene?"

"Yes it is, Your Honor," he mumbled.

"Well? What happened?"

Deputy Breaux looked over his shoulder as if someone were watching him.

"Not sure I should say. Pastor Don didn't want anyone to be alarmed until we knew more. I mean to say, not that he wanted anyone to be alarmed afterwards either—"

"Get to the point," Celia interrupted.

Breaux cleared his throat and stared at his inexpertly-shined shoes.

"It seems when Pastor Don came into the church this morning, he found Pastor Chad."

"What's so unusual about that?" Celia demanded. "Where else would he expect to find Pastor Chad, if not at his place of employment?"

On the far side of the church, a motorboat zoomed along the bayou. Loud laughter and whoops rang from the boat. When the noise had died away, Mary Alice spoke.

"I think the deputy is saying he was dead, Celia."

"That's correct, ma'am." Breaux sounded relieved that he wasn't the one who had to say it.

Celia blinked, speechless.

"Who was dead?" Celia croaked, finally.

"Pastor Chad, your honor. The new youth minister."

"I see." Celia placed her hands on her hips. "And is it possible he died of natural causes? Putting crime scene tape everywhere is simply going to get people all riled up"

Breaux shrugged.

"His face was all smashed up. Half caved in, and his nose was all the way over on one side. Hard to see how that could be natural causes."

"Oh dear," Mary-Alice gasped.

"I see. And have you identified a suspect?"

"No, ma'am. Your honor. Everyone liked Pastor Chad, as far as any of us can tell."

"Is that so."

"There wasn't no murder weapon either. None that we found, anyway."

"I see. Well. Carry on, Deputy."

The women left Deputy Breaux standing in front of the empty church.

"That explains why Pastor Don seemed so glum this morning when I met him," Mary-Alice said.

Celia didn't respond. She was scowling, deep in thought. Finally, she said,

"That Yankee's gotta have something to do with this."

"What Yankee?" Mary-Alice asked.

"Sandy-Sue Morrow. Marge Boudreaux's great-niece. Calls herself Fortune, as if the name Sandy Sue's not good enough for her."

"Do you mean the tall blonde girl who helped save us from the fire?"

"Mary-Alice, that woman's brought nothing but trouble with her. Since the day she arrived in Sinful—"

Another motorboat zoomed by, cutting close to the bank and splashing Mary-Alice with murky bayou water. Some even got on her sparkly tennis shoes. She didn't mind too much, though. It was ferociously hot and humid out, and the water was cool. As the boat sped away, Mary-Alice saw dozens of fish popping out of the water in its wake.

"Celia," Mary-Alice asked, "whatever are those fish doing? I've never seen such a thing. They're jumping like popcorn."

"Oh, those? Well, they're...just a minute."

Celia pulled out her cell phone to look up the answer to Mary-Alice's question.

"Ouch!" Celia exclaimed.

"What is it, Celia?"

"My phone." Celia cradled the phone in her shirt and gingerly typed something in. "It's hot. Something must be wrong with the battery. Anyway, they're called Asian carp.

They were introduced to fish farms around the South in the 1970s."

The two women continued to stroll down the gravel road as Celia read the entire Wikipedia entry on Asian carp in her most authoritative tone. Mary-Alice nodded and smiled encouragingly. It was better than hearing her complain about Fortune Morrow.

CHAPTER 6

Mary-Alice's real estate agent drove over from Mudbug the next morning at Mary-Alice's request. Mary-Alice appreciated Celia's kindness in trying to help her find a new house. But she realized that Celia was trying to be kind to too many people at once, including the lady who was trying to unload her termite-ridden teardown. Sinful's real estate inventory was limited enough to cover in a single morning, and by lunchtime, Mary-Alice had found her new home: the old Cooper place, only fifty yards from the shops on Sinful's main street. It needed some minor renovations, but the owners were willing to do a rent-to-own, and Mary-Alice could move in right away. Despite its central location, it was set back from the main street, which gave her some privacy. Once you got past the overgrown yard and went inside, you could tell that it was rather grand in its own way.

Mary-Alice signed the papers over lunch at Francine's and bid farewell to her agent.

Celia will be so happy for me, she thought.

Oddly, when Mary-Alice told Celia the news in person later at Celia's house, Celia did not seem happy for her. In fact, Celia curled her lip and scoffed that the old Cooper place was "pretentious" and "a monstrosity." Mary-Alice was briefly stung by Celia's reaction. Upon reflection, however, Mary-Alice realized that Celia didn't want her to move out, and was acting gruff to disguise her true feelings.

That afternoon Mary-Alice bought a pie from Francine's as a thank-you gift. She collected her things from Celia's house and left the pie on the kitchen counter. Celia gave her a halfhearted hug goodbye, but did not help her carry her things to her car. This only confirmed Mary-Alice's theory that Celia secretly wanted her to stay. Mary-Alice was touched by Celia's devotion.

The old Cooper house needed a new coat of paint and a few other fixes, but it was fundamentally in good shape and was clean enough to move right in. Mary-Alice was delighted to find that sitting at the kitchen table, she could see out to the main road and watch the citizens of Sinful going about their business. She even saw two people she recognized. The tall Yankee girl, walking with that handsome deputy sheriff who looked like he should be on the cover of a romance novel. They made a nice-looking couple, she thought.

Mary-Alice loved watching people. She didn't need scandalous gossip—really, the last couple of days in Sinful had produced an embarrassment of riches in that department—but she liked knowing what was going on. Joe Arceneaux hadn't cared for her curiosity. She'd always had to be careful not to ask her late husband too many questions, or let on that she knew something he didn't. Either one would set him off.

But Joe Arceneaux was long gone, and Mary-Alice had a new house and a new life. She would have liked to celebrate with Celia, but Celia's evening was once again going to be taken up with a GW meeting. It was kind of Celia to offer to get Mary-Alice into the group, but Mary-Alice wasn't sure she'd enjoy having to go to so many meetings.

She heated up a frozen spaghetti dinner in the microwave,

pulled out one of her new books from Harriet's, and had a pleasant time reading and eating at her kitchen table. It was *Passion's Promise*, the one that her new friend Gertie had written. Mary-Alice was surprised at how risqué it was—Gertie seemed like such a lady!—and even more surprised when she finished it in one sitting, not noticing that the daylight had completely disappeared outside.

Mary-Alice closed the book, set it on the table (she'd have to get some bookshelves), and switched on the porch light. She was in the habit of watching a show before she went to bed, but her television had melted in the fire back in Mudbug, and she had yet to buy a replacement.

Then she remembered that she had her grandson's tablet, the one that his lawyer had insisted wasn't his. She'd bought a charging cable for it at the General Store (honestly, was there anything you couldn't get at the General Store?) optimistic that she'd be able to figure out how to work it. She drew the curtains shut (a little fragile from sun exposure; they'd have to be replaced), retrieved the tablet, sat back down at the kitchen table, and started it up. Once again, she clicked on the single, yellow eye. At some point, she would have to figure out how to choose her own movies.

At first, the window opened greyish-black. There were some shuffling sounds, and then a whoosh. A flushing toilet? What kind of silly film was this?

Mary-Alice swiped her finger around the screen, looking in vain for some kind of control panel that would let her change the movie. The screen flared to life with an image of a fan suspended from a Wedgewood blue ceiling, as if someone had rested the camera lens-up. Now there was a hubbub of voices. Mary-Alice could pick out a few phrases.

"Approve the minutes."

"Agenda items."

"Mary-Alice Arceneaux."

What?

An electronic device had just called her name.

Mary-Alice pressed the "off" button on the side of the tablet until the image collapsed into black. Her heart was pounding. She had been through a lot lately: the move from Mudbug to Sinful, the house purchase, her grandson setting her house on fire. She hadn't been getting all the sleep she should. Mary-Alice hoped that this was only temporary and that she wouldn't end up like poor Marceau Mirande, who slept in the doorways of downtown Mudbug and got into arguments with parking meters. Mary-Alice was not above getting help. She would visit the doctor first thing tomorrow.

CHAPTER 7

Sitting in Doctor Broussard 's waiting room wasn't helping Mary-Alice's nerves any. The local news was playing on the television. The top story was the mysterious murder of Chad Cruz, 32, who had died of blunt force trauma to the face. The murder weapon, the newscaster stated ominously, had not been found. Mary-Alice remembered hearing somewhere that the mantra of local television news was "if it bleeds, it leads." That certainly seemed to be true here. Mary-Alice had feared that Sinful would be dull. Well, that was one thing she could cross off her worry list. The local minister's murder was exciting enough for the New Orleans stations to cover.

The TV screen flashed photos of the crime scene, thankfully with the worst details pixelated out. Almost against her will, Mary-Alice found herself staring at the television. Why did the room look familiar?

It was her nerves. That was all. Good thing she was here to see the doctor. As if on cue, a receptionist in pink scrubs came out and called her name.

Doctor Broussard was a mature man with a grave demeanor. Mary-Alice found his presence comforting. She hopped up onto the patient table with its crinkly layer of paper. Honesty was often the best policy, Mary-Alice thought, but she wasn't certain that total disclosure is necessary. Why ruin poor Dr. Broussard 's day with unpleasant details about her grandson?

To her surprise, Doctor Broussard already seemed to know the whole story: that Mary-Alice's grandson had hacked into Celia's computer to get his hands on the town's funds, and then, when threatened with exposure, he'd set Mary-Alice's house ablaze with herself and Celia inside.

"I don't mean to be presumptuous, Mrs. Arceneaux," Doctor Stewart apologized. "But this was in the news, and that the extreme stress you've experienced certainly has some bearing on your well-being."

"And now I'm hearing voices," Mary-Alice conceded.

"How have you been sleeping?"

"Sometimes well. Sometimes not so well."

"I wouldn't become alarmed just yet, Mrs. Arceneaux. Auditory hallucinations can be a result of sleep deprivation or stress, and you've had plenty of both. Do you have a social support network?"

"I'm sorry, Doctor? I'm not sure what you mean by that."

"Who are your friends and family?"

Mary-Alice sighed and looked at her delicate hands resting in her lap.

"Joe, that was my husband, he passed away years ago. My son and daughter-in-law as well. Now my grandson will be going away for a very long time."

"I'm sorry to hear that, Mrs. Arceneaux. My deepest sympathies."

Mary-Alice brightened.

"I suppose I still have Celia, my cousin by marriage. Celia is my social support network. Doctor Broussard, is everything alright?"

Doctor Broussard ended his coughing fit with an elegant throat-clearing.

"You know, Mrs. Arceneaux, your cousin will have many demands on her time as mayor-elect, especially with this audit of the election results going on."

"There's an audit of the election results? Whatever for?"

"Well, I'm sure I couldn't say." Doctor Broussard fumbled for his prescription pad.

"No, please tell me," Mary-Alice pleaded. "I hate not knowing what's going on. Celia never said anything about an audit."

Doctor Broussard cleared his throat again.

"Well, I, ah, how shall I put this? Our most recent mayoral election appears to have been marred—or made more interesting, depending on your point of view—by votes cast on behalf of several long-departed citizens of Sinful."

"Are you saying that dead people voted?" Mary-Alice's blue eyes widened.

"It appears so. And they voted for your cousin, I'm sorry to say. I don't believe I'm betraying any confidences here. This has been a matter of public knowledge since the election."

The scrap of Celia's phone conversation that Mary-Alice had overheard suddenly made sense. Pastor Don must have been catching young Pastor Chad up on local politics when he'd said,

Here in Sinful, we don't deprive someone of their right to vote just because they've passed on.

Celia had heard the conversation and was furious with both men. Furious enough to batter one of them to death? Mary-Alice immediately put the thought out of her mind. It was absurd. Celia was physically no match for a young, healthy man in his early 30s.

"Aside from social support, Doctor Broussard, do you have any other advice for me?"

Dr. Broussard cracked a kind smile, the first of the visit.

"Catch up on your sleep. Take some time to relax and look around our beautiful town. Welcome to Sinful, Mrs. Arceneaux."

"Oh, call me Mary-Alice, please. Doctor Broussard, who do you think killed Pastor Chad?"

Dr. Broussard looked up sharply, then shook his head.

"I have no idea. Lately, I don't know what's going on around here."

CHAPTER 8

Mary-Alice took Doctor Broussard's recommendations to heart. She strolled along the bayou that afternoon and took in the sights of Sinful, which were already becoming familiar: the butcher shop, the General Store, Francine's Diner, the Baptist and Catholic churches facing each other across the narrow road. Mindful of the importance of her social support network, Mary-Alice made a luncheon appointment with Celia for the following day.

Celia accepted, but made sure to let Mary-Alice know that she had to eat quickly, as her mayoral duties consumed practically all of her time.

That night, Mary-Alice was in bed by nine.

Mary-Alice arrived at Francine's Diner the next day at noon, right on time. Celia came ten minutes later ("so terribly busy, not a moment to myself!") and it was another twenty minutes before a table became available. They were finally seated, and placed their meal orders with the sweet-natured but high-strung young waitress named Ally. Only then did Mary-Alice get down to brass tacks.

"Celia, I'm ever so grateful that you're putting in a good

word for me with the GWs. It's so important for ladies our age to have a social support network. I wonder if I might inquire how my application is coming along?"

Celia paused, as if hesitant to deliver unpleasant news.

"Well, you're still under consideration," Celia said finally, with a strange note of satisfaction.

Under consideration? Mary-Alice was confused. Celia herself had suggested membership to Mary-Alice, and wasn't Celia the one in charge? Maybe Celia didn't have quite as much pull as Mary-Alice had thought. It did not occur to Mary-Alice that Celia might be stringing her along to make herself feel important.

"What do you think my chances are, Celia?" Mary-Alice asked.

Celia regarded her cousin-in-law with a gaze that could only be described as pitying.

"I couldn't say, Mary-Alice. I simply couldn't say."

Mary-Alice was a little put out by Celia's evasiveness, but she let it go. She had always looked up to Celia, for one reason: Celia had stood up to her bullying husband Max. Mary-Alice had never dared confront Joe Arceneaux. Not even in the early days of their marriage, before Joe lost his job in the 80s oil bust. And certainly not after, when they'd moved to the smaller house in Patterson, and Joe would sit out in his lawn chair next to the Bayou Teche and drink all day. Celia had an inner strength that Mary-Alice very much admired.

CHAPTER 9

After lunch, Mary-Alice trudged across to the General Store to pick up some groceries. At the sight of the old Cooper house—her house!—Mary-Alice perked up. Things were turning out well for her, she reflected. She had a lovely home right in downtown Sinful. And things with Celia would work themselves out, after this election audit was over with. Celia was very busy just now.

Mary-Alice paused at the glass door of the General Store to peruse the posted announcements. There were used boats and trucks for sale, yard and handyman services, and boat repair. A poster featuring Mister Twister fishing lures was faded to a blue shadow of its former Kodachrome glory. She nudged the door open and went in. Inside the General Store, the air was about twenty degrees cooler than outside and fragrant with chewing tobacco and beef jerky.

Mary-Alice spotted the back of a blonde head over by the motor oil display. It was that Yankee girl, the one who had been with Gertie and Ida Belle that terrible afternoon. Mary-Alice didn't like to think about what might have happened if the three women hadn't come by to rescue Celia and her from the burning house. What was the young lady's name? Fortune. That was it. Easy enough to remember, under the circumstances. Mary-Alice had never properly thanked her for rescuing them, and supposed now was as good a time as any. She wound her way around the aisles. At barely five feet tall, Mary-Alice was shorter than the shelves and invisible to the casual observer. Mary-Alice didn't mean to sneak up on Fortune, and she would sooner die than eavesdrop on someone's private conversation, but entirely against her will, she happened to overhear something strange.

"They showed up yesterday," Fortune was saying into a phone that she held close to her face, obscured by a curtain of bleach-blonde hair. "An Amazon box. No, it was perfect. There are so many of these going through the mail now, the postman didn't think anything of it. Yes, even here. Come on, Harrison, that ship has sailed. The Company hired Amazon Web Services to build our cloud. No, I'm not joking. Ask Morrow if you don't believe me."

The young lady was obviously preoccupied. Mary-Alice would talk to her later. As she turned to leave, the sole of her tennis shoe squeaked ever so faintly on the floor.

"Gotta go." Fortune was facing Mary-Alice now, towering over her like a giant. She must be over six feet tall, Mary-Alice thought. Maybe even seven feet tall. Mary-Alice wondered what they were feeding young girls these days.

"Hello." Mary-Alice stepped back so she could make eye contact without getting a crick in her neck. "I never had a chance to thank you for what you did that afternoon for Celia and me. I believe you saved our lives."

A broad smile lit up the young lady's face. She has beautiful teeth, Mary-Alice thought. Her family must be well-to-do. And she's lovely. She could have her pick of husbands. But she's close to thirty, no ring, lives by herself, and flirts with that handsome deputy. And then Mary-Alice realized:

She must be starting over. Just like me.

"Thanks. It's what I live for. I mean, as a school librarian, I don't get to go out and be a hero in the real world very often. It was a lucky coincidence we just happened to be in the neighborhood."

Mary-Alice noticed that Fortune's hair looked a little bumpy at the roots—the telltale sign of grown-out hair extensions. Fortune had lovely bone structure and didn't need to hide behind all of that fake hair. She was probably insecure, Mary-Alice realized, and shy. Add to that the fact that she was a Yankee, the poor thing was probably having trouble making friends. It would only be neighborly to spend a minute or two chewing over the latest news.

"Did you hear about Pastor Chad?" Mary-Alice whispered. "Such a shock. It's even been on the New Orleans stations."

Fortune nodded and began to rummage through a bin of electronic components.

"You wouldn't expect this kind of thing in a peaceful town like Sinful," Fortune said.

"And according to the television, no one knows anything," Mary-Alice continued. "No murder weapon. No suspect. No motive. No clues."

"I know," Fortune said absently. "And no idea who's next."

"Next?" Mary-Alice stammered. With all of the excitement, it had been easy to forget that there was still a killer on the loose.

CHAPTER 10

Mary-Alice went to Mass with Celia on Sunday morning, but she declined to join the post-church race to Francine's Diner. Francine's banana pudding was heavenly, and Mary-Alice knew very well that there wasn't enough of it for everyone. But she didn't care for the cutthroat competition that emerged as the Baptists and Catholics raced to be first to the Promised Land. Mary-Alice strolled at a dignified pace as Celia and the other Catholic ladies sprinted ahead as if they were being chased by the Grim Reaper on roller skates. They enjoyed a slight advantage in terrain, as the Catholic church was on the same side of the street as Francine's. The Baptist church was across the way, backing up to the bayou, which made for a longer distance for the Baptist ladies to cover. But they had Fortune on their side. She led the pack with a sort of effortless speed walk. Her legs were so long that racing her would be like trying to outrun a giraffe. Ida Belle, too, was amazingly spry for her three score and ten.

Old people were "spry," Mary-Alice reflected. Young people were "fit." She herself was firmly in "spry" territory. Mary-Alice was feeling rather philosophical after listening to Father

Michael's homily. Without referring to Pastor Chad's murder directly, Father Michael had ruminated eloquently on the transience of life.

We are but a shadow, Father Michael had said, a vapor that appears for a little while and then vanishes away.

The older ladies in the congregation had seemed more concerned about Francine's banana pudding vanishing. Before Father Michael had finished saying his last "amen," half of them were already out the door.

One of the Catholic ladies (not Celia, oddly) had saved Mary-Alice a spot at their table. But the Baptists had gotten to Francine's Diner first, and sequestered all of the banana pudding. The Catholics were left to console themselves with fluffy pancakes soaked in melted butter, juicy chicken fried steak, and biscuits smothered in savory gravy.

Mary-Alice tucked into her pancakes happily, having taken Father Michael's message to heart. Life, she realized, was too short to feud over little things. In his dying moments, did Pastor Chad wish he had elbowed more old ladies out of the way for a bowl of banana pudding? Mary-Alice thought not.

Mary-Alice didn't have a chance to talk to her cousin until after breakfast, as they were walking back up to the church to get their cars.

"Celia," Mary-Alice asked shyly, "I was wondering, have you heard anything about my becoming a member of the GWs?"

Celia put on a thoughtful face and gazed up at the green-gray sky.

"Your application is still under discussion," she said finally. "Some in the group say you haven't yet proven yourself."

Mary-Alice wondered what she would have to "prove." As far as she could see, all the GWs did was lose the banana pudding race every Sunday and have a lot of meetings the rest of the week.

"We do have a meeting this afternoon," Celia said.

"Are you allowed to have business meetings on Sunday?" Mary-Alice gasped.

"Only in case of emergency and with the permission of the mayor. Who is me, of course. I will attempt to sway them in your favor, Mary-Alice, because you're family. I wouldn't hold out much hope for immediate admittance, but I will make a plea for you to reapply in a year's time as permitted under our bylaws."

Mary-Alice felt a mixture of relief and disappointment. As grueling as the GWs meeting schedule sounded, she disliked feeling left out. The thought crossed her mind, briefly, that Celia might be making up all of these "bylaws" on the spot.

CHAPTER 11

Mary-Alice arrived home with a sense of satisfaction. She had done everything on the day's to-do list. She'd gone to Mass and had lunch with the GWs at Francine's. She was free to spend the afternoon as she pleased. She still had books to read; her craft basket awaited in the spare room (she made glow-in-the-dark glasses holders, her own invention); and although she still hadn't bought a television, there was the tablet with the strange movies. She scolded herself for being afraid of the thing. She owned it, not the other way around! And it hardly seemed scary at all on a sunny Sunday afternoon.

Mary-Alice went to her pantry, where she had stored the frightening machine. She hesitated—would the device call her name again? Well, and what if it did? She brought to mind Doctor Broussard's comforting explanation. What she had heard had been a simple "auditory hallucination," a perfectly natural result of stress, and not a sign that she was cracking up.

Mary-Alice took the tablet down from the top shelf, propelled by defiance and a strong dose of curiosity. She set it on the dining room table.

Then she poured herself a tall glass of sweet tea and added a dash of Sinful Ladies' Cough Syrup to steady her nerves. Ignoring the other icons on the screen, Mary-Alice once again pressed the yellow eye.

Immediately the device emitted a hubbub of voices. Women's voices. The screen flickered to life and focused, and again, Mary-Alice found herself looking at a ceiling fan.

The image jumped as someone rapped the table.

Then, unmistakably, as she stared at the whirling walnut-grain fan blades, Mary-Alice heard Celia's voice:

"This meeting of the God's Wives is now in session."

Mary-Alice's tea glass paused halfway to her mouth. She stared at the tablet in disbelief, snapping out of it only when she realized she was pouring ice-cold tea into her lap.

No wonder her grandson's lawyer had disavowed any knowledge of this device. The boy was already in trouble for stealing Celia's personal information and using her credentials to hack into Sinful's bank accounts.

Mary-Alice realized he'd been using this tablet to spy on Celia. Now she knew why she'd heard the device speak her name earlier. She wasn't cracking up at all. Celia must have mentioned Mary-Alice in conversation. (Probably putting in a good word for her with the GWs.)

Mary-Alice knew she should stop watching, but her curiosity wouldn't let her. She stared at the image of the rotating ceiling fan and wondered whether she would hear her name again.

She did.

"I don't know why you wanna make Mary-Alice wait another year," said a voice that sounded like it had been rough-ened by years of cheap bourbon and three packs a day.

"I like Mary-Alice," someone else said.

"Me too," agreed Bourbon and Smokes. "And if we don't get her into the God's Wives now, the Sinful Ladies'll grab her."

"Is she eligible for the Sinful Ladies?"

"I believe she is. Didn't her husband pass on a while back?"

"Come on, Celia, why are you holding this up?"

Celia? Celia was the one holding up her nomination?

Mary-Alice was numb.

Celia had encouraged her to apply to the GWs. Mary-Alice wasn't exactly champing at the bit to join, but now she felt confused. And a little hurt.

Celia finally spoke.

"As leader of the God's Wives, I must maintain strict impartiality. I can't favor Mary-Alice just because she's my cousin."

The room broke out in a loud hubbub, and Celia had to spend some time shushing everyone so she could continue speaking.

"Listen, there is a certain order that must be maintained. Mary-Alice needs to learn her place. I mean, I like Mary-Alice too, but she shouldn't be allowed to come in, buy the biggest house in town, and start walking around like she...she... owns the place."

"Why Celia, you're not jealous of Mary-Alice, are you?"

"How dare you, Beatrice! That's a dollar in the swear jar."

"The swear jar? But I didn't—"

"A dollar, Beatrice."

Mary-Alice heard the zip of a wallet and the crinkling of bills. Beatrice, determined to get her money's worth, muttered a very rude swear word.

"Why is this thing so hot?" Celia barked. Suddenly the camera tipped up, and Celia's giant, frowning face filled the screen. Mary-Alice squeaked with fright and flipped the tablet face-down.

CHAPTER 12

Mary-Alice's unintentional peek into the GWs meeting had left her feeling jumpy and out-of-sorts. A walk would be just the thing, she thought. It was late afternoon, and just cooling off. Mary-Alice sprayed herself liberally with Bombshell perfume to ward off mosquitos, pulled on her bejeweled tennis shoes, and looked around for a safe place to store the tablet. Now that she knew it was a spying device, she wondered whether she could get in trouble simply for possessing it. She remembered hearing about a woman in Minnesota who was fined a quarter-million dollars for sharing her music files. She dropped the troublesome tablet into her bag without really thinking about it, and started walking.

Mary-Alice avoided walking on Celia's street, where she knew the GWs were meeting and talking about her. She held her head high and walked without thinking about it, toward the edge of town. The stroll was quiet, with only the soothing bayou sounds of frogs, crickets, and an occasional, distant, barking dog. She was in outer Sinful now, about a mile from the city center. The houses were farther apart here, separated by browned but well-trimmed lawns and ancient shade trees.

There was no sidewalk here; Mary-Alice crunched along a single-lane road paved with loose gravel and shells. Mary-Alice realized that dusk had come on quickly, and there were no streetlights. She would have to turn back soon, although she wasn't in any hurry to get home.

As she was passing a large, dark-colored Victorian house, she heard a woman yelling. Mary-Alice paused. Was someone in trouble? The noise was coming from behind the house.

Mary-Alice remembered how grateful she was to have been rescued. Without another thought, she sprinted toward the back.

Gertie Hebert was hanging by her knees from a low tree branch, her short skirt flipped completely upside-down, exposing her camo underwear. She was trying to pull herself up, but with no success. Ida Belle stood underneath Gertie, holding up a cell phone. The light from the phone illuminated Gertie from below and cast wild shadows around the backyard as Gertie flailed her arms.

"Use your abs!" Ida Belle shouted. "Remember the technique!"

"Do you need help?"

Ida Belle turned to the sound of Mary-Alice's voice. Gertie lost her knee-grip on the branch and dropped on top of Ida Belle. Ida Belle's camera went flying toward the back porch, just in time to plop into the pitcher of iced tea Fortune was carrying.

"I'm terribly sorry," Mary-Alice stammered as Fortune plucked Ida Belle's phone out of the tea and shook it dry.

"It's not your fault, Mary-Alice." Ida Belle's voice was muffled, as she was still stuck under Gertie. "Gertie needs to learn to concentrate."

"Ida-Belle was just spotting Gertie," Fortune said. "This happens all the time. They'll be fine. Why don't you join us for a glass of tea, Mary-Alice?"

"We have some Sinful Ladies' Cough Syrup to mix with it."

Gertie was back on her feet now, dusting herself off. Ida Belle stood and looked up warily, as if another elderly lady were about to drop out of the tree without warning.

"Why don't we go inside?" Fortune said. "These mosquitos are eating me alive."

Mary-Alice followed Fortune, Ida Belle, and Gertie into the dark blue Victorian house. Inside, it was clean and surprisingly modern. A little bare for Mary-Alice's taste—not a floral or frill anywhere in sight—but neat and tastefully furnished. It was nicer, if Mary-Alice were to be honest, than Celia's house, with its avocado appliances and the macramé owl hanging in the guest room. Mary-Alice supposed that Celia hadn't redecorated in a while.

"This is your house, Fortune?" Mary-Alice exclaimed. "Why, it's lovely!"

"It belonged to my late great-aunt Marge. You're right, it is lovely." Fortune poured Mary-Alice a glass of tea and held up a little bottle of Sinful Ladies' Cough Syrup by way of offering it. Mary-Alice nodded enthusiastically. If ever there was a day for an extra helping of Sinful Ladies' Cough Syrup, it was today.

"Oh, Gertie," Mary-Alice said, "I've been meaning to tell you, I bought *Passion's Promise* at Harriet's bookstore and I simply couldn't put it down. I read it in one sitting. Are Ida Mae and William real people? By the time the book was over I felt like I knew them. Imagine, a romance seventy years in the making!"

"Well actually, it's funny you ask that—" Gertie began.

"So what brings you out this way, Mary-Alice?" Ida Belle interrupted.

"I was just out for a walk. It was quite by accident that I stopped by here. I had a terrible shock this afternoon, you see. Where do I begin? Oh, dear, I'm sorry. You don't want to hear my troubles."

"Of course we do, Mary-Alice," Fortune said kindly. "You've been through a lot lately. I'm impressed that you're holding up as well as you are."

"It's Celia," Mary-Alice said. "Oh, dear, I feel so disloyal. She is my cousin, and she's helped me out so much—"

"How has she helped you?" Ida Belle scoffed. "By blaming you for your grandson's crimes, and holding them over your head?"

"She's not the person I thought she was," Mary-Alice said quietly. "She's been talking me down behind my back. And it's got me wondering what else she's capable of."

"Oh, I can tell you the answer to that," Gertie said. "She's capable of anything but gratitude and kindness."

"What exactly do you mean, Mary-Alice?" Ida Belle leaned forward. "What exactly is Celia capable of, in your opinion?"

"Do you know how everyone has been saying that no one had a motive to murder poor pastor Chad? Well, Celia did."

Ida Belle sat up straight and exchanged a glance with Gertie.

"I heard her on the phone, you see. I'm afraid I'm rather quiet, and I do overhear things, although I don't mean to." She shot Fortune an apologetic glance. "Celia was angry that Pastor Don and Pastor Chad were laughing about all the dead people who voted for her in the mayoral election. It seemed like such a small thing, certainly not worth killing someone for. But Pastor Chad was found dead the very next day, wasn't he? And now Celia is saying bad things about me. That I don't know my place, and I was getting above myself buying the old Cooper place. I mean, those aren't big things, are they? But neither is having a laugh about the election. And now Pastor Cruz is dead. What if I'm next?"

Fortune handed Mary-Alice a clean paper napkin. Mary-Alice didn't realize until that moment that tears were rolling down her powdered cheeks.

"Do you know," Mary-Alice gasped, "I never really put all of this together until just now. But it's true. I am afraid of my own cousin. It sounds ridiculous, doesn't it?"

"Not at all," Gertie said.

"We wouldn't put anything past Celia," Ida Belle added.

"Maybe we should call the sheriff," Fortune suggested.

"No, please. I'm afraid--Oh dear, I should just stop talking."

"Who told you that Celia was saying those things about you?" Fortune asked.

"Well, that's the thing, you see. No one told me. I'm going to show you something now. Can I trust you?"

Gertie, Ida Belle, and Fortune all nodded. Mary-Alice reached down for her purse, pulled the tablet out, and set it on the kitchen table. She opened what she now realized was her grandson's snooping software.

The four women watched the blades of a ceiling fan whirl around on the screen while a woman's voice read a list of names and dues status.

"We're watching a meeting of the GWs," Mary-Alice explained. "The God's Wives."

"We call 'em the Got No Lives," Ida Belle said.

"It's okay, Mary-Alice," Gertie assured her. "They call us the Geritol Mafia. So we're even. When was this recorded?"

"It's not recorded. It's live. This meeting is going on right now."

Ida Belle leaned closer.

"This is fantastic, Mary-Alice!"

"It's not fantastic. This was one of the devices my grandson

47

was using to spy on Celia. He left it in my car. I don't think I'm supposed to have it."

"You're right," Fortune said. "The four of us probably broke about a dozen state and federal wiretapping laws just watching that ceiling fan spinning around. It looks like your grandson turned Celia's cell phone into a hot cam. From what I can see, Celia takes her phone out during meetings puts it face-up on the table. Probably to take notes."

"A hot cam?" Mary-Alice repeated. "How do you know that?"

"She reads a lot of techno-thrillers," Ida Belle said. "As a librarian. She's around books all the time."

"You have techno-thrillers in the elementary school library?"

"Kids these days," Gertie said. "Am I right?"

"Well, 'hot' is right," Mary-Alice said. "Celia kept complaining that her battery kept heating up."

"Interesting," Fortune said. "Here's some good advice. If you feel your phone getting hot, don't talk about anything more controversial than the weather. Maybe not even that. I, uh, read that too. In the library."

"So what else did you see, Mary-Alice?" Gertie asked eagerly. "Not just some dumb old GW meetings, I hope."

"I think I saw the room where Pastor Chad was found. That's another reason I'm wondering about Celia. If what I'm seeing is the view from her phone, that means she was in that room."

"The auxiliary room in the Baptist Church?" Fortune asked. "How do you know it was the same room?"

"I saw it on the TV news. I recognized the file cabinet. Celia must have been in there. But why? What was she doing?"

"Should we take this to the deputy sheriff?" Gertie asked.

"Take what?" Fortune shot back. "Illegally-obtained evidence? Mary-Alice, I know you didn't ask to have that thing drop into your life, but I'm telling you, you should drop it out of your life as soon as you can. If I were you I'd throw it into the bayou tonight and never look back."

Mary-Alice thought Fortune was a little bossy. But maybe Yankees were just like that. At least Fortune meant well, and that was the important thing.

"Do you think Celia did it?" Mary-Alice asked.

"I don't know," Ida Belle said carefully. "It seems this Pastor Chad might have had a gambling problem."

"He did?" Mary-Alice brightened. "So maybe it had nothing to do with Celia. Maybe the timing was an unfortunate coincidence."

"Do you think we had another mob execution?" Gertie said.

"Another mob execution?" Mary-Alice faltered. "Good gracious."

"Or it could be a serial killer," Gertie suggested.

"A serial killer?" Mary-Alice looked pale.

"Celia's meaner than a snake," Ida Belle said. "No offense. But we're not sure she's capable of cold-blooded murder."

Mary-Alice let out a relieved sigh. "Perhaps I was overreacting—"

"Celia's not physically tall or strong enough to have caused the fatal injury," Fortune said. "Not unless she was standing on a stepladder and swinging a handbag full of buckshot. More tea?"

Mary-Alice caught a glimpse of her reflection in the black window. She didn't relish the idea of walking a mile or more in the dark, but the sooner she started back, the sooner she'd be safe and home.

"Oh dear, I've let the time go by." Mary-Alice stood.

"It's 1955," Fortune said.

"I'm sorry? Did you just say it's 1955?"

Now she was time traveling? Mary-Alice wondered how much stranger her day could get.

"She means five minutes to eight," Ida Belle explained. "Nineteen hours and fifty-five minutes."

"Yes, five minutes to eight. That's what I said."

"Thank you so much for the tea. I really should go."

"Listen, Mary-Alice," Ida Belle said. "If you need anything, or if you find anything else out, give me a call." Ida Belle pulled out a business card and handed it over.

"You have a card, Ida Belle?" Fortune exclaimed. "I didn't know you had an actual card."

Mary-Alice examined it. It was porcelain blue, with a cheery floral border.

Sinful Ladies' Society. Ida Belle. No title, no last name. Just a phone number.

"That's my cell," Ida Belle said. "Only for emergencies. Including emergency orders of Sinful Ladies' Cough Syrup."

"Sinful Ladies' Society," Mary-Alice read aloud. "Are you all members?"

"I'm not," Fortune said.

"Yet," Ida Belle added.

Curiosity overcoming politeness, Mary-Alice asked,

"What does a person need to do to get in?"

"Only never-married women or those who have been widows over five years may apply," Gertie said.

Mary-Alice nodded and tucked that bit of information away. She was eligible. Joe Arceneaux had passed away ten years ago. Of course, Celia would be furious…

"Come on, Mary-Alice," Gertie said. "I'll drive you home. You shouldn't be walking alone in the dark."

CHAPTER 14

The next morning, Mary-Alice was awakened by impatient knocking on her front door. The doorbell wasn't working. Something else on her to-fix list.

Celia stood on the porch.

"Good morning," Mary-Alice gulped. She wondered whether the "hot cam" went both ways. Had Celia seen Mary-Alice spying on her? No, that was impossible. Why did she feel so on edge, then, as if she were about to be found out?

"Aren't you going to ask me in, Mary-Alice?"

Mary-Alice glanced down at the red Piggly Wiggly shopping bag Celia was holding and wondered what was in it. A murder weapon? No, that was ridiculous. She was just letting her imagination run away with her.

"Perhaps we can sit out on the front porch?" Mary-Alice asked brightly.

"Don't talk nonsense, Mary-Alice. It's a hundred degrees out here and humid as a gorilla's armpit."

Celia pushed her way past Mary-Alice into the house and bustled into her kitchen.

Mary-Alice stayed by the front door. She wasn't sure what Celia was up to. Or whether gorillas really had sweaty armpits.

"Celia," she called after her cousin. "I'm not sure this is the best time."

"This won't take a moment," Celia called back. "You worked as a bookkeeper, so this is right up your alley. I just need you to look over these cash flow statements."

"I suppose that's okay, then," Mary-Alice muttered. She followed Celia into the kitchen. Celia had already taken the papers out of her red Piggly Wiggly bag and spread them out all over Mary-Alice's kitchen table. Mary-Alice silently scolded herself for being paranoid.

"You should know that your name came up at the latest meeting of the God's Wives." Celia stepped back to allow Mary-Alice access to the table. "I fought very hard for you, but some of the members felt that you weren't yet a proven quantity."

"I'm sure you did everything you could," Mary-Alice said. "Celia, these are cash flow statements. What did you want me to look for?"

Mary-Alice was annoyed with Celia for lying to her about the GWs meeting, but relieved that at least she didn't seem to be trying to murder anyone.

"I want you to tell me if you see anything unusual. Like excessive spending. Or embezzlement."

Mary-Alice examined the papers.

"What exactly am I looking at here, Celia? I can't tell you very much if I don't know where these came from."

"I'm not at liberty to discuss the details."

"I can see that these are cash flow statements, but I need to know what kind of business this is. Otherwise, I can't really give you an opinion."

"Fine. It's a church, Mary-Alice."

"The church? Does Father Michael know you have this?"

"Please. I've already said too much."

Mary-Alice sat down at the table and sorted the statements by month. Then she took out a separate pad and made notes. Celia paced impatiently behind her, and then without asking, went to Mary-Alice's fridge and helped herself to a glass of sweet tea. She didn't offer to get one for Mary-Alice.

"Starting about a month ago," Mary-Alice said, "I see an increase in money spent on postage. That's really the only thing that stands out to me."

"How much money?" Celia asked.

"Over the past month, it amounts to twelve hundred five dollars and forty-nine cents. The previous two months were four hundred and fifty-one dollars and twelve cents, and three hundred ninety-eight and eight cents. But I don't have a whole year here, so I can't do a seasonally-adjusted—ouch!"

Celia snatched the sheet that Mary-Alice was reading from, dealing Mary-Alice a tiny paper cut.

"So it could be embezzlement?"

"Oh, Celia, I wouldn't want to—"

"But there was a large increase in the amount spent on postage. Compared to previous months."

"Yes, I suppose there was."

Celia swept the papers back into her bag and beamed triumphantly.

"Gertie and Ida Belle are gonna blow a gasket when they find out I solved it."

"Solved what?" Mary-Alice asked.

"Why, Pastor Chad's murder. Celia the Sleuth. Ha! Sheriff's not open for another hour, so how about we go get ourselves some breakfast?"

"Well, actually, Celia, I have a lot of—"

"My treat."

Astonished, Mary-Alice followed Celia over to Francine's Diner.

CHAPTER 15

After breakfast, Mary-Alice drove out to Mudbug to buy herself a television. By dinnertime, she had it all set up. Her natural optimism had rebounded; things were finally falling into place. The tablet was back up on the top shelf of her pantry, forgotten for the moment.

Celia was no murderer, Mary-Alice had realized, to her great relief. Just a snoop and a busybody, and was that really so bad? Mary-Alice didn't see what the Catholic church's postage expenses had to do with the murder of the Baptist youth minister, but Celia seemed happy about what she'd turned up, so Mary-Alice was happy for her.

She reheated the leftovers from that morning's breakfast at Francine's and sat down to watch her new television. A summer storm was pelting rain against the windows, which made it all the cozier to be indoors. Feeling celebratory, she fixed herself a glass of sweet tea with a dash of Sinful Ladies' Cough Syrup. She didn't have cable hooked up, and wasn't even sure whether it was available in Sinful, but for now, she had her choice of several over-the-air stations. She flipped around and settled on the local news. There she saw something that nearly made her drop her tea.

Footage from earlier that afternoon showed a photograph of Pastor Don, with the caption "Person of Interest in Youth Minister Murder." Pastor Don, who had never shown Mary-Alice anything but kindness, and had saved her untold money and heartache by warning her off the purchase of a termite-ridden house. Mary-Alice turned up the volume and listened, her eyes wide.

According to the report. a "source" had provided evidence that Pastor Don had been stealing from the church. The theory was that Pastor Don had murdered Pastor Chad when the younger man had threatened to expose him.

The cash flow statements that Mary-Alice had examined that weren't from the Catholic church. With dawning horror, Mary-Alice realized what she had witnessed the first time she opened that program on the tablet: The cell phone flashlight illuminating the room, the camera-jarring steps over to the file cabinet, the dropped phone and the swearing— a theft in progress. Celia had walked in and grabbed a handful of the Baptists' cash flow statements.

"No! Pastor Don didn't steal anything! The theft only started last month! It was Pastor Chad!"

Mary-Alice realized she was shouting at the television, and clapped her hand over her mouth.

She clicked off the television and rested her head in her hands. Her cheery mood had utterly drained away. She tried to organize the facts:

Celia had been in the Baptist church, poking through the file cabinet. Mary-Alice had seen that on her grandson's tablet.

And the next morning, in the same room, Pastor Chad was found bludgeoned to death.

The pieces fell into place.

Pastor Chad must have interrupted Celia as she was plundering the papers. Maybe Celia was trying to dig up embarrassing information on the two pastors, but then Celia panicked and killed Pastor Chad. And then she managed to pin the murder on Pastor Don.

Mary-Alice shuddered. It was one thing to dispose of someone from a distance. But to hit him in the face, hard enough to kill…

No. Fortune had said that Celia was too small to have bludgeoned Pastor Chad to death. Unless she had a stepladder and a handbag full of buckshot.

Mary-Alice picked up her phone to call Celia, and then set it down again. This was exactly how people get killed in movies, Mary-Alice realized. And anyway, what was the point? Celia would deny any wrongdoing, and try to make Mary-Alice feel guilty for even questioning her.

Mary-Alice's heart ached for poor Pastor Don. Then she had a terrifying thought: If Celia had brought the paperwork to law enforcement, she might have told them that Mary-Alice was the one who had looked it over. What if the police came calling, searched her pantry, and found that tablet?

Mary-Alice buried her face in her hands, too devastated to cry. She had so been looking forward to starting her new life in Sinful. Now she was stuck with twenty years of mortgage payments, in a town where her only family was a homicidal sociopath. To top it all off, she had an illegal wiretapping device sitting in her pantry.

Well, there was one thing she could do. Get rid of that tablet.

The rain had eased up to a sprinkle. The leaves in Mary-Alice's front garden glistened darkly as she hurried down the porch steps, the tablet concealed under her jacket. She crunched along the side of the wet gravel road on the bayou side, then hurried through a gap between two houses to walk directly alongside the bayou. When she spotted a patch of water that looked particularly dark and deep, she'd drop the tablet in without even breaking her stride. Even of someone spotted her, all they'd see is someone out for an evening walk. And if anyone heard a splash, why, it could be a frog, a fish, or a gator.

A roar tore through the peaceful night. A motorboat zoomed by, leaving whooping and hollering of adolescent voices hanging in the air. As the boat passed, she saw a scrawny silhouette hanging off the back, waving a net. In the wake of the motorboat, alarmed fish popped up out of the water.

"Got one!" the silhouette yelled, startling Mary-Alice so badly that she dropped the tablet right into the water.

Well, it was out of her hands now, and that had been her plan all along. She watched the fish jump, across the width of the bayou, gleaming silver against the dark water. Some were quite close, and she could see that they were much bigger than she—

Ouch!

Mary-Alice stared at the hefty carp flailing in the mud as her shoulder burned with pain. She felt a shameful urge to kick the stupid fish back into the bayou. As if it had read her mind, the carp flipped itself into the dark water and wiggled away to safety.

Mary-Alice couldn't move her left arm. The pain was overwhelming. The fish had smacked right into her, and it was huge —thirty pounds if it was an ounce. She dropped her bag on the ground and with her uninjured right arm managed to retrieve her phone.

9-1-1? No, she didn't want to be a bother and risk diverting an emergency vehicle from a real emergency. Doctor Broussard's office? It was certainly closed by now.

She dug into the bottom of her purse and fished out Ida Belle's card.

There was no answer. She felt a drop of water, and then another. Within seconds, Mary-Alice was standing in a downpour.

The Baptist church wasn't far from where she stood. If she could get inside, she'd be dry, and have a place to sit down…

Her phone rang.

"Sorry I couldn't pick up right away," Ida Belle said. "We were right in the middle of—Mary-Alice, are you okay?"

"Well," Mary-Alice faltered.

"Where are you? We'll be right there."

"If you're sure it's not too much trouble," Mary-Alice gasped. "I'm right behind the Baptist church. I think I dislocated my shoulder. Oh, and Ida Belle. I believe I found the murder weapon."

CHAPTER 16

Tuesday dawned bright and shiny, a perfect post-storm day. The nice folks in the emergency room had popped Mary-Alice's shoulder back into place and sent her off with an immobilizing sling and a little bottle of powerful painkillers. Mary-Alice was feeling peppy enough to meet Fortune, Ida Belle, and Gertie for breakfast at Francine's.

"Thank you again for rescuing me. Again." Mary-Alice beamed as she took her seat.

"Well, you were right," Ida Belle said. "Pastor Chad's fatal injuries were consistent with a blow to the face from a blunt, airborne object. Like a big ol' carp."

"We looked it up," Fortune added. "They can jump out of the water at fifteen miles per hour. And they've caused serious injuries before."

"We talked the medical examiner into taking another look at the body," Ida Belle said. "Looks like Pastor Chad was hit by the fish just about where you were. He managed to get inside the church before he died of his injuries."

"There were fish scales stuck in the poor man's hair," Gertie added.

"So what about Pastor Don?" Mary-Alice asked.

"Off the hook, with an apology from Sheriff Lee," Ida Belle said.

"Celia's the one who should really apologize," Gertie said. "She came in barging up to Lee with some crazy story about Pastor Don stealing money and killing Pastor Chad, and she threatened to fire everyone in the sheriff's department if he didn't make an arrest pronto."

"Celia can do that?"

"Sure can," Ida Belle said. "Until the recount's done, she's the mayor."

"Celia told me you and Gertie would 'blow a gasket' when you found out that she solved the crime." Mary-Alice took a shy sip of sweet tea. "Are you detectives?"

"We're just concerned citizens," Ida Belle said with a perfectly straight face. Gertie nodded, looking equally solemn. Fortune tried not to choke on her tea.

"But you know so much about what's going on in Sinful," Mary-Alice said. "You always seem to be ahead of Celia. It's...remarkable."

"We know people." Gertie shrugged. "And we're nice to them. A little kindness goes a long way."

Mary-Alice took a deep breath.

"I want to join the Sinful Ladies' Society," she declared. "I believe I qualify. I am a widow and a law-abiding...er, a reasonably well-behaved citizen."

"Mary-Alice," Ida Belle said kindly, "you are a sweet, kind lady. But to be a Sinful lady, well, it requires a certain toughness. A willingness to do whatever it—"

"Oh, come off it, Ida Belle," Gertie snorted. "It's the Sinful Ladies' Society, not Seal Team Six. Mary-Alice, dear, I hate to ask, but when and how did you lose your husband? Only because sometimes you think you've lost one, and then he shows up years later."

Mary-Alice nodded. "Like what happened to Celia. I understand. I'm certain he's gone. It was ten years ago. Joe was relaxing in our backyard, next to the bayou."

After Joe lost his job, all he did was relax in the backyard. And after a day spent drinking and nursing his grievances, he would take his disappointment out on Mary-Alice.

One sunny April Sunday afternoon, Mary-Alice was washing the dishes, her eye still throbbing from the punch Joe had landed the night before. A sudden motion in the backyard made her look up, just in time to see a twenty-foot bull gator rise out of the water. In in a single motion, the alligator pulled Joe Arceneaux and his lawn chair down into the Bayou Teche and out of Mary-Alice's life for good.

Mary-Alice dried her hands, picked up the phone, and reported the incident to the police. Then she called her insurance company.

Mary-Alice realized that the three women were watching her expectantly.

"Gator got him," Mary-Alice said.

"That's horrible," Fortune exclaimed.

"It was over in a second. I don't think he felt a thing."

Ida Belle and Gertie nodded understandingly. Fortune looked from one to the other.

"I'm sorry, but is that as normal as you seem to think it is? People just get eaten by alligators here?"

"That surprises you?" Ida Belle asked. "After we just had someone murdered by a flying fish?"

"Mary-Alice," Gertie said, "I'm sorry to hear about your husband, and I think you'd be a wonderful addition to our society. What do you think, Ida Belle?"

Ida-Belle looked skeptical.

"Sure. I guess."

"Congratulations, Mary-Alice!" Gertie reached over and clasped Mary-Alice's hands in her own, getting a big smudge of gravy on her sleeve in the process. "Welcome to the Sinful Ladies' Society."

"Now you're going to have to keep an open mind about things if you're going to hang with us," Ida Belle said. "I mean, sometimes a Sinful Lady has to break a rule or two. And no offense, Mary-Alice, but you come off like kind of a goody two-shoes."

Every night, after Joe had drunk himself into a stupor and staggered back into the house, Mary-Alice would go out back to collect Joe's empty beer cans. And move Joe's lawn chair a quarter-inch closer to the water's edge.

He'd never noticed.

"No offense taken, Ida Belle." Mary-Alice smiled. "I think you'll find I can rise to the occasion."

BAYOU BUSYBODY

CHAPTER 1

Mary-Alice Arceneaux awoke to the happy whirring and banging of construction in her kitchen. The crew liked to show up early, while it was still cool. Mary-Alice could scarcely blame them. The old Cooper place sat right on the bayou, and by mid-morning, the humidity was nearly intolerable. Mary-Alice was not in the least put out that she couldn't use her kitchen. It gave her an excuse to stroll over to Francine's Diner for breakfast.

Mary-Alice had recently moved to Sinful, Louisiana, and so far she was pleased with her decision. She had come from Mudbug, about an hour's drive away. Mudbug had two restaurants, a roller rink, and its own historical society. But Mary-Alice was ready to leave the hustle and bustle behind. To stop and smell the swamp lilies, if you will.

Mary-Alice's one disappointment had been her cousin Celia. Celia was a lifelong resident of Sinful, and Mary-Alice been looking forward to having family nearby. But Celia had just been elected mayor and was busy with her new duties. Fortunately, Mary-Alice had no trouble making new friends. She was agreeable and curious and above all, a good listener.

Celia did not approve of Mary-Alice's new friends. This did not trouble Mary-Alice; Celia disapproved of most people.

Francine's Diner was a short walk from Mary-Alice's front door. Mary-Alice had already made the trip several times. Francine's served excellent food and was the only dining establishment in town. She spotted three of her new friends sitting at a booth near the back. Gertie, Ida Belle, and Fortune still had their menus on the table, meaning they hadn't yet placed their order. Mary-Alice hesitated by the front counter before anyone noticed her. Mary-Alice's mother had taught her so well how to be "ladylike," she was practically invisible. Even her sequined tennis shoes and henna-red hair couldn't make her conspicuous. If one did happen to notice Mary-Alice, the impression was of a festively-decorated mouse.

Gertie noticed Mary-Alice first and waved her over to their table. Like Mary-Alice, Gertie and Ida Belle were in the prime of life (that is to say, on the sweet side of seventy). The third woman (girl, really), was the grand-niece of their late friend Marge. She was visiting from the Northeast to take care of her aunt's estate. Her name was Sandy-Sue Morrow, but everyone called her Fortune.

Fortune Morrow was an odd one, even for a Yankee. She was a children's librarian, with none of the serene temperament one would expect. She crackled with a pent-up energy that reminded Mary-Alice of a downed electrical line. She used military-sounding phrases like "Alpha Mike Foxtrot" instead of "goodbye." When she met someone for the first time, she gave them the up-and-down as if she were sizing them up. Mary-Alice concluded Fortune had read a few too many spy thrillers in her spare time.

"What's good today?" Mary-Alice picked up a menu. From the way the women's conversation had stopped cold, she suspected they had been talking about her cousin Celia.

"Everything," Fortune sighed. "I can't decide."

"That's why we need a plan of attack," Ida Belle said, "I get the strawberry waffle. Fortune, you get the ham and biscuits with redeye gravy, and Gertie'll order the shrimp and grits. And now Mary-Alice is here, we can order one more."

Gertie brightened.

"The crab Benedict! Is that alright with you, Mary-Alice? Then when Almira shows up, if she shows up, there'll be plenty for all of us."

"Of course." The thought of so much food made Mary-Alice feel overwhelmed, but she was happy to be included in the breakfast plan. And who was Almira? As much as Mary-Alice enjoyed the women's company, their conversation often made her feel like she'd missed an entire reel of a movie.

"Good. It's settled."

Ida Belle waved Ally over to place their breakfast order. Ida Belle was bossy, but in a good way. She got things done. Ida Belle was the chief of the powerful Sinful Ladies' Society, a cabal of widows and old maids who more or less ran the town of Sinful. Gertie was Ida Belle's second in command.

Fortune's role was a little harder to figure out. She was too young to be an official member of the Sinful Ladies' Society (the minimum age was 40). And while the SLS officially forswore the company of men, Fortune seemed to spend a lot of time with the handsome deputy sheriff.

"Who's Almira?" Mary-Alice asked when Ally had taken their breakfast order.

"A writer friend of Gertie's," Ida Belle said. "She's coming to Sinful with her family."

"A writer? How exciting!" Mary-Alice clapped her hands. "How long is she staying?"

"She's not visiting," Gertie said. "She's moving here."

Mary-Alice noticed Fortune's worried expression. She was probably imagining Gertie's friend was a Russian undercover agent or something. Well, it was no crime to be peculiar, thank

Heaven. Because if it were, Mary-Alice had several harmless acquaintances who would be behind bars.

"Here she is now. Almira!" Gertie stood and waved.

A solemn-looking woman with a bleached-blonde pixie cut glanced around Francine's lunchtime crowd. Her tense features relaxed when she caught sight of Gertie.

Ally came hurrying over with a fifth chair and scooted it over to the end of the booth.

"Morning, ladies. We met at the A.R.E.A. conference, right?"

"Yeah, I remember you," Ida Belle said.

"Nice to see you again," Fortune added.

"What's the area conference?" Mary -Alice asked.

"The American Romance and Erotica Authors conference," Gertie explained. Ida Belle snorted, and Fortune suppressed a smile.

"That sounds so exciting." Mary-Alice's circle had expanded to include another writer. Who knew the tiny town of Sinful would be such a stronghold of The Arts?

Ally arrived at the table balancing four gigantic plates.

"What can I get for you?" she asked Almira when she'd placed the breakfasts on the table.

"Nothing for me, thanks."

Almira watched Ally hurry off.

"I shouldn't spoil my appetite. My husband's expecting me to have lunch with him."

Mary-Alice was good at spotting unhappy marriages, having lived through one herself. Ten years earlier, a hungry bull gator had climbed up out of the Bayou Teche to find Joe Arceneaux sleeping off a hangover in his favorite lawn chair. Within moments, Mary-Alice was a widow.

She'd had to act sad, of course. But even now, all she felt was relieved.

Gertie asked Almira about her latest book, which cheered her up. Soon the conversation was moving from one writerly topic to the next. Gertie wrote romances in a genre she called "seniorotica," featuring mature protagonists. Almira's genre was "literary romance," which sounded very elegant. Almira started to tell a juicy story about a self-help author they both knew and disliked, who set out to take revenge on a reviewer. Just as she was getting to the confrontation in the craft beer aisle, she stopped.

"Here's my lunch date." Almira aimed a strained smile at the middle-aged man approaching their table.

Dr. Whitbread was fair-skinned to the point of translucency. His eyes were pale blue and his hair colorless. He was what Mary-Alice's mother would call a "boiled blonde."

Almira glanced at her watch. "Geoff, honey, I lost track of the time. Gertie, Ida Bell, Fortune, er...I'm sorry, Mary-Ann?"

"Mary-Alice," Mary-Alice said.

"Mary-Alice. This is my husband, Dr. Geoffrey Whitbread."

"Your last name is actually White-bread?" Ida Belle snickered.

"Ida Belle!" Gertie scolded.

"What? His name is White bread, didn't she just say? And look at him! Come on, it's kinda funny. Right, Geoff?"

Ida Belle dealt Dr. Whitbread a friendly punch in the arm.

"The name is actually *Whit*bread." The man gave Ida Belle a patient smile and rubbed his bruised bicep. "A good old Anglo-Saxon name. Although some of my students seem to prefer the alternate pronunciation. Almira, honey, you're making us late. Rochelle's waiting in the car."

"I'll be right out, sweetheart." Almira's small store of joy had evaporated. Her expression as she watched her husband leave the restaurant was pure resentment.

"Rochelle is your son's wife?" Gertie asked.

"Yeah. She's been staying with us while Tristan's deployed. I didn't think she'd want to move down to Sinful with us, but here she is."

"You don't get along with your daughter-in-law?" Ida Belle asked. Almira shrugged.

"She's not exactly my biggest fan. She has no problem with Geoff, though. Those two get along great. Anyway, duty calls. Gotta go."

Almira edged between the crowded tables of the diner. On her way out, she pushed the door so hard Francine's customers looked up from their breakfasts to see what the angry jingling was about.

"Almira married her writing professor," Gertie explained. "And then her writing career took off."

Ida Belle nodded. "Bet he didn't like that much."

"It's like the plot of A Star is Born," Mary-Alice said.

"Isn't it funny, Mary-Alice?" Gertie grinned. "You thought you'd escape drama by moving to Sinful."

Fortune smiled knowingly, and Ida Belle snorted.

"Oh, I wouldn't trade it for anything," Mary-Alice declared. "I love it here. And I'm living right downtown in one of Sinful's historic homes. It's so much fun."

"Not as much fun as watching Celia Arceneaux turn five shades of green when you moved into one of Sinful's most distinctive homes."

"Oh, I know now that Celia was upset about the old Cooper place, but I certainly didn't mean to show anyone up."

"That's what makes it even better," Ida Belle said. "All you did was buy a nice old fixer-upper, and you got Celia spitting nails. Sorry, Mary-Alice, I know Celia's your cousin, but she is a mean, petty woman and you're far too nice to her."

Mary-Alice preferred to think the best of people, especially when they were family. But even she had to admit the evidence was not in Celia's favor. So powerful was Celia's hatred of Ida Belle, Gertie, and the rest of the Sinful Ladies' Society that Celia had founded a rival group. They called themselves the "God's Wives," which Mary-Alice thought was irreverent. Mary-Alice liked hanging out with the Sinful Ladies' Society anyway. But tact demanded she keep this a secret from Celia for the time being. Best not to poke the bear. Especially when the bear was the acting mayor.

Mary-Alice thought it would be lovely if one day they could all get along. But Celia had been feuding with Gertie and Ida Belle for decades, and longstanding traditions don't change overnight.

"All of this literary talk's made me hungry," Ida Belle declared. "I think it's time for dessert."

"So soon after breakfast?" Mary-Alice had indulged rather liberally in strawberry waffles, fluffy biscuits drenched in gravy, and creamy grits. She found the prospect of dessert daunting.

"We're grown-ups," Ida Belle countered. "Who's gonna tell us no?"

"My jeans," Fortune muttered.

"That's what elastic waistbands are for." Gertie picked up the hand-drawn table tent listing the desserts on offer.

Mary-Alice bought a box of brownies on the way out of Francine's. The sweet treats weren't for her own consumption. After the breakfast she'd just had, she was sure she wouldn't be able to eat for a week.

The old Cooper place wasn't visible from the main road. Someone who took the trouble to turn down the long, gravel driveway would not be impressed with what lay at the end. The house had fallen into disrepair over the past century or so. Celia had come right out and declared it looked like a dump.

The interior wasn't much better. The kitchen was stripped to the studs and filled with noise, dust, and sweaty men who wore their pants too low. But coming through the front door always perked Mary-Alice up. She saw the possibilities. The house had good bones and in the real estate agent's words, needed only a few nips and tucks.

Mary-Alice could already see her new kitchen taking shape.

The dreary green walls had been repainted the color of butter. The wall tiles were going up now, a dazzling arrangement of aqua, red, and sunshine yellow.

"It looks like a parrot," Celia had sniffed. "Mark my words, Mary-Alice, you're going to get tired of those garish colors. You should have brought in a professional decorator. I could have helped you if I didn't have so many more important things going on."

Celia's own interior featured avocado appliances, a carpeted kitchen, and macramé owl wall ornaments. It was either hopelessly dated or on the cutting edge of fashion (Mary-Alice suspected the former). In any event, Mary-Alice was certain she would not have liked Celia's ideas, and was glad Celia had been too busy to help her.

Mary-Alice knocked softly on her kitchen door frame. The foreman stood, rubbed his hands on the sides of his pants, and came out to the dining room

"Good morning, Mister St. Clair."

"Call me Boon. Please. There's not a problem, is there?"

"Oh, no. The tile is looking wonderful. I just wanted to let you know I got you and your men some of Ally's peanut butter brownies, to keep your energy up. Please help yourself. Whenever you like."

"Miz Mary-Alice, you are spoiling us. After this job, I don't think I'll be happy working anywhere else."

Mary-Alice beamed.

"Well, I do plan to keep you all busy for a while. Don't forget, there's cold sweet tea for you out here in the mini-fridge."

Mary-Alice would never engage in any sort of improper behavior, and most certainly not with a hired man. But she did enjoy her little chats with Boon St. Clair. It was always best to be kind, and to stay on good terms with people. Where was the harm?

CHAPTER 2

The next morning, Mary-Alice decided to vary her routine. She said good morning to Boon and the crew, then took a can of Coke and a day-old brownie out to the back porch. It was cooler right on the water. She got comfortable, opened her laptop, and started a new unit in her online computer course. She was still a member of the Crafting Circle and the Historical Society, but Mudbug was now an hour away. She wanted something to keep her mind active, and the self-paced class filled the bill.

When it got too hot to sit outside, Mary-Alice put away her laptop and went in to check on the kitchen. Boon needed her input on a few things, so they spent some time discussing joints and fittings and grout lines.

By the time she was finished talking with Boon, it was already noon. The brownie had been tasty, but no one would call it a substantial breakfast.

Mary-Alice was surprised at how deserted Francine's Diner appeared. Most of the tables were empty. There was no sign of Gertie, Ida Belle, or anyone else she knew. The only person she recognized was Ally, who was busy waiting tables.

"Sit anywhere you like, Aunt Mary-Alice," Ally called to her from the ordering counter. Mary-Alice chose a seat close to the window. If there was no one to eat with, at least she might see something interesting going on outside.

Ally came over with a menu and a glass of water.

"Hi, Aunt Mary-Alice. Missed you at breakfast. Not a problem with the remodel, I hope?"

"No, the kitchen is coming along splendidly. I didn't want to get into a rut. So I thought I'd try doing my computer lessons in the morning and having lunch here."

"Aw, that's great, Aunt Mary-Alice. Are you learning how to send emails and surf the internet?"

"Not exactly. Right now I'm learning about packet-switching. Ally, dear, where is everyone? I hope I'm not missing out on any excitement."

Ally sighed.

"I guess excitement is one word for it. No, Aunt Mary-Alice, you are not missing out. What happened was, Aunt Celia and Gertie really got into it this morning. And I guess they ended up drawing a crowd."

"Oh, dear."

"Exactly."

Celia could be a terror when she got riled up, Mary-Alice knew, and Gertie was as stubborn as a rock.

"Do you know what it was about?" Mary-Alice asked.

Ally pulled her order pad out of her apron pocket.

"Something to do with the City Hall flagpole, Aunt Celia's underwear, and the First Amendment. Apparently the sheriff's involved. You know, just another day in Sinful. I just try to stay out of it. Are you ready to order, Aunt Mary-Alice?"

"Oh, my goodness, I haven't even looked at the menu yet. Something light, I think. I ate so much yesterday, I thought I'd pop. What do you recommend?"

"The shrimp salad's is on the lighter side. And Francine's

crispy catfish with fried potatoes and greens is amazing. Fish is fresh."

"The catfish sounds lovely. I'll have that."

Mary-Alice smiled and handed Ally her menu.

"Oh, and I'd like to get something sweet to go. For the workmen. Do you have something without peanuts? Boon, the foreman, is allergic, but this whole time he's been too polite to say so."

"I'll pick out something for you and leave it at the counter. Tea, coffee, or Coke?"

"Sweet tea please, thank you, dear."

Mary-Alice was worried about Gertie. She considered ordering her lunch to go so she could rush over to City Hall and make sure her friend was okay. But Ally had told her sheriffs were on the scene, so perhaps it was best to leave things to them. She was still debating with herself when Celia herself pushed through the front door of Francine's.

Oddly, Celia didn't seem upset. In fact, she was beaming.

"Ah, there you are, Mary-Alice." Celia sped over to Mary-Alice's table and slid into the booth opposite her.

"Hello, Celia. Won't you join me for lunch? I've only just ordered."

Mary-Alice was relieved to see Celia unharmed. The sheriff must have stepped in before things got too out of hand. So Gertie must be okay too.

"You know, Mary-Alice, I was right. What this town just needs some strong leadership. And today, it got some."

"Why, what happened?"

"That horrible woman's finally gotten what's coming to her. And her little Yankee, too. Ally!"

Ally came scurrying over, order pad in hand.

"Hi, Aunt Celia. What can I get you?"

Ally didn't ask Celia where she'd been, or what she'd been up to. Which meant Celia had to make some effort to bring it up.

"Oh, I couldn't possibly eat a thing after all that excitement. Maybe just a slice of peach pie, if you have it. Warmed, with vanilla ice cream. Not too hot, I nearly blistered my tongue last time. And coffee. With cream. And a side of fried potatoes, just so I have something on my stomach. Thanks, dear."

"And you're still fine with the catfish, Aunt Mary-Alice? Anything else with that? Dessert?"

"So it's *Aunt* Mary-Alice, now? Well, isn't that something. Ally, you know she's not really your aunt, right? Her Joe was cousin to my Max, is all. No blood relation."

Ally cleared her throat.

"Peach pie, warmed, a la mode, coffee, side of fried potatoes for Aunt Celia. Crispy catfish special for Aunt Mary-Alice, and you got your sweet tea. Anything else?"

"Oh. Ally. You're still here. Well, I might as well give you both the news at once. Gertie and that skinny Yankee are leaving Sinful."

Allie's eyes widened.

"Are you talking about Fortune? Aunt Celia, what did you do?"

"Me? I didn't do anything. Except press charges."

CHAPTER 3

"Press charges?" Mary-Alice faltered.

"You can't just let people go around disturbing the peace and disrespecting elected officials. I won't even go into the disgusting details of what that woman—"

"Did you send Fortune and Gertie to jail?" Ally demanded.

"Not exactly jail." Celia sounded a little disappointed. "The next-best solution. Anger management camp. And it's a good thing, too. You should've heard the things those two...well, I'm a lady, and I won't repeat it, but mark my words, it was disgraceful. I'm surprised you didn't hear the ruckus all the way over here. Ally, don't look at me like that."

Ally strode over to the counter, ripped the page off her pad, and impaled it on the check spindle with a good deal more force than necessary.

Celia seemed baffled her tale of triumph wasn't meeting with more approval. Having lost half her audience, Celia turned back to Mary-Alice.

"I know you like to be friends with everyone you meet, Mary-Alice, you're like a pathetic little puppy sometimes,

77

honestly. But those women are a terrible influence and I'm glad you'll have a few days free of them. The only bad thing is Ida-Belle isn't going with them. Now I would never dream of telling you what to do, but if you were to ask my advice, I'd tell you to stay far away from those three. Far away."

Mary-Alice didn't know what to say. She knew she should try to stay on good terms with her cousin, but she felt loyal to Gertie, Ida Belle, and Fortune. Fortunately, Celia didn't wait for Mary-Alice's reply.

"Anyway, I'm happy to share a meal with you when I can, like today, but you can't expect me to keep you company all the time. As you know, the mayor's office comes with great responsibility. You'll have to learn to make friends on your own."

Mary-Alice nodded. She wondered how much time it could possibly take to manage the affairs of a town with a population of 253. But she was secretly relieved Celia's duties would be keeping her occupied.

"Well, Celia, I'll certainly miss your company, but I suppose I'll keep busy with my lessons and my remodeling. Oh, the kitchen walls turned out the loveliest shade of yellow—"

"Now don't tell me you're still frittering away your life savings on that run-down old money pit. I don't like to be a snob, Mary-Alice, but when people find out that the poor soul living in that old shack is an Arceneaux…"

In fact, Celia had been complaining to anyone who would listen that the old Cooper place was far too grand for Mary-Alice. If Mary-Alice wasn't careful, Celia declared, people would think she was getting above herself. But although Celia's reasoning was inconsistent, her determination to put others in the wrong was unwavering.

"I suppose as long as you're spending all your time and savings on your little renovations, you'll be staying out of trouble and away from bad company. So that's a mercy, at least."

"You always have such good advice for me, Celia. Oh, look. Here's Almira. My goodness, what happened to her?"

Almira Galvez-Whitbread was soaking wet. Her hair lay flat on her head. Specks and sticks clung to her clothes, and her feet were caked in mud.

She stood by the front door, perhaps afraid to track mud onto Francine's immaculate floor.

"I need help." Almira spoke so quietly, Mary-Alice could barely hear her.

Celia and Mary-Alice stood up at the same time: Mary-Alice to assist, Celia to confront the undesirable who had disrupted her lunch.

"What is going on here?" Celia stomped over to confront the woman. Mary-Alice followed her.

"Please." Almira ran her hand through her hair and then pulled it away, as if she was surprised to find it was wet. "I just—"

"I am the mayor of this municipality." Celia's delivery was so effortless it sounded as if she had been practicing the phrase in the mirror. "And I'll thank you not to disturb the peace. If you have an incident to report, you may do so at the sheriff's office."

Almira blinked, and looked from Celia to Mary-Alice and then back to Celia.

"There's a sheriff?"

"It's right over there, you Yankee nitwit," Celia boomed, pointing over Almira's shoulder.

By now all the diners had stopped their conversations and set down their utensils. The ones who were unlucky enough to be facing the wrong way had turned around to watch the show.

"Next to the butcher shop," Mary-Alice added. "It's easy to miss if you don't know the town. Celia, maybe we should walk her over."

Celia glared around the diner.

"What are you all gawking at? I suppose I'll have to deal with this too. You people won't be happy until you've worked me to death. Come on, let's get this over with."

"Excuse me? Aunt Celia? Aunt Mary-Alice?" Ally came running up with the check and a bakery box. But Celia had already marched Almira halfway across the road. Mary-Alice stood alone.

CHAPTER 4

"Thank you, Ally." Mary-Alice drew two twenties out of her purse. It was enough for both breakfasts, the oatmeal raisin cookies, and a nice tip for Ally. Mary-Alice dropped off the cookies at her house, then hurried over to the sheriff's office.

Mary-Alice found Celia and Almira in the reception area, seated on opposite ends of a wooden bench. Mary-Alice sat between them. She tried not to make a face at the swampy stench coming off Almira's clothes.

Behind the counter sat a woman with an apricot-colored beehive and glittering green eyelids. She looked up, gave Mary-Alice a wink, and then went back to work. The tapping of her keyboard was the only sound in the room.

Finally, Deputy Breaux emerged from the back, looking harassed.

"Sorry, Madam Mayor, I mean your honor," he babbled, "I was out at the Swamp Bar, I mean, I was on a call, I wasn't at the Swamp Bar..."

Celia stood up.

"Better late than never. You can take it from here, Deputy.

This woman claims her husband's missing. Come along, Mary-Alice."

"Can she stay?" Almira blurted out.

"Me?" Mary-Alice was surprised. She didn't think she had made much of an impression on Almira.

"I just, Gertie's not picking up her phone, and I…"

"Of course I'll stay with you." Mary-Alice patted Almira's soggy shoulder. "If that's what you'd like."

"Suit yourself, Mary-Alice. Just don't blame me when he turns up tomorrow with an empty wallet and a hangover."

The woman with the beehive looked up from her computer and watched Celia stalk out of the sheriff's station.

"Don't worry about Celia, hon. She hates being upstaged."

"Oh, my. I certainly didn't intend to upstage anyone." Least of all Cousin Celia, whose tender ego, Mary-Alice knew, required special handling.

Deputy Breaux led Almira and Mary-Alice down the hallway and into a small office. Once they were all seated, he pulled a small notebook and pen from his shirt pocket and looked expectantly at Almira.

"Just go? Okay. It was Geoff's idea to rent the boat."

Breaux wrote, and then paused.

"And who is Geoff, please?"

"My husband. Geoff Whitbread. He's a writer. You might have heard of him."

Breaux shook his head.

"Anyway, he wanted to pack us some sandwiches and beer, rent a boat, and just explore."

"And you agreed."

Almira nodded.

"I did. I mean, it's pretty quiet here, there's not much else to do. I wasn't crazy about the idea, though. I get seasick."

Deputy Breaux looked up from his writing.

"Ma'am, why did you agree to lunch on the water if you get seasick?"

Almira shrugged.

"I didn't want to seem ungrateful. I can't remember the last time Geoff planned something for us. I mean, he packed us a picnic lunch. The last time that happened was, oh, I don't know, *never.*"

Almira blinked quickly and looked at the ceiling.

"So we parked somewhere, I couldn't even tell you where, got in the boat, and at first it wasn't that bad. The water was really calm. So we ate our sandwiches and opened a couple of beers, and we were just floating along. I was watching the trees that grow up from the water, you can see where the trunks split into roots. What are those called?"

"Cypress," Mary-Alice and Deputy Breaux said in unison.

"Cypress. I'll have to remember that. Anyway, I was wondering, should I take a picture with my phone? And then I heard Geoff make this kind of, I don't know, snort? I turned around and he stared back at me and then just...tipped over sideways into the water. Next thing I know it's dark, I'm in the water, the boat's upside-down and I'm stuck underneath."

"You capsized," Breaux suggested.

"Yeah. Can someone turn that down? It's freezing in here."

An ancient fan rattled away on the file cabinet, pushing the muggy air around. Mary-Alice got up and switched it off. Deputy Breaux fetched a blanket. Mary-Alice helped him drape it around Almira's shivering shoulders.

"Thanks. That's better. Anyway, so I'm stuck under the boat, it's dark and I can feel things bumping against my legs. I don't know if it's fish or alligators or debris or what, but it was, you can imagine, it was scary. I felt for the edge of the boat and pushed myself down into the water. That was harder than I thought it would be, but it was because I had my life vest on. Finally, I popped up on the other side. And Geoff was gone, he wasn't anywhere, it was just me hanging onto an upside-down boat. Floating. By myself."

"Was your husband wearing a life vest, Ma'am?"

Almira closed her eyes and shook her head.

"I tried to get him to wear it. He laughed at me. Because the river's not very wide—"

"River?" Deputy Breaux interrupted. "What river?"

"The one right out there that runs behind this building. I followed it back into town. It's a good thing I—"

"Oh, you mean the *bayou*." Breaux relaxed.

Almira looked perplexed.

"It's a bayou? Not a river? Isn't a bayou like a swamp?"

"Well this one here's a bayou," Breaux explained.

Almira pulled her hand through her hair, exposing dark brown roots.

"Whatever. Bayou. Anyway. I made it to shore, I thought I was safe when I reached the trees, but the ground was so soft, I felt like I was getting sucked down into the mud. But I saw these big stones scattered around, so I walked on them and then I realized they were gravestones."

"Sounds like you came up on the cemetery," Breaux said. "It's been flooding every so often, especially after Katrina."

"Geoff would've loved the scene. A woman who'd just escaped death, picking her way through a flooded graveyard. Stepping on the headstones to save herself from sinking into the muck. Ugh. Why didn't I make him wear his life jacket? Sure, it would've ruined our afternoon, me being the nagging wife that he hates, but I guess our afternoon was ruined anyway. Wasn't it?"

Breaux examined his notepad.

"Anything else you can remember?"

Almira shook her head and sniffled. Breaux scrambled to retrieve a box of tissues while Mary-Alice gently rubbed her back.

"He likes his tuna salad with jalapenos, but I like mine plain. Just tuna and mayo." Almira pulled out a tissue and blotted her eyes. "He made my sandwich without jalapenos, the way I like it. He did that for me."

"Did you and your husband have any disagreements recently?" Deputy Breaux clearly did not like having to ask this question.

Almira shrugged.

"No. I mean, nothing big. Just the usual married couple stuff."

CHAPTER 5

It was nearly sunset by the time Mary-Alice and Almira left the sheriff's office.

"May I drive you home, dear?"

Almira pulled the scratchy brown blanket tight around her.

"Yes," she said, finally. "Thank you."

Mary-Alice started walking in the direction of her house. Almira followed her.

"Is there someone I can call?"

Almira shook her head.

"It's just Rochelle at home. My daughter-in-law. Tristan's not coming home until tomorrow."

"Tristan?"

"Our son. He's in the Air Force."

"Goodness, you must be very proud. I didn't know you had a grown son."

"Yeah, I was young. Only twenty-one when he was born."

Mary-Alice had married Joe Arceneaux when she was nineteen. "Better late than never" had been her mother's comment on the timing.

Mary-Alice turned off the main road toward her house.

Almira hesitated, then followed. Mary-Alice supposed the driveway did look a little spooky, with the shadows lengthening and the cypress trees looming on either side. She made a note to ask Boon St. Clair about getting lights installed.

"Almost there, dear. Watch where you step, it's a little bumpy after the last rain. How did you meet your husband?"

"I was a sophomore in Professor Whitbread's women's literature class. He was thirty-two and married. He had us reading Virginia Woolf and Charlotte Perkins Gilman and all this first-wave feminism stuff, and yet we managed to enact this perfect patriarchal cliché. You know, I had no sympathy for his wife. Not back then, anyway. Karma, huh?"

Mary-Alice nodded. While she didn't know all the references Almira was making, she understood the gist.

"There's nothing new under the sun, is there? Father Michael said it just last Sunday. Ecclesiastes, I believe. Ah, here we are."

Mary-Alice switched on the light. Her dark-green Oldsmobile 88 gleamed under the carport's fluorescent tubing. Lumber and paint buckets were stacked against one wall and covered with a translucent tarp.

"Mary-Alice, can you stay for dinner? It's just going to be me and Rochelle. I don't think I can face her by myself."

Almira looked greenish and wretched in the harsh light. Mary-Alice could read the faded letters stenciled on the rough blanket. *Calcasieu Parish Emergency Services*. The poor woman.

"That's very kind. Just a minute." Mary-Alice fumbled in her purse. "Let me make a quick call."

Mary-Alice walked a discreet distance away and started to dial Gertie's number. But just as the phone started ringing, Mary-Alice recalled Celia had sent her out of town. And Fortune, too.

She called Ida Belle next. Fortunately, Ida Belle answered her phone. Unfortunately, she was even more brusque than usual.

"Oh, Ida Belle," Mary-Alice faltered. "You sound like you're busy. I don't want to bother you."

"Mary-Alice! Sorry, I thought you were Gertie. I wouldn't have used that kind of language if I'd known it was you. What's going on?"

"Gertie's friend Almira seems to have lost her husband in the bayou."

"Aw, crap. She had to do that now?"

"She's asked me to drive her home and stay for dinner. I just wanted to let you know what happened and where I was going to be."

"You think she bumped him off and you're next?"

"Well I didn't really think of that—"

"Nah, it's good to be cautious. Are you gonna be alone with her?"

"Her daughter-in-law will be there."

Ida Belle grunted, and Mary-Alice heard what sounded like a struggle, followed by the snap of a latch being forced shut.

"Ida-Belle, are you packing? Are you leaving town?"

"Packing? I have no idea what you're talking about."

"Celia told me she sent Gertie and Fortune to anger management camp. You're going to go and try to get them out, aren't you? That's why you're packing! Oh, are you bringing a gun?"

Ida Belle waited a few moments to respond.

"Mary-Alice," she said finally, "your powers of observation are worthy of the Sinful Ladies' Society. Your discretion, on the other hand—"

"Oh dear, I didn't mean to be nosy."

"No, no, nosy is good. Nothing wrong with nosy. Just don't go saying things out loud. Can anyone hear you?"

Mary-Alice glanced at Almira, who was now shaking out the blanket, unaware it was as dry as it was going to get in the bayou humidity.

"No," Mary-Alice whispered. "No one can hear me."

"All right, listen to me, Mary-Alice. Maybe you're right. This thing wasn't an accident."

"Oh no, I never said—"

"So it's not the worst idea in the world to keep an eye on this Almira woman. Gertie likes her, but Gertie doesn't always have the best judgment."

Mary-Alice heard a grunt that sounded like Ida Belle was dragging something heavy. Like a suitcase.

"So where's her house? Just in case you disappear, I have to know where to tell the sheriff to look for your body."

Mary-Alice put her hand over the phone and walked over to Almira, who was now folding the damp blanket.

"Almira, where are you staying?"

Almira set the blanket on the ground, patted her pockets, and then closed her eyes and sighed.

"It's gone. My phone. My purse. I need to replace all my credit cards. Wait. I think I can remember it."

Almira told Mary-Alice a street name and number.

Mary-Alice scurried away and repeated the address to Ida Belle.

"That's not far from Marge's place. Fortune's place, I mean. Yeah, okay. Worst case, you make a break for it and it's only a mile or so back to your house."

"Thank you, Ida Belle. And safe travels."

"Hmph," said Ida Belle.

Mary-Alice hung up and returned to Almira.

"Almira dear, I would be delighted to join you for dinner. Here, let me help you in"

CHAPTER 6

Almira balked at the idea of climbing into Mary-Alice's spotless car. Mary-Alice brought out a bath towel to protect the seat and assured Almira the upholstery was dirt-proof.

Mary-Alice's mother would not have approved. She claimed Cleanliness was next to Godliness and would have judged the filthy husband-stealing Yankee in the passenger seat to be far from both. But Mary-Alice did not think it would be right to leave Almira to fend for herself.

"Well, I *would* have given her a ride," Mary-Alice imagined explaining to Saint Peter as he weighed out her life's works. "But I just had my car detailed, and how was I supposed to know she'd get run over in the dark?"

Mary-Alice made sure they were both buckled in and set her phone's GPS to the address Almira gave her. Mary-Alice was glad she had a navigation system to guide her down the narrow gravel roads. Sinful had no streetlights, and the blue dusk was fading fast to black.

After they had been driving for a few minutes, Almira spoke.

"I wonder if I need to let Danny know."

"I'm sorry?"

"Danny. Geoff's business partner."

"Business partner? I thought your husband was a professor."

"He's an entrepreneur, too. Have you heard of 'Solutions for Authors'?"

"I don't believe so, no."

"They provide services for writers, like editing and uploading, and charge them an arm and a leg for it. The business has done so well, they're gonna sell it and make a bundle. Geoff thinks our share is going to be around three million."

"Goodness. Well, that says something nice about Sinful, doesn't it? You can live anywhere you like, and you chose to move here."

"Yeah. That was really Geoff's decision. Not mine."

"Oh. Was Geoff—I mean, is Geoff from around here?"

"Not even close. But he thought moving here would re-ignite his creativity. He was going to be the second coming of Faulkner or something. And that's all that matters, isn't it? That *Geoff* gets to arrange his life however he wants. I'm just along for the ride. Never mind that I don't even have a driver's license...sorry. I'm rambling. Mary-Alice, I really appreciate that you're here. Thank you."

"You're very welcome, dear. You've been through a lot today. What will you tell your daughter-in-law?"

"I don't think I'm going to say anything. We don't know what happened yet, and Tristan's not coming in until tomorrow. If Geoff doesn't turn up by then, then I guess we'll have to talk about it."

"Your destination," announced the GPS voice, "is on the left. This concludes your navigation."

As soon as Almira let herself out of the passenger seat, the front door flew open and a young man bounded down the porch steps. He grabbed Almira around the waist and lifted her into the air. Panicked, Mary-Alice pulled out her phone to call the police. But then the young man kissed Almira's cheek and set her down.

"I wasn't expecting you tonight," Almira laughed.

"Is Dad with you?"

"Dad's not here, baby. Oh, Mary-Alice, come meet my son. Tristan."

Mary-Alice did as Almira asked. As she was coming around the car she saw a woman standing in the doorway at the top of the porch steps. Neither Almira nor her son seemed to notice her.

"Ma'am, pleased to meet you." Tristan's handshake was perfect, firm but not crushing. He was exceptionally good-looking. Mary-Alice could see he had Almira's honey complexion and full mouth. His golden hair and light eyes were his father's contribution.

"A pleasure to meet you," Mary-Alice said, and then she turned to address the silent woman at the top of the steps.

But the doorway was empty.

"Will you be alright now, Almira?" Mary-Alice asked hopefully. "I don't want to intrude on your reunion."

"Oh no, don't leave. Please stay for dinner."

"Please join us, Miz Mary-Alice," Tristan echoed. "It's too quiet out here. We could use the company. And I'd like to learn more about Sinful."

"Oh. Well, thank you. It would be a pleasure."

Tristan walked Almira up the steps, his arm around her shoulders.

Mary-Alice put on a cheery smile and followed them inside. She would have been perfectly happy to run back to her car, hop in, and head for home. But she wouldn't dream of doing something so impolite.

"What a beautiful home," Mary-Alice exclaimed. Under no circumstances would she have said anything different. The house appeared to have been fitted out as a long-term rental, decorated less to delight the eye than to avoid offense. The palette ranged from beige to brown; the furniture was serviceable and forgettable.

"I'm glad we're renting," Almira said. "These old places are total money pits. Okay, everyone hang tight, I'm going to go take the quickest shower ever."

"Rochelle, baby," Tristan called out, "We got a dinner guest. Come meet Mary-Alice. She's a local, so she can give us the inside scoop."

A young woman appeared in the living room. Mary-Alice thought she might be the silhouette from the doorway.

"How do you do, dear?" Mary-Alice smiled and extended both hands. "I'm afraid it would be false advertising to call me a local. I've only just moved over from Mudbug."

"Hey," the young woman muttered.

Almira's daughter-in-law had not been blessed with much in the way of wit or charm. She was pretty enough, with an unobjectionable figure, and thick, dark hair that hung past her shoulders. But she was hardly the wily Jezebel Mary-Alice had expected from Almira's description.

"Whatever you're cooking smells delicious," Mary-Alice said.

Tristan reached over and pulled Rochelle into a hug, which didn't seem to make her any less glum. The couple put Mary-Alice in mind of a golden retriever hugging a cat.

"Too bad Dad's not home yet." Tristan nuzzled his wife's neck. "Rochelle made fish and chips. I know he won't wanna miss that. You're awesome, baby."

"I'll go set another place."

"Oh dear, I'm intruding," Mary-Alice fretted. "Really, I don't need to—"

"Don't worry, Miz Mary-Alice" Tristan laughed. "She's talking about me. I wasn't planning to be back until tomorrow. If Dad's late, he'll just have to make himself a sandwich or something. Too bad. You snooze, you lose."

CHAPTER 7

"The table's all set," Rochelle said. "I guess we can eat."

They went through to the dining room. Dinner had been set out family style on the table, with bowls of fried fish, coleslaw, green beans, and biscuits.

"Thank you for getting dinner ready, Rochelle." Almira came through the door, wearing a clean t-shirt and jeans and looking refreshed. Her hair was wet and neatly combed. "That was very helpful of you."

Tristan pulled out chairs for each of the three women, starting with Mary-Alice and ending with his wife. Then he sat down himself and passed the green beans to Mary-Alice.

"So Mom, what were you going to tell me outside?"

Almira reached the serving tongs toward the fried fish platter and then paused.

"Well, today we—Rochelle, did you do this batter spicy or plain?"

"Plain. Sorry, Almira, I know you like the spicy kind."

"No, no, don't worry. Plain is perfect. I'm the one who can't handle spicy, remember?"

Rochelle's eyes widened.

"I know it's counterintuitive," Almira laughed.

Rochelle stared at Almira, burst into tears, and ran from the table.

"Mom!"

"What? What did I say?"

"You made her feel stupid again."

"Tristan, all I said was—"

"Remember what the counselor told us? Mom, I love you, but Rochelle is my wife, and I have to stand with her."

And then Tristan was gone, leaving Mary-Alice and Almira at the table.

"Well. I think it's time to open the wine."

Almira stood up and disappeared through a side doorway.

"Red or white?" She called out.

"You choose, dear. Anything is fine with me."

Mary-Alice and Almira were sipping a decent red wine when Tristan returned to the dining room.

"Everything okay?" Almira asked.

"Mom, she's a mess. Look. You can't just—"

"Tristan, I can't just what?"

"You treat her like she's stupid. That's what."

"Stupid? Rochelle is obviously not *stupid*. She managed to get you to marry her, didn't she? What did I say that upset her so much? All I said was I can't handle spicy food."

"Well, maybe it was the way you said it. See, now you're rolling your eyes."

Almira leveled her gaze at him.

"Tristan, sit down."

He did.

"Your father is missing."

Tristan looked from his mother to Mary-Alice and back to his mother.

"What do you mean missing? How? When's the last time you saw him?"

Almira told her son the same thing she'd told Deputy Breaux.

He jumped up and pulled out his phone.

"You don't believe me?" Almira asked.

"I never said that, Mom. I'm just gonna call the sheriff and see if there's any new developments."

From Tristan's side of the conversation, it was clear there had been no new developments.

Tristan sat back down, his boyish good humor gone. Talking with the sheriff's department had made the situation real.

"Mom. What happens to the business if Dad doesn't come back?"

Almira turned her palms up.

"Geoff should have signed the papers. I mean, I think he did…"

Tristan blinked.

"Mom, you left it to him? Don't you remember what happened with the life insurance?"

Mary-Alice wondered whether there was any way she might sneak out undetected. As she was one of only three people in the dining room, she realized this was probably not realistic. Instead, she helped herself to another piece of fried fish.

"That's not fair, Tristan. When the insurance thing came up it was a busy time, and I can't imagine he'd make the same mistake twice…oh, geez, who am I kidding. I'd better go check."

Almira got up and left again, this time through a different door.

"Sorry, Miz Mary-Alice. I guess you caught us at a bad time. It's not every day a person's father goes missing."

"Oh, no, I understand, dear," Mary-Alice reassured him. "I truly do. I was with your mother when she made the report to Deputy Breaux. This must be very difficult for all of you."

Almira returned, looking greenish under her platinum hair.

"The papers are still there," she said.

"What does that mean, they're still there?" Tristan's handsome jaw tightened and he stood so quickly he almost knocked his chair backward. He reached back and managed to grab it before it toppled over. "He didn't send them in? Did he at least sign them?"

"No. They're still sitting in the sign-me folder on his desk. With the signature sticky thing telling him where to sign. No, he didn't even sign them."

"Mom, don't you remember what the lawyer said? If anything happens to Dad, Danny gets everything."

"I know." Almira drifted over to the dining table and sank into her chair like a ghost. "I remember Geoff was joking about it. Sweetheart, I'm sure your father will be fine. He's a strong swimmer. He'll come back when he wants to. Mary-Alice, you haven't eaten a thing. Tristan, come sit back down. We're making our guest uncomfortable."

"Oh, not at all," Mary-Alice stammered.

Tristan pulled his chair out and sat down.

"My leave is only a week. Dad better turn up before then."

CHAPTER 8

Geoff Whitbread turned up the next morning.

Mary-Alice learned about it first from Boon St. Clair, when he came in with his crew. She heard it again from Walter when she stopped over at the General Store to pick up tea and sugar. By the time she got over to Francine's Diner, the entire dining room was abuzz with the news.

Mary-Alice glanced around Francine's dining room. At first, she saw no one she knew well. Gertie and Fortune were still paying their debt to society. Ida Belle wasn't there either. Probably off to spring the other two, Mary-Alice thought.

Then she spotted her cousin Celia by herself at a booth, talking on her phone. Before she could look away, Celia caught her eye and motioned her over.

"Mary-Alice, did you hear the latest?" Celia exclaimed as Mary-Alice eased into the booth. "Stumpy Pitre went out bass fishing last night, and you'll never guess what he caught."

Mary-Alice had already heard the story twice, but she didn't want to be a spoilsport. Fortunately, Celia didn't leave her the option.

"That woman's missing husband, that's what. Stumpy pulled

him right up out of the bayou like he was an old tire. I knew it wasn't going to end well the minute that woman showed up here yesterday looking like ten miles of bad road. I didn't say anything. But I knew."

"You were simply being tactful," Mary-Alice assured her. "The mayor has to keep morale up."

"Exactly. Now you know me, Mary-Alice, I'm not prejudiced and I treat everyone with fairness. A woman in my position can do little else. But I'm telling you, these Yankees come here and bring nothing but trouble with them, and that's a fact."

Ally came up to their booth.

"You're right, Aunt Celia. It was very inconsiderate of that man to drown in our bayou like that. Morning, Aunt Mary-Alice. What can I get you both for breakfast? We have fried catfish and eggs on special."

When Ally had taken their order and left, Celia leaned over the table.

"I could tell that woman was hiding something," she whispered. "I wouldn't be surprised if she drowned her husband herself. Not that some of them don't deserve it, mind you. But frankly, Mary-Alice, she scared me. That's why I got out of there so quick, even though she begged me to stay. I'm very sensitive to other people, and can't be around that kind of…well, I hesitate to call it evil, but you know me. Honest to a fault. I call things as I see them."

Mary-Alice did not call things as she saw them, not when doing so would cause embarrassment to someone else. Mary-Alice's recollection of the previous day was entirely different from Celia's. But she would not have said so for the world.

"So what happened after I left?" Celia continued shamelessly.

"Well, I drove Almira home." Mary-Alice chose her words carefully. She had no wish to air the bereaved family's dirty laundry. "And I met her son and her daughter-in-law."

"There are more of them?" Celia asked greedily. "What were they like?"

"I was only there for a short time, so I didn't really...why, here they are now."

Celia cranked her head around to see Tristan and Rochelle coming through the front door of Francine's Diner. They stopped at the front counter. Ally went over to greet them, glanced around the full dining room, and shook her head.

"We have room at our booth," Mary-Alice suggested.

"Do you know what, Mary-Alice? We have room at our booth. Let's not make the poor things wait."

"That's a good idea, Celia." Celia's hospitality may have had more to do with curiosity than compassion, but Mary-Alice was glad to encourage it regardless.

Mary-Alice was the only person at the table who had met everyone, so she made introductions.

"We are both so sorry for your loss," Celia simpered.

"Where is Almira?" Mary-Alice asked.

"Mom's back at the house. She wanted to be alone. She's upset. I mean, we all are."

Mary-Alice wondered whether he was keeping his wife and his mother apart on purpose. It was probably not a bad idea.

"We still can't believe it," Rochelle's nose and eyelids were pink.

"Miz Celia," Tristan asked, "are you new in town too?"

"Oh, no," Celia tittered. "I am a proud, lifelong resident of Sinful. And I also happen to be the mayor of this fine municipality."

Celia went on to enumerate Sinful's abundant virtues. Most of these, she implied (but did not state outright) were due to her leadership. At least she refrained from taking credit for Sinful's mild weather, historic churches, and picturesque cemetery.

"It is a beautiful place," Tristan agreed. "But after what happened to Dad, I don't think we'll be staying too long. Dad was really the one who was hot on moving here. Mom wants to leave, like, yesterday."

Celia shot Mary-Alice an "I told you so" glance. She then assured the couple that their departure would be regretted. Sinful, Celia declared, was a friendly town, brimming with Southern hospitality.

A more cynical observer than Mary-Alice might have seen Celia's charm offensive as a ploy to wring the latest gossip out of the bereaved couple. And perhaps enjoy the company of a handsome young man. After meeting Tristan, Celia no longer seemed worried about the ongoing invasion of Sinful by hostile forces from the North.

But Mary-Alice refused to entertain such an unworthy interpretation. That is, until Celia invited the young couple on a personal guided walking tour of Sinful's downtown.

"Miz Mary-Alice," Tristan asked, "are you coming too?"

Celia interrupted before Mary-Alice could accept the invitation.

"No, Mary-Alice is very busy with her home remodel. She bought the old Cooper place, and I reckon she bit off a little more than she could chew, isn't that right, Mary-Alice? Nothing wrong with living simply and within one's means, that's my philosophy. Well. Shall we?"

Tristan shook Mary-Alice's hand and thanked her for her help the previous night.

"It was nice to see you again, Miz Mary-Alice" Rochelle added, as she offered her own hand. The young woman's voice was hoarse, and Mary-Alice realized she had barely spoken.

Celia led the way out of Francine's Diner, and the young couple followed her. Tristan placed a protective arm around his wife as they walked the gauntlet of gawking customers. Their difference in size was striking. Tristan was well over six feet tall, broad-shouldered and well-built. Rochelle was petite, only a little taller than Mary-Alice herself.

Mary-Alice remembered Joe Arceneaux holding her like that. It was usually after he'd noticed another man looking at her or worse, trying to talk to her. At first, Mary-Alice had been flattered by her husband's possessiveness.

She reproved herself for wallowing in the past. Joe Arceneaux was long gone, and Almira's son seemed like a perfectly nice young man.

Mary-Alice took her time enjoying her tea—she might as well, she reasoned, since Celia had stuck her with the bill again. When she finally headed to the front counter to pay. Ally sped over to meet her.

"Don't worry about it, Aunt Mary-Alice. It's taken care of."

"Celia paid?"

"Aunt Celia?" Ally snorted. "Of course not. No, *he* paid for everyone. Good looking and nice manners too. Oh yeah, and married, of course."

"Ally, you're such a lovely girl. I know you'll find someone. Oh, do you suppose I can buy something sweet for my workmen?"

Ally disappeared into the kitchen and returned with a stack of three white bakery boxes.

"Something for everyone. Fudge brownies, iced blueberry squares, and oatmeal-raisin cookies with no nuts."

Mary-Alice brought the bakery boxes back to her house and set them on the dining room table. Air conditioning was in her remodeling plan, but right now the climate indoors was infernal. Mary-Alice poked her head into the kitchen and invited the men to help themselves to the treats.

Boon put down his tools and came out to the dining room. He didn't have any particular question for Mary-Alice, so he thanked her for her thoughtfulness. Then he treated her to a general update on the crew's progress since that morning.

Mary-Alice politely (and reluctantly) cut the conversation short. Contrary to what Celia had said, Mary-Alice's remodeling project did not require her to be there. As much as she enjoyed chatting with Boon, she could tell her presence distracted him and slowed things down.

She took a few minutes to freshen up, and then stepped outside and started walking. The midday humidity was less suffocating outdoors than it had been inside her house, but only slightly.

Mary-Alice had no particular destination in mind. She hoped a long walk would help her set her thoughts in order. Geoff Whitbread's death was a tragedy. But was it murder? If the mission of the Sinful Ladies' Society was to keep the affairs of Sinful running smoothly, did it include investigating crime? And Mary-Alice was only a provisional member of the SLS. Should she get involved at all, or simply mind her own business and hope things held together until Ida Belle and Gertie returned?

Mary-Alice paused in front of City Hall, site of the dustup that had gotten Gertie and Fortune banished to anger management camp. It was quiet now. On the city's new easy-rise pole, the Stars and Stripes and the pelican-in-her-piety fluttered peaceably in the sluggish breeze.

Mary-Alice pulled out her phone and punched in Ida Belle's number. On the face of it, the case seemed unremarkable. A middle-aged man had gone boating on the bayou, suffered a heart attack, and died. It was the kind of thing that happened every day.

Except the dead man was about to get a three million dollar payout.

CHAPTER 9

Ida Belle's phone clicked over to voice mail. Mary-Alice couldn't think of any message to leave, so she left none. She kept walking and punched in Gertie's number next. It went straight to voice mail too. They'd probably confiscated the phones at anger management camp. So it wasn't any use trying to call Fortune.

Mary-Alice put her phone away and headed over to Harriet's Books. She loved getting lost among the tall shelves and inhaling the aroma of scented candles and old paper. Harriet herself was a delight, always ready to chew over the latest gossip.

The first time Mary-Alice came into the store, Harriet had shared a rumor about the mayor's cousin's grandson going to prison for computer fraud. Mary-Alice had replied that the rumor was true. She herself was that very cousin. And her grandson, to her great disappointment, was indeed a guest of the state. Bonded, perhaps, by mutual mortification, Harriet and Mary-Alice had gotten on splendidly ever since.

Harriet was glad to see Mary-Alice and eagerly shared the latest Sinful news. Mary-Alice heard Harriet out and did not interrupt her. No one who says "stop me if you've already heard this" really means it, after all. The well-mannered conversationalist is obliged to act attentive at all times. Even if she has to sit through the same story four times in a single day.

"Now I'm as open-minded as the next person," Harriet concluded. "But our Yankee visitors seem to be bringing in a lot of their own bad luck lately, don't you think? I mean, that Fortune Morrow is a nice enough girl, but look at how much trouble we've had here since she's moved in."

Mary-Alice examined the display of flower-topped pens on the counter.

"Now Harriet, I don't like to be contrary, but if you recall, Fortune helped save my life. And Celia's too. The fact that those women were in Mudbug that night, and just happened to be driving right past my house when it went up? Well, I'd call that pretty good luck, wouldn't you? By the time the fire trucks got there it would have been too late."

"Oh, I'm terribly sorry, Mary-Alice. You're right. I forgot Fortune was there. I wasn't thinking."

Mary-Alice patted Harriet's hand.

"Don't worry, dear. I understand. We're all in a state over what happened to this poor man."

"I can't imagine what Stumpy is going through right now," Harriet fretted. "Think of it, going out for a nice night of bass fishing and pulling up a body. And I heard the man had a wife. How terrible for her."

"Yes, her name is Almira. She's a friend of Gertie's. And she was on the boat with her husband when it capsized."

Harriet's eyes widened.

"Oh, dear. And Celia's just sent Gertie away to anger management camp. That poor woman, losing her husband just when her only friend is out of town. I'm sorry, Mary-Alice, I know Celia's your cousin, but honestly, that woman doesn't know the difference between mayor and dictator. Although you know what they say when there's a suspicious death. It's always the spouse, isn't it? Mary-Alice, do you think the marriage was...troubled?"

"Why, I couldn't say."

Which did not mean that Mary-Alice didn't have an opinion. Mary-Alice did not like Professor Whitbread. She did not expect his wife had, either. He was thoughtless, condescending, and horribly selfish. He moved his family away from everything they knew, to help his writer's block. He neglected paperwork that would have ensured his family's financial security. He refused to wear the life vest that might have kept him alive.

But it was bad manners to kick a person when he was down, let alone when he was dead. And even the worst people had their redeeming qualities.

"Almira told me he packed a picnic lunch for them to take on their boat ride," Mary-Alice said. "And he fixed her sandwich just the way she liked it. I thought that was sweet. My Joe, rest his soul, wouldn't have done that for me, not in a million years."

Mary-Alice didn't like to visit Harriet's without buying something. She purchased a bouquet of flower pens and a blank journal.

"Are you going to start keeping a diary?" Harriet asked as she rang up Mary-Alice's purchases. "How about a gardening journal? Do you know, Sinful's in Climate Zone 28, ideal for camellias. I love camellias, don't you?"

"I do, and that's a wonderful idea, Harriet. I could write a gardening journal."

Mary-Alice had no intention of writing a gardening journal. She would use the blank book to take notes on important events. Geoff Whitbread's death, she thought, would be a worthy topic. She might call her journal "The Sinful Chronicles."

Feeling a renewed sense of purpose, Mary-Alice left Harriet's bookstore and headed down the main road toward the edge of town. She found herself turning onto the even narrower lane to the Sinful Cemetery. This was where Almira had pulled herself up onto shore after her boat capsized. Or so she'd told Deputy Breaux.

Mary-Alice pulled out her new notebook and one of her new pens, which was crowned with an enormous silk sunflower. She wrote:

Sinful cemetery at the far end of town. Looks to be in poor repair, possible flooding, one road but also boat access as bayou runs behind the treeline where the swamp begins. The ground is spongy.

Mary-Alice hesitated. Should she stick to observable facts, or include her thoughts as well? What would a real detective do? She wondered whether she should have asked Harriet for a book about how to be a detective. Had she done so, Harriet would certainly have noticed, and the news would quickly be all around Sinful. No, that would not have been wise.

Mary-Alice hit upon a solution. She would write down the facts first and then add her thoughts and opinions. She would label them so she would know which was which when she re-read her notes.

Thoughts:

I wonder whether the Sinful Cemetery will end up like the one Beulah Monroe from Crafting Circle was telling us she'd seen out in Leeville, where you could only get to it by boat. She was telling us how the water lapped around the rectangular stone tombs which stood like islands. There was an infant's one, which she said looked terribly lonely, out there in the water.

Mary-Alice wondered whether Celia had a plan for saving Sinful Cemetery. Some of the gravestones looked to be from before the War Between the States, and it would be a shame to let them get washed into the bayou. As mayor, Celia seemed to love calling meetings and digging up arcane laws to enforce, but she didn't seem to pay much attention to things like roads and water and cemeteries.

Mary-Alice was inspecting a tipped-over gravestone so worn she could barely read it when her phone buzzed in her handbag.

It was Celia calling.

"Mary-Alice, when I was showing those two young people around Sinful, we happened to walk past the old Cooper place —excuse me, I suppose I should be calling it the new Mary-Alice Arceneaux place—and your construction crew was making a terrible mess out in your carport. I wanted to give you a warning, and not issue a citation right away. Because you're family, Mary-Alice, and you're new here, I figured you simply didn't know any better."

Mary-Alice didn't roll her eyes—Mary-Alice would never roll her eyes—but she couldn't help gazing heavenward.

"Mister St. Clair already arranged the permits, Celia. And I do recall his assuring me the carport enclosure had been approved. So I don't believe I'm in violation of any of Sinful's statutes. Did you check with him?"

"Well, that's the same story he tried to give me. And it's one thing to obey the letter of the law. But the mess he was making, why it was disgraceful, and right downtown where everyone could see it."

Arguing was quite out of character for Mary-Alice, but even she had a limit.

CHAPTER 10

Mary-Alice pressed the phone to her ear with one hand. The other she placed defiantly on her hip.

"Celia dear, you can't see my house from the main road."

"Now I know what I saw—"

"If you saw anything, it wasn't from the main road. You would have had to go around the stand of cypress in the front, and then all the way down the driveway. Which winds back and forth so you can hardly see ten feet ahead of you. Don't you remember complaining about how it made you feel dizzy and closed-in? Anyway, since you did go all the way down to the house, you know the crew had all the permits they needed."

"Really, Mary-Alice, do you expect me to go walking onto an active construction site and interfering with every little detail? Just how much free time do you think I have? I have an entire city to run, you know."

Mary-Alice closed her eyes and rubbed her temple with her free hand.

"What would you like me to do, Celia?"

"Just do your part to keep Sinful the way it is. We don't need a bunch of people moving in, ignoring building codes and next thing you know it's just like Mudbug, full of slums and urban blight."

Mary-Alice refused to respond to this absurd slur on her former town. Mudbug, population 502, was scarcely the teeming hellscape Celia was making it out to be. She was probably just jealous that Mudbug had two restaurants and its own historical society.

Mary-Alice noticed mud oozing up around her sequined tennis shoes. With some hesitation, she stepped onto an old headstone. Mary-Alice was no more superstitious than the next person, but standing in the cemetery was giving her the creeps.

"By the way, Celia, are Tristan and Rochelle still with you?"

As obnoxious as Celia could be, continuing a conversation with her seemed preferable to being alone with the dead.

"I walked them home. The boy didn't want to leave his mother alone for too long. Thoughtful, don't you agree? And you'd think he'd be falling to pieces after losing his father, but he's so stoic. It's the military training. Mary-Alice, I have to say, I know some people around here don't care for Yankees, but you know me, I believe people should get the benefit of the doubt."

"Of course. That's kind of you, Celia."

Mary-Alice was not surprised. It was easy to get the benefit of Celia's doubt if you were young, charming, and male.

"And little Rochelle's nice enough. She puts me in mind of my daughter, although she's nowhere near as pretty. You remember Pansy, don't you?"

"Yes, I do, Celia. Such a lovely girl."

"She was too good for this world, Mary-Alice."

Mary-Alice remembered Pansy as a troublemaking boyfriend-stealer who grew up to be a professional escort and blackmailer. But Mary-Alice had to allow for Celia's maternal feelings.

"That mother, now, I know you stayed with her for her

interrogation with Deputy Breaux and drove her home and all. But I didn't care for her."

Mary-Alice stepped across to the next toppled headstone, and then the next. She wondered how it must have felt for Almira, escaping from a capsized boat and making it to shore, then having to hopscotch across a cemetery.

"Honestly, what a drama queen that woman is, sulking in her house like that. I mean to say, Mary-Alice, you and I both lost our husbands, and you don't see either of us carrying on like that."

"I suppose not." With one hand pressing her phone to her ear and the other extended for balance, Mary-Alice darted over the half-sunken headstones. They reminded her of rotten teeth in a decaying skull.

"What are you doing, Mary-Alice?" Celia demanded. "It sounds like you're running up a flight of stairs."

"Just out for a walk." Mary-Alice stepped onto the gravel road. The shell pieces crunched comfortingly under her muddy sneaker.

"Well, I don't trust that woman, maybe it's just my intuition. I think her daughter-in-law's afraid of her, truth be told. And the bleached-blonde hair. She looks like a mulatto Tinkerbell."

"Celia!"

"Well, she does. She's not fooling anyone with that color."

"I don't believe she's trying to fool anyone, Celia. Sometimes people simply like a color and want to wear it on their hair."

"Listen, I can't spend the whole day chatting. Some of us have responsibilities and full schedules. Now don't forget to talk to your workmen. It would be a shame to see that big remodeling job shut down just because people didn't clean up after themselves."

"Thank you for the notice, Celia. I'll have a talk with them."

By the time Mary-Alice walked back to her house, the workmen had left. She went over to Francine's Diner and bought a two boxes of Ally's fanciest brownies. It was, she felt, the least she could do for the crew after this afternoon's run-in with Celia. A rumble in her stomach reminded her she'd been out walking most of the day, and had probably burned quite a lot of calories. She bought a third box for herself.

Mary-Alice trudged down the driveway toward her house. Which was invisible from the main road, just as she had said to Celia.

Mary-Alice's problem was not unsightly construction. It was Celia's horror of being upstaged. Mary-Alice would have to humor her. A less patient person might have allowed herself to be drawn into a feud, but Mary-Alice would have no part of such a thing. She would not be one of those people who boycotted family gatherings and went to their graves holding on to some long-ago grudge.

In any event, she had bigger fish to fry. She fixed herself a plate of brownies, poured a cold glass of sweet tea, pulled out her new journal, and sat down at the dining room table.

The first page was already filled with her notes from the Sinful Cemetery. She turned it, gently pressed the journal open, and wrote:

The Case of the Disappearing English Professor

Victim: Geoff Whitbread

Victim's occupation: Professor (retired?), business owner.

Marital status: Married.

And then, a phrase she had read many times in murder mysteries:

Cui bono?

Who benefits?

1. Business Partner Danny.

Geoff had disappeared before signing the papers, Danny would get everything when the business sold. Or so Almira seemed to think.

Means: Unknown. How could he have done it?

Motive: Money

Opportunity: Where was he? Where is he now?

Almira had the opportunity. She was the last one to see him alive. How did she benefit?

2. Wife Almira.

Means: unknown. (Cause of death? Will there be autopsy?)

Motive: Jealousy? Anger? Money? (If money why hadn't Almira checked on paperwork having to do with company sale) (What about life insurance?)

Opportunity: Yes

Mary-Alice frowned and twirled the sunflower pen. Business partner. Wife. Who else?

3. Daughter in law Rochelle.

Means: Unknown (see above).

Motive: To get back at Almira? (Seems excessive).

Opportunity:

4. Son Tristan

Means: Unknown (as above)

Mary-Alice popped the last bit of brownie into her mouth and daintily wiped her fingers with a folded paper towel. Once her house was in order she would buy proper napkins.

"She doesn't care for me," Almira had said of her daughter-in-law. "She has no problem with Geoff, though. Those two get along great."

What if they had gotten along too well for Tristan's liking? Tristan had struck Mary-Alice as a little possessive.

Motive: jealousy.

Almira had been surprised to see her son. She'd been planning on his arriving the following day.

Opportunity: Showed up in Sinful earlier than expected.

Thought: Is his mother protecting him?

Thought 2: What if Almira is not telling the truth about what happened? Changes everything.

She only had Almira's word about Geoff falling off the boat and into the bayou. What if he'd been killed somewhere else?

Or what if it had happened just as Almira had said? Maybe there was no foul play involved at all, and Mary-Alice was wasting her time.

She glanced at her watch. Nine o'clock, well past her bedtime. Mary-Alice was exhausted and confused. It was time to ask for help.

She pulled out her phone and called Ida Belle's number.

To her surprise, Ida Belle picked up in the middle of the first ring.

"This better be important," Ida Belle hissed.

"I'm terribly sorry, Ida Belle, it's just, this case is so confusing. The husband disappeared in the bayou, and it turns out he never signed the papers and now his partner gets everything, and Celia said the daughter-in-law was afraid of her, and we don't even know that he really—"

"Talk to Myrtle. Sheriff's station. Probably there now. Gotta go."

"Who? Oh, Myrtle."

Myrtle Thibodeaux, night dispatcher at the sheriff's office, and member in good standing of the Sinful Ladies' Society.

Mary-Alice smiled as she placed her phone and her journal back into her bag. Ida Belle had just given her the green light.

Mary-Alice grabbed a box of brownies and stepped outside. She wasn't used to walking around Sinful at night. At least Mudbug had a few streetlights. The humming and chirruping of nocturnal creatures filled the air. This was not the time to linger. Mary-Alice sprinted up the driveway, onto the main road, past the butcher shop, toward the light over the front door of the sheriff's station.

She found Myrtle Thibodeaux seated in the spot previously occupied by the woman with the apricot beehive. Myrtle rose to greet her.

"Well if it isn't my favorite Arceneaux. And are these Ally's brownies? Goodness, Mary-Alice, are you trying to bribe me? Whatever you want, the answer is yes. Let me make us some fresh coffee."

"Well, if you're not too busy…"

"Look around, Mary-Alice. We got the place to ourselves. The usual Friday Night customers don't really start coming in till after midnight. It's early yet."

Mary-Alice waited while Myrtle brewed a fresh pot into the glass decanter. Mary-Alice was more of a tea drinker, but she liked the idea of coffee. Drinking bad coffee in the sheriff's office as the fluorescent lights hummed overhead seemed like something a real crime investigator would do.

Myrtle returned with two brimming Styrofoam cups and set them down. Mary-Alice pulled out her notebook and went over all her thoughts and observations concerning Geoff Whitbread death

When she had finished, Myrtle took a gulp of coffee and cleared her throat.

"You put a lot of thought into that, Mary-Alice. I am impressed. But I'm not entirely convinced it wasn't just bad luck."

"I suppose it could have been natural causes," Mary-Alice conceded. "But the man was about to collect three million dollars from the sale of his company."

"Well, that is an impressive number. Here's another one. Did you know Louisiana is third in the nation for rate of deaths from drowning? It's not exactly unusual."

"No. Goodness, that sounds high."

"Only Alaska and Hawaii are ahead of us. Mary-Alice, these kinds of accidents happen all the time. And according to the wife, the man wasn't even wearing his life jacket."

"But Almira told Deputy Breaux he made a funny sound and fell into the water."

"Consistent with losing his balance. Which would be pretty likely if he was intoxicated. They were drinking beer, according to the report."

Mary-Alice felt deflated.

"So you think there's nothing to investigate here?"

Myrtle helped herself to another brownie.

"Now I wouldn't say that. Not at all. I'm just saying we shouldn't let ourselves get carried away. Don't start making accusations unless we're on solid ground. Slow and steady wins the race."

A twinkle appeared in Myrtle's eye.

"Clyde Lowery found a phone washed up on the bank this afternoon, and brought it in. He was real disappointed when his only reward was a thank-you."

Mary-Alice's eyes widened.

"You think it belongs to Almira's husband?"

"I believe the vic went by 'Professor Whitbread', not 'Almira's husband'. But yes, it was definitely his. It had one of those permanent sticky labels on it."

"Of course it was probably too water-damaged to find anything useful."

"No, it was sealed up in a waterproof case. In fact, that's how Clyde found it in the first place. It was jammed up against the bank caught in a bunch of debris. He said he saw something shiny, thought it might be valuable. But it was just the plastic."

"Did you check it for text messages or phone calls?"

Myrtle glanced around, although there was no one else in the station.

"Tried. But it was password-protected."

"Where is it now?"

"Sheriff Lee said there was no point to our keeping it, as there wasn't any evidence of a crime committed. So we got in touch with the wife. Deputy Breaux ran it back to her earlier this evening."

Mary-Alice helped herself to yet another brownie, more out of anxiousness than out of hunger.

"So Almira has the phone now. I don't like to go around accusing people of killing their husbands. But couldn't you have held onto it and gotten some kind of expert to look at it?"

"Yeah, good luck getting a judge to sign off on that warrant. Listen, Mary-Alice. You seem to be on good terms with this Almira. Ida Belle and I think the best thing for you to do is observe, but quietly. If she voluntarily shows you the phone or anything else, take advantage of the opportunity."

"You talked to Ida Belle?"

"Yep. And she says to tell you, passive observation only. Don't do anything that could put you in danger. If there's any real investigating to do, best to wait until Ida Belle comes back with Gertie and Fortune."

"Wouldn't you say listening and observing is real investigating?"

"Aw, don't take it like that, Mary-Alice. All we mean to say is keep yourself safe, that's all. We like you, and we don't want to lose you."

A rough crackle echoed through the sheriff's station.

"What do you know, our first customer of the night. Sorry Mary-Alice, gotta take this one."

Myrtle lifted her headset onto her head; the conversation was over.

CHAPTER 12

The delivery company had told Mary-Alice to expect the truck to arrive sometime between seven and four. It was only seven-thirty, and Mary-Alice was already feeling restless. As excited as she should have been about her new side-by-side refrigerator, all she could think about was the dead man's phone.

Looking in on Almira was out of the question. If she wasn't there to sign for the delivery, the truck would turn right around and drive back to Lake Charles. She'd have to stay in town.

Mary-Alice headed over to the General Store, glancing back now and then lest the delivery truck appear without warning. She reached the General Store, pushed open the door, and nearly choked with astonishment.

"Well hey, there!"

Almira Galvez-Whitbread turned from the beverage display and strolled over to Mary-Alice.

"Almira, dear, how are you? What a lovely surprise."

Mary-Alice reached up and embraced the younger woman.

"Oh, Mary-Alice. It's so nice to see a friendly face. This has been absolutely…"

She lowered her voice.

"Listen. Where can you get a bottle of wine around here? I can't find any here, and I don't really want to ask. I mean, I feel like I'm already under the microscope."

Mary-Alice glanced at Almira's empty handbasket.

"You won't find wine within the city limits. Sinful is a dry town."

Almira's brow creased.

"Seriously?"

"I recommend you stock up on Sinful Ladies' Cough Syrup. Do you see the display by the counter?"

Almira lifted her head and squinted.

"Those little bottles? Why would I want...oh."

"I hear it goes well with coffee."

"Perfect. Hey, thanks."

Almira walked over and started moving bottles of Sinful Ladies' Cough Syrup from the display to the counter.

Mary-Alice completed her shopping as quickly as she could. When she was done, she found Almira waiting for her outside.

"Thanks again for the tip, Mary-Alice. Listen, can I take you to breakfast? Is there anywhere else besides that diner?"

"I'm afraid I can't go far this morning. I'm waiting for an appliance delivery. Why would you want to go someplace besides Francine's? Don't you like the food?"

"No, I mean, it's great, but isn't there someplace else? Not a Starbucks, but like an independent coffee shop?"

"Why would they need one? You can buy coffee at Francine's. I suppose if you wanted something different you could go out to Mudbug."

Almira looked down the narrow gravel road and ran her hand through her white-blonde hair.

"Is Mudbug walking distance?"

"No. It's an hour's drive. Almira, why don't you join me for a glass of tea on my porch? I have to apologize for not having a proper kitchen, but if I do get my appliances today, it shouldn't be long."

"Know what? A glass of tea on the porch sounds great. I'd love that."

As they walked back to the old Cooper place, Mary-Alice started to have second thoughts. She didn't have the stomach for this cloak-and-dagger stuff, she thought. How on earth could she ask a possible murderer about her dead husband's phone?

But for Mary-Alice, curiosity was a stronger motivator than fear.

"I heard they found your husband's phone," Mary-Alice said as they sat down on the back porch. It was a humid, overcast day. The buzzing and splashing sounds of the bayou mingled with the jackhammering noises from the kitchen.

"They did." Almira seemed neither offended nor surprised. She reached into her shopping bag, pulled out a bottle of Sinful Ladies' Cough Syrup, unscrewed the top, and emptied half of it into her tea. She sipped the tea, coughed, recovered, and then took another sip.

"Are you all right, dear?" Mary-Alice asked.

Almira closed her eyes and sighed.

"Whoever the Sinful Ladies are, they have my everlasting gratitude. And these little bottles are so pretty."

Then, to Mary-Alice's surprise, Almira produced a shiny, clear plastic case containing a black phone. She slid down the zipper and shook the phone onto the table.

"Here it is. Someone found it and turned it in to the sheriff. I've been carrying it around in my purse. I don't know why. It just adds extra weight."

Mary-Alice lowered her glass of iced tea onto the crate table between the two chairs.

"Is there a password?" Mary-Alice asked.

"Yeah, but I know it."

Almira tapped on the screen and then handed the phone to Mary-Alice.

"This is the messaging app. There's a few texts with me, and a couple with Danny. His business partner."

"I'm so sorry, Almira. This must be very difficult."

Mary-Alice wondered whether the phone would contain any helpful clues. She knew wasn't going to find a signed text message saying, "Dear Geoff, I am coming to drown you in the bayou."

"I'll tell you what's difficult." Almira drained her glass of tea and refilled it from the pitcher "I feel like I'm losing my mind. Where are all messages to Rochelle?"

"Your daughter-in-law?"

"I know for a fact those two were texting each other all the time, but there's nothing. Not a single message. Either to or from."

"Maybe they weren't really—"

"And don't tell me he had another phone. I saw him. He used this one. He didn't even try to hide it. He told me I was the one who was being unreasonable."

Almira picked up the phone and drew her arm back as if to toss it into the bayou. Mary-Alice grabbed Almira's wrist.

"Almira, please. Clyde Lowery took the time to turn it in to the sheriff when he could've just kept it for himself, and then they went to the trouble to return it to you."

"I guess it wouldn't be good Southern manners, would it?" Almira scoffed.

"Oh dear." Mary-Alice released her grip. "I suppose manhandling one's guests isn't terribly good manners either. Please accept my apologies."

That made Almira laugh. Which made Mary-Alice blush.

Almira clapped Mary-Alice's shoulder and stood.

"Listen, I think I hear your truck pulling up. That's my cue to get going." She zipped the phone back into its case and tucked it into her purse.

"If you don't mind waiting, I can drive you home after they've unloaded the appliances."

Almira shook her head.

"Nice of you to offer, but I could use the walk."

Mary-Alice saw Almira off at the front door and then went to greet the deliverymen. It was only then she realized her heart was pounding.

CHAPTER 13

Early Sunday morning, Mary-Alice was jolted awake by her phone ringing.

"Mary-Alice, are you up? This is Myrtle"

"Myrtle?"

Mary-Alice sat up and rubbed her eyes.

"Myrtle Thibodeaux. From the sheriff's station."

"Of course I'm awake, Myrtle. Otherwise I wouldn't be talking with you. Why are you at the sheriff's station?"

"I'm working. Sorry, I know it's a little early, but I thought you'd want to know—"

"You're working on the Sabbath?"

"It's the sheriff's office," Myrtle laughed. "Do you think criminals observe the Sabbath?"

"Well, if they don't, they certainly should."

"Listen, I got something for you. The business partner. Danny."

Mary-Alice was wide-awake now.

"You looked into Almira's husband's business partner?"

"You didn't think we just brushed off your concerns, did you, Mary-Alice?"

"Well, actually, it did seem a little like—"

"His name's Daniel Chan. And he's squeaky clean."

"But now Almira's husband is dead, he gets everything from the sale of their company. Doesn't he?"

"Well, for one thing, he's been over in California for the past two weeks, meeting with investors. No way he could've made it out here himself to drown his business partner."

"He could he have paid someone to do it for him, though. Couldn't he have?" Mary-Alice got out of bed, switched on the light, and went to her closet to find something to wear to Mass. She wasn't going to get back to sleep anytime soon.

"See, that's the thing. We found an email from him to his lawyer—"

"You saw his email? Myrtle, you can do that?"

"Forget what I just said. Let me rephrase. When Danny learned about Geoff's death, he did the right thing. I forget what the exact legal verbiage is, but he's told his lawyer to split the proceeds from the company sale with the victim's survivors. Just as if Whitbread had signed the papers."

"So the business partner has no motive. Not a money motive, anyway."

"Exactly. Now, he might have been having an affair with the wife."

"Myrtle!"

"Hey, it happens. Anyway, I thought you'd like to know we checked it out. I think what we have here is a tragedy, not a crime."

"Thank you, Myrtle. I appreciate your following up."

Mary-Alice arrived at Mass just as it was starting, and slipped into a pew in the back. The pew's only other occupant was a dapper man in a tailored gray suit. He flashed Mary-Alice a friendly grin. Mary-Alice smiled back and sat down. Her cheeks felt warm; she hoped the man couldn't see her blushing. Who was he? And why did he look familiar?

Mary-Alice followed the order of worship from muscle memory. She stood, sat, kneeled, and sang as appropriate, occasionally stealing sidelong glances at the man in the suit. Celia was in front next to the side exit, ready to sprint as soon as Father Michael said the last "Amen." Mary-Alice was not up to participating in today's banana-pudding race. It seemed irreverent in light of the recent tragedy. Mary-Alice had never enjoyed competition. Losing was no fun, and winning made her feel guilty.

Also, she thought she might like to stick around and say hello to the man in the suit. Something about him appealed to her, although she couldn't say what it was.

When the service was over, the man in the gray suit stood and approached her.

"Miz Mary-Alice." He flashed a grin, and Mary-Alice recognized him. It was Boon St. Clair, the construction boss in charge of her kitchen remodel. My, he looked nice in a suit.

"Mister St. Clair." Mary-Alice beamed and clasped his hand. "How lovely to see you. I didn't know you worshiped here."

"You've probably never seen me because I sit in the back. I've seen you ladies running out the door the second Mass is over."

"Oh, dear, I didn't think anyone noticed."

"Is Francine's banana pudding really that good? I don't believe I've ever had the opportunity to try it. Someone else always seems to get to it first."

Mary-Alice glanced at the vacant front pew. Celia and her posse had already raced out the door in hopes of getting to Francine's before their Baptist rivals. Most of the other parishioners had followed them outside to cheer them on.

"The banana pudding is tasty. But I didn't have the heart for it today."

"Miz Mary-Alice, would me the great honor of joining me for breakfast? I can't guarantee banana pudding, but I imagine Francine's has something reasonably tasty."

Ally seated Mary-Alice and Boon at a quiet table near the back, far from Celia and her glum crew. (The Baptist ladies had gotten there first and ordered all the banana pudding). Boon got biscuits with sausage gravy. Mary-Alice, hoping for something on the lighter side, ordered a tuna-and-tomato salad, which turned out to be massive. Nothing on Francine's menu, Mary-Alice realized, was on the "lighter side."

As they tucked in, Boon asked Mary-Alice how she liked Sinful. Mary-Alice said she liked it very much, and intended to stay indefinitely. Which Boon might have already guessed, she added, from the scale of her remodeling project.

"So you're not one of those house-flippers, like on TV?" he asked, with a wink.

"Heavens, no. Sinful is lovely. At first I was afraid it would be a little dull, but it's every bit as exciting as Mudbug. In fact, more so."

"Oh, you can say that again." Boon set down his coffee cup and assumed a confidential tone. "You might not know this, but we've had some strange goings-on this summer. Including a couple mysterious deaths."

"You don't say."

"There's that new family in town, the White Breads? Well, they were only here maybe a week, and they lost the father in the bayou."

"Yes, I know. I was just talking to the poor man's wife yesterday. She's quite distraught."

Mary-Alice had decided this was the explanation for Almira's delusional rant about nonexistent text messages. And her attempt to chuck her dead husband's phone into the bayou. Grief can make people do strange things, Mary-Alice knew.

"Well, I imagine she's even more distraught now. Did you know they found a dead raccoon on their property yesterday?"

"Oh, dear. How did you hear about it?"

"Ran into Cornelius's boys yesterday out at the dump. They were the ones went out to clear it."

"Oh, poor Almira. It must have happened after I spoke to her yesterday. Do you think someone left it as a warning? Or a threat?"

Boon shook his head.

"Nah. Looked like it'd gotten into some rat poison. I mean, I won't go into detail, Miz Mary-Alice, specially not over a nice meal, but there's ways to tell, know what I mean? Unlucky critter just happened to expire in those poor folks' backyard. "

Mary-Alice set her fork down slowly.

"Did you say poison? Where is the poor creature now?"

Boon, chuckled, apparently moved by Mary-Alice's tender-heartedness.

"Well, I reckon it's still at the dump. Don't suppose it got up and walked away. Mary-Alice, what do you say to a peach cobbler with ice cream? Got some room for dessert?"

Mary-Alice nodded, but her mind was already elsewhere.

CHAPTER 14

As soon as it was polite to do so, Mary-Alice took her leave of Boon. He was good company, but she had more urgent matters on her mind. She'd see him Monday morning in any event.

She hurried home and called Myrtle Thibodeaux. Myrtle's shift at the sheriff's office was over, so there was no point in going there.

Myrtle wasn't picking up. She was probably asleep. Mary-Alice tried Ida Belle, and then Gertie. Both went straight to voice mail. She might even have called Fortune, had she known her number. She had so many ideas bouncing around inside her head. It would have been nice to talk it all through with some-one. She'd have to do her best by herself.

She pulled out her journal and her sunflower pen, sat down at the dining room table, and began to write.

A dead raccoon found in Almira's yard. Poisoned. Maybe husband was killed by poison?

Autopsy?

Were they going to perform an autopsy? Had they done one already? Even if they had, Mary-Alice had it on good authority (a murder mystery she'd read recently) that they didn't screen for everything.

She couldn't barge into the sheriff's office and demand Geoff Whitbread's remains be tested for exotic poisons. But she could call in an anonymous tip.

"Sinful sheriff's office," said the voice on the phone.

"Uh, good afternoon. I'm an... unidentified citizen. I'd like to report a possible crime of poisoning."

"Mary-Alice Arceneaux, is that you?"

"Oh dear, I..."

"Why, I recognized your voice. It's Tilly. You got something on that Yankee family, hon? I was a little worried about you when you offered to drive that woman home. Thought we might never see you again. She was a strange one, wasn't she? Of course, you can't expect someone to be at her best at a time like that, can you?"

"Oh, Tilly, yes, what a nice surprise." Mary-Alice had been struggling to recall the name of the apricot-haired woman. "It's just a hunch, nothing more, but I was wondering if there was going to be an autopsy of the man who passed on? Can they check for...uh, poisons?"

The line went quiet for a moment, and Mary-Alice was afraid Tilly would laugh at her. She didn't.

"Oh, Mary-Alice, that ship has sailed, I'm sorry to say. His family's already claimed the body. Not this family. His parents. They brought the remains back to Connecticut for cremation."

"Oh, dear. Here's the thing. You see, I was just having lunch at Francine's with Boon St. Clair—"

"I know, I heard. Sinful's most eligible widower. You go, girl! Don't let Ida Belle know, though, she'll kick you right out of the Sinful Ladies' Society. So you think the vic was poisoned?"

"I believe it's possible. May I tell you what I know?"

Mary-Alice wasn't going to be one of those people who coyly kept their suspicions under wraps until they were 100%

certain. People who did that in murder mysteries invariably got killed before they could reveal the truth.

"Certainly. You go right ahead."

"Boon told me the family found a dead raccoon in their backyard."

Mary-Alice pressed her phone to her ear and began pacing back and forth in the dining room.

"Oh, I know. They called it in to the sheriff. Those folks are not ready for country living if you ask me."

"Well, Boon said he thought the raccoon had been poisoned. What if it ate something it found around their house? What if his sandwich had poison in it? And the raccoon found the leftovers?"

"But Mary-Alice, I remember. He was the one who made the sandwiches. Remember? He liked his tuna salad without jalapeno peppers and she liked them with. Or the other way around, I can't recall. But you could tell them apart, that's the point. Are you saying he poisoned himself? Set his family up with life insurance money or something?"

Mary-Alice shook her head.

"No, it doesn't seem likely. Maybe it wasn't the sandwiches, then. The beer? Maybe something slow-acting that wasn't even with them on the boat? Then the raccoon found whatever it was, ate or drank it, and died."

"Or maybe the wife was lying," Tilly said. "We only have her word for it that he packed the lunch. Mary-Alice, let us take it from here. You lay off snooping for a while."

"Lay off? Why?"

"Because if the murderer finds out you know she killed her husband, you're gonna be next."

Mary-Alice had been so excited by her insight, it hadn't occurred to her she might be in danger herself. It was also pretty clear who Tilly thought the murderer was.

"What should I do?"

"I'd say just lay low and pretend you don't know anything. It's one good thing about being a lady of a certain age. People aren't inclined to be wary of us. We're just harmless busybodies."

Mary-Alice sank into a chair.

"Harmless Busybody. I believe I can manage that. Oh, someone's at the door."

"I bet it's Boon St. Clair," Tilly giggled. "Now take your time answering. You don't want to seem too eager. Men like it when you're a little hard to get."

Mary-Alice plugged her phone into the wall charger so it wouldn't run out of battery. She closed her journal and dropped it back into her purse. Then she smoothed her hair, sucked her teeth to make sure there weren't any unsightly specks, and made her way to the front door.

But it wasn't Boon calling on her. It was Almira.

CHAPTER 15

"Almira!" Mary-Alice exclaimed. "Did you walk all the way into town?"

"Yep. Can I come in?"

"Know what?" Mary-Alice said briskly. "My kitchen's still in pieces, and I was just going to pop over to Francine's for a cup of coffee and a piece of pie. Won't you join me? My treat."

Almira plopped down on the porch swing.

"I'm sorry to just show up without calling. I guess with Gertie still on the inside, you're the only friend I have in town. Sure. I'll come to Francine's with you. Don't you need to bring your purse or something?"

"Oh look at me, so forgetful. Hang on, I won't be a minute."

Mary-Alice rushed back into the house and grabbed her bag, and the women started up the driveway toward the main road.

"Almira, are you quite all right?"

"Tristan and Rochelle are having a huge fight. I had to get out of there."

"I'm terribly sorry. It's been such a difficult time for everyone."

If Ally was surprised to see Mary-Alice at Francine's again, she didn't show it.

"Afternoon Aunt Mary-Alice, Miz Almira. Will anyone else be joining you, or just you two?"

"Just us, Ally dear."

Mary-Alice slid into one side of the small booth, and Almira plumped down on the other side.

"It's just been nonstop." Almira pulled her hands through her hair. "First this thing with Geoff. Then Rochelle finds a dead raccoon in our backyard and it freaks her out so badly, my son has to call 9-1-1. And now? Turns out I was right all along about the text messages."

"You were?" Mary-Alice glanced around the crowded restaurant. She hoped Almira wasn't going to start hallucinating about text messages again. That would be embarrassing.

"Yeah, that's why my son's having a blowout with his wife. He found messages on her phone. Between her and Geoff."

"But you told me you didn't see any messages on his phone."

"He must've deleted them. Like the experienced philanderer he was. He knew how to cover his tracks. Poor little Rochelle, she was a noob."

"Oh. He deleted the text messages." Mary-Alice was annoyed with herself for not having thought of this simple explanation. But then, neither had Almira. "What did the messages say? If you don't mind my asking, that is."

"No idea. My darling daughter-in-law pulled out a meat tenderizer and smashed the phone to splinters. Whatever was on there had to be pretty bad, though. Tristan…I don't think I've ever seen Tristan so angry. If Geoff wasn't already dead, I honestly think Tristan would—"

Ally appeared at their booth with her pad and pen at the ready. Almira was resting her face in her hands, so Mary-Alice ordered for both of them.

"One coffee, one sweet tea, and two peach cobblers, please."

Ally nodded, shot a concerned glance at the top of Almira's bleached-blonde head, and hurried away.

"But you already knew," Mary-Alice said gently. "About your husband and your daughter-in-law."

Almira nodded, still covering her face. Mary-Alice moved the napkin dispenser over to where Almira could reach it. Almira pulled out a napkin and blew her nose.

"I'm so sorry, dear."

"I have to let it go. He's gone. It's over. I mean he's dead, how much more over could it be? Oh yeah, speaking of that, Mary-Alice, do you know where I can donate this? It was stupid of me to try to throw it into the water. It's a perfectly good phone. Someone might get some use out of it."

Almira placed the phone on the table.

"As a matter of fact, yes. There's a woman in my crafting circle back in Mudbug who collects old phones for the women's shelter. I'll be visiting next week and I'll bring it to her if you like."

"If you don't mind?"

"Not at all, dear. Oh look, here's our peach cobbler."

Mary-Alice really did intend to donate Geoff Whitbread's phone. And she would.

But first, she had to recover the missing text messages. Geoff Whitbread had deleted his text messages to hide his affair. Perhaps he was hiding something else, too.

Mary-Alice set up her laptop on the dining room table. Geoff's phone, she noticed, used the same connector as her own. She plugged it in with her cable.

Mary-Alice's computer class had not taught her how to retrieve deleted text messages, specifically. But she had learned how generous people could be with information. If you didn't know the answer to something, you could almost certainly find it online.

Mary-Alice couldn't understand people like Celia, who

pined for the "good old days." She loved living in a world where you could type the words "retrieve deleted text messages" and have your answer appear like magic. Mary-Alice quickly found a downloadable program that suited her purpose, and got to work.

Mary-Alice's second call was to the sheriff's office. The first was to Almira.

CHAPTER 16

Geoff Whitbread wasn't supposed to die.

The recovered text messages confirmed what Almira already knew. Geoff Whitbread was having an affair with his daughter-in-law. They also contained something else: a murder plot.

Geoff wanted Rochelle. But he didn't want to divorce Almira. Divorce would mean splitting his three million dollar payout with her. So he came up with the idea of an "accidental" death.

Rochelle executed the details. She was the one who packed the picnic lunch that Geoff would take out on the boating trip. Geoff liked his tuna salad with jalapeno peppers, and Almira preferred hers without. Keeping the poisoned sandwich separate from the harmless one should have been easy.

Except Rochelle wasn't a good listener. And maybe she was a little prone to stereotyping. Somehow, she got it in her head that it was her Latina mother-in-law who liked jalapenos in her tuna.

So Rochelle mixed rat poison with the jalapeno tuna, used enough of the mixture to make the death sandwich, and threw away the rest.

When Almira came home with Mary-Alice, Rochelle would have already known something was wrong. She must have realized her mistake when Almira mentioned she couldn't tolerate spicy food. This was why Rochelle had become so upset. She knew then she'd poisoned her lover.

And she might have gotten away with it, had it not been for an unlucky raccoon and a curious busybody.

Mary-Alice related the whole story to Gertie, Ida Belle, and Fortune over a welcome-back lunch at Francine's.

"I should have figured it out sooner," Mary-Alice said. "I was married to a selfish man. Joe Arceneaux would never have made a picnic lunch in his life. And neither did Geoff Whitbread."

"Well, you did some good work," Ida Belle reached over and clapped Mary-Alice on the shoulder.

"Agreed," Gertie beamed. "Almira's cleared, and that terrible daughter-in-law's headed to prison. Mary-Alice, I'd say you have the makings of a real Sinful Lady."

"I love working with the Sinful Ladies' Society," Mary-Alice said shyly. "But I might want to stay an affiliate member for now. I'm not sure I qualify for full membership."

"What are you talking about?" Ida Belle objected. "You meet the age limit, you've been a widow for ten years—"

"In fact, I hate to hurry off, but I have an appointment this afternoon down in Lake Charles."

"An appointment?" Ida Belle demanded. "What on earth is in Lake Charles?"

"The last day of the home remodeling show. Ah, Boon, here you are."

Boon St. Clair, dressed in his dapper Sunday suit, greeted Ida Belle and Gertie, and then leaned over the booth to offer his arm to Mary-Alice.

Gertie, Ida Belle, and Fortune watched the couple exit Francine's, still arm-in-arm.

"You wouldn't consider—" Gertie began.

"Absolutely not. You know as well as I do what the presence of men does to a woman's rational thinking processes. Just look at how Fortune is around Carter LeBlanc. Her brain turns to mush. She's obsessed."

"Hey, I'm right here. And I am not obsessed."

"I do see your point, Ida Belle." Gertie stole a sly glance at Fortune. "When we were at anger-management camp, Fortune kept yelling out Carter's name in her sleep. I almost requested a transfer to another barracks."

"Gertie, that is a lie."

"Still, Mary-Alice didn't do too badly on this case, did she? In fact, I believe this calls for a toast. Hand over your coffee cups, ladies." Gertie reached into her bag and pulled out a bottle of Sinful Ladies' Cough Syrup.

THE VANISHING VICTIM

CHAPTER 1

Mary-Alice Arceneaux picked at her strawberry waffle and stared out the window of Francine's Diner. There was nothing wrong with Francine's strawberry waffle. It was crisp and fluffy, soaked with sweet strawberry syrup and crowned with real cream, whisked with vanilla and a sprinkling of powdered sugar. But Mary-Alice's mind wasn't on breakfast. She was thinking about Boon St. Clair.

Mary-Alice liked Boon a lot. But the handsome widower happened to be working for Mary-Alice, supervising her kitchen remodel. Getting involved with a hired man--well, it simply wasn't done. Worse, ever since Boon had begun to call on Mary-Alice, he hadn't charged her for any work. They had never discussed it; the bills simply stopped coming. Mary-Alice believed Boon's intentions were good (Mary-Alice generally believed the best of everyone). But accepting the free work put her in an awkward situation. Not only was she was in Boon's debt, but if something went wrong, she couldn't complain. Not that the work had been anything but impeccable so far, but what if a problem did come up?

Neither could Mary-Alice imagine confronting Boon to

insist on paying. That would be throwing his gift back in his face. She would rather die.

"More tea, Aunt Mary-Alice?" Mary-Alice hadn't heard Ally approach her table. The young waitress stood over her holding a sweating pitcher of iced tea. "Can I box up that waffle for you?"

"No thank you, darling. I'm just taking my time. Enjoying a nice, leisurely breakfast."

I can't possibly tell anyone back in Mudbug about Boon, she thought. They wouldn't understand. I hardly understand it myself.

Mary-Alice gazed out the window, across the white, crushed-shell road off toward the General Store. Had she possessed x-ray vision, she could have seen her own house farther down, through the trees. The old Cooper Place was at the end of a long drive, its back porch jutting out over the bayou. Boon and his crew were there now, scraping up yellowed linoleum and pulling down termite-eaten cupboards.

Mary-Alice loved her new home in the heart of Sinful, steps from Francine's Diner.

I should be looking forward to getting my new kitchen, Mary-Alice thought. But here I am, so vexed that I can scarcely stomach Francine's strawberry waffle. Ida Belle would scold me for letting myself get muddle-headed about a man, and she would be right. But Gertie? Now I believe Gertie might understand.

Mary-Alice took out her phone and dialed Gertie Hebert's number. Keep your voice down, she reminded herself. People that shouted into their phones in restaurants reminded her of old Marceau Mirande, who paced the streets of Mudbug yelling out orders to his banker. The only difference was that poor Mister Mirande didn't have a phone.

Just as Gertie picked up, a crash reverberated from the kitchen.

"Mary-Alice?" Gertie called out. "Is this you? Are you okay? What's going on?"

"I'm fine," Mary-Alice whispered. The dining room had gone quiet. "I'm at Francine's."

A large, disheveled man stumbled out into the dining room. Mary-Alice thought he might be in his fifties, and judged he might once have been handsome. Right behind him was Francine, red-faced and brandishing a long wooden spoon. Mary-Alice had never seen Francine so angry.

"Victorin Lowery," Francine hissed, "so help me, if you made my soufflés collapse you are a dead man."

"But Francine, honey," he slurred, "I was just looking for a li'l drink, that's all—"

"A *dead* man, Victorin. *Feet pue tan!*"

Francine shook the spoon and glared as the man staggered out toward the front door. A wave of boozy body odor assailed Mary-Alice as he lurched past her table.

"*Cooyon!*" Francine muttered as the glass door swung shut. Then she turned and strode back into the kitchen.

"Mary-Alice. Mary-Alice! What happened?"

As the hum of conversation resumed, Mary-Alice told Gertie about Francine's intruder.

"Who was he?" Gertie asked.

"Victor, I believe his name was? The poor man was in just awful shape, I can tell you that. He absolutely reeked of liquor."

"I believe you've just seen Victorin Lowery," Gertie said.

"Do you know him?"

"He's our town drunk. One of 'em, anyway. It's strange that he's decided to bother Francine. What's he hoping to find in a diner in the middle of a dry town?"

"Well, there's cooking sherry," Mary-Alice said. "When he went past I saw he was holding a bottle, hidden halfway up the sleeve of his jacket. Francine was behind him, so she couldn't see. I didn't believe it would have been right for me to get involved, so I didn't say anything at the time."

"Well, that's a step up for him. Walter had to ban him from the General Store. He was shoplifting bottles of Sinful Ladies Cough Syrup. After Walter locked those away, Victorin started stealing mouthwash."

"What a terrible thing to be a slave to drink. Oh, Gertie, I remember what I was calling about now. I wanted your opinion on a personal matter. If it's not too much trouble, of course."

"Sounds like it's something we should sit down over. I'm at Fortune's. Come on over."

Mary-Alice pulled up to Fortune Morrow's dark blue Victorian house, the one that had belonged to Fortune's late Aunt Marge. Mary-Alice knew Marge Boudreaux by reputation. She had been a founding member of the Sinful Ladies' Society. People spoke of Marge as being "ahead of her time," which was more polite than coming right out and calling her crazy.

Fortune herself was a little "ahead of her time," Mary-Alice mused as she climbed the porch steps. Fortune was a former beauty queen, who could act a perfect lady one minute, and cuss like a soldier the next. She worked as a children's librarian and was still unmarried at 28. But Fortune had a good heart, and that, Mary-Alice believed, was what mattered.

And to be fair, Fortune was a Yankee, which probably explained everything.

Gertie answered the door.

"Is that what I think it is?" Gertie cast a greedy look at the pink bakery box Mary-Alice was holding. "Come on in, and let's get that box open."

"Is Fortune here?" Mary-Alice asked as she followed Gertie into the house.

"She had to take a call. It might be a while." Gertie set the box on the kitchen table and opened it. "Francine's blueberry cheesecake squares. These are just my favorite. I'll get some plates. Oh, Mary-Alice, honey, your blouse!"

Mary-Alice looked down to see a purple smear of blueberry topping on her flowered shirt.

"Oh, mercy. Do you think Fortune has any club soda to hand?"

"Marge used to keep her cleaning supplies in the closet at the end of the hall. You might find some stain remover there."

Mary-Alice went down the hallway in her usual quiet way. As she passed a closed door, she heard Fortune's voice. Mary-Alice didn't mean to eavesdrop, but she couldn't help but hear.

"Well, of course I hated it at first," Fortune was saying. "I mean, a whole summer in Stinkhole, Louisiana with a bunch of —no, I wasn't going to say that. Look, Harrison, I was wrong, okay? I'll admit it."

Mary-Alice wondered what Fortune was talking about. She had lived in the state all her life, and had never heard of a town called Stinkhole. Mary-Alice opened the closet at the end of the hallway. Amidst bleach bottles and tins of brass polish, Mary-Alice found a package of stain wipes. She pulled one out and headed back to the kitchen, scrubbing at the stain.

"I've made real friends here, Harrison," Mary-Alice heard as she passed the closed door again. "Yeah, I just met an Arceneaux who's not pure evil, believe it or not. Name's Mary-Alice. I don't know, some kind of distant cousin. No, she doesn't know."

Mary-Alice hurried back to the kitchen before she could hear any more. She felt embarrassed at her eavesdropping, but at the same time, curiously exhilarated. Fortune Morrow was talking about her! Mary-Alice wondered what Fortune had meant by "not pure evil" and decided it must be some kind of Yankee compliment.

Mary-Alice and Gertie had just finished setting up the kitchen table when Fortune came in.

"Hey, Mary-Alice, nice to see you." Fortune shot Gertie a

quizzical look. Apparently, Gertie had invited Mary-Alice over without telling Fortune. "Are those blueberry cheesecake squares? Awesome. Don't mind if I do."

Fortune popped an entire square into her mouth and then licked her fingers. Mary-Alice thought this oddly un-beauty-queen-like.

"So what's up? Did you just stop by to fatten me up?"

"Well, as a matter of fact, I was hoping to ask your advice about a delicate matter--" Mary-Alice began. A hammering on the front door cut her short. Fortune sprang up and opened the door.

Ida Belle stood in the doorway clutching her shoulder. Her white hair was in large plastic rollers. Under her hand, a red stain spread on her yellow t-shirt.

CHAPTER 2

Mary-Alice went for her handbag and pulled her mobile phone out.

"My heavens! I'm calling 9-1-1."

"No," Ida Belle cried. "No phone calls. Gertie, fetch me some disinfectant and a butterfly bandage. I'll be fine."

Gertie laid a first-aid kit on the coffee table as Ida Belle sank into a chair. Mary-Alice noticed that the kit appeared to be well-used. Bandage boxes and rolls of gauze had been opened, the iodine was nearly gone, and the tube of antibiotic ointment was all squeezed out. Mary-Alice wondered why the first-aid kit contained a bottle of Sinful Ladies' Cough Syrup.

"Ida Belle's tougher than she looks." Gertie took out the cough syrup, unscrewed the top, and poured it over Ida Belle's shoulder. Ida Belle closed her eyes and went a little pale. "Ida Belle, you remember that to-do we had in Muang Khua? Mary-Alice, Fortune, you should've seen her. Stitched herself right up. No painkillers or anything."

"Where?" Mary-Alice asked.

"A nightclub," Ida Belle muttered through clenched teeth.

"Nightclub," Gertie agreed. She took out a pair of tweezers

149

and began peeling the bloody shreds of fabric away from the wound.

"Ida Belle, you should see a doctor." Fortune plopped down on the side of the couch closest to Ida Belle's chair. Gertie hovered behind Ida Belle, tending to her shoulder like a white-haired ministering angel.

"No doctor," Ida Belle whispered, and then perked up. "Say, do I smell blueberry cheesecake squares?"

"Hold still, Ida Belle," Gertie scolded.

Fortune disappeared into the kitchen and returned with the blueberry squares.

"Why ever don't you want to see a doctor, Ida Belle?" Mary-Alice asked.

"Just killed a man. If you're going to be nosy about it."

"Fine, I'll play along," Fortune leaned forward. "Who'd you kill, Ida Belle?"

"*Whom* did you kill," Gertie corrected Fortune as she fussed with Ida Belle's shoulder.

Ida Belle opened her eyes. "I need something to drink."

Mary-Alice stood up to get Ida Belle a glass of water, but Ida Belle used her good arm to grab the cough syrup. She took three solid chugs and handed the empty bottle back to Gertie. Mary-Alice sat back down.

Ida Belle wiped her mouth on the sleeve of her good arm and began.

"Well, I was in my garage working on my bike, just minding my own business. I had the door open, of course, and I heard a noise. When I looked up, who do you suppose it was? It was that drunk Lowery, and he was poking around our cough syrup."

"How did he know that was our cough syrup?" Gertie cried. "Those boxes were supposed to be labeled Quilting Supplies."

"When you say 'that drunk Lowery,' do you mean Victorin Lowery?" Mary-Alice asked.

Ida-Belle gave her a sharp look.

"That's him."

"He caused quite a fuss at Francine's this morning," Mary-Alice said. "Francine chased him right out of the kitchen with a wooden spoon in her hand."

"It's true," Gertie confirmed. "I heard the whole thing this morning when I was on the phone with Mary-Alice."

"Why, Ida Belle, after Francine ran him off, he must've decided to try your place next," Mary-Alice said.

"Bad move on his part."

"Anyway," Ida Belle continued, "I grabbed my shotgun. Just to scare him off, you understand. But instead of clearing out, he came right at me. Well, I tried to aim for somewhere below his knees, but just as I squeezed the trigger he dropped down on his haunches and it seems he got a shot in before he died. My, those blueberry squares do look good. Gertie, would you mind passing me just a taste?"

Gertie grabbed a blueberry square and stuffed it in Ida Belle's mouth.

"And you just left him there?" Gertie dabbed at Ida Belle's shoulder, making her wince. "Did you remember to close your garage door, at least? So people don't walk by and see a dead body lying there?"

Ida Belle said something through her mouthful of blueberry cheesecake square, which Mary-Alice didn't understand.

"Ida Belle, you're hurt," Mary-Alice said. "At least we should fetch you a doctor."

"You didn't do anything wrong," Fortune added. "It was self-defense. You have nothing to worry about."

"I don't want anyone poking around my garage. And no offense, Mary-Alice, I know she's your cousin and all, but I cannot put my trust in our local justice system what with Celia in charge. That woman reminds me of Pol Pot, only with less compassion."

"Well, you have to do something, Ida Belle," Gertie said. "Or you're going to have a big, smelly problem on your hands."

"We need to call the sheriff," Mary-Alice insisted. "Whenever people have a chance to call the police and then they decide not to, things end up very badly for them."

"Another insight from your mystery novels?" Ida Belle snapped.

Mary-Alice's rouged cheeks flushed even pinker than usual; Ida Belle was right. Just about everything Mary-Alice knew about crime and the justice system came from the books she had read.

"Ida Belle!" Gertie scolded. "That was uncalled-for. Mary-Alice is only trying to help."

"Well, I'm sorry, Mary-Alice. I'm just not having the best day right now, as you may have noticed."

"You have to admit, Mary-Alice has a point," Gertie said. "If you shoot someone and you don't report it, it makes you look guilty. Like you have something to hide."

Ida Belle widened her eyes at Gertie.

"Something to hide? You mean like boxes of moonshine disguised as quilting supplies stacked in my garage? In the middle of a dry town? Whose mayor has hated me since high school?"

"Since elementary school, actually," Gertie said.

"How's the shoulder?" Fortune asked.

Gertie stepped aside, giving Mary-Alice a clear view of the wet, red patch blooming on the neat square of gauze. Mary-Alice felt lightheaded and quickly looked down at her folded hands.

"Never better," Ida Belle said. "I'll just rest here a while and then I'll be on my way."

Gertie placed her hands on her hips.

"Is that so? You're fixin' to walk on out of here with a bloody piece of gauze stuck to your shoulder and no shirt on?"

"Take anything you want from my closet," Fortune said.

"Don't get me anything pink," Ida Belle hollered after Gertie. Then to Fortune:

"I'll stay here 'til dark. Then we can load up some cleaning supplies in your Jeep, and you three can drive me home and help me clean up. We can weight the body and dump it in the bayou. I only got one good arm, so I can't lift anything, but I can supervise."

"I have a better idea," Fortune said. "We can...Wow. I forgot I had that."

"I said I didn't want anything pink!" Ida Belle complained, as Gertie popped a hot-pink flowered poncho over her head.

"It's perfect. It keeps you covered and you don't have to move your arms." Gertie pinned Ida Belle's hair rollers back into place. "What's the plan now?"

"How about this?" Fortune said. "Gertie, you drive Ida Belle back to her house. I'll call the sheriff and report Ida Belle's injury. When the sheriff shows up, I'll tell him Ida Belle asked Gertie to drive her home. That'll give you time to clear your moonshine out of the garage. Then when the sheriff goes over there to talk to you, Ida Belle, tell him what you told us. He was an intruder, you felt threatened, and you shot him. And whatever you do, don't touch the body and don't step in the blood."

"I suppose that'll do," Ida Belle said. "Not that I'm in any position to argue. Fortune, when you call, see if you can't get Deputy Breaux."

"Why is that?" Mary-Alice asked.

"Well you know we have two deputy sheriffs in Sinful," Gertie explained. "There's Carter LeBlanc, who is not only extremely good-looking but also highly intelligent and perceptive. And then there's Deputy Kyle Breaux. He's...very nice."

Ida Belle refused all offers of help and made it down Fortune's front steps by herself, bracing herself with her good arm.

Fortune stood at her front window and watched until Gertie's ancient Cadillac had pulled out and lumbered off down the road. Then she took out her phone and made a call.

"I'd like to speak to Deputy Breaux, please," Fortune said. "Deputy Breaux, this is Fortune Morrow. Very well, thank you. Listen, I'm calling to report that Ida Belle had an intruder on her property, and she's injured. Seems he shot her. Well, she's not really in a condition to talk right now. Gertie's doing first aid. No, she doesn't want an ambulance. Yes, Marge Boudreaux's old place. We'll be waiting here. Thank you, deputy."

Fortune hung up and turned to Mary-Alice. "Do you want something to drink? Coffee? Tea?"

"I'd love a glass of tea if it's not too much trouble."

"We're not doing anything wrong, you know," Fortune called from the kitchen. She came back with two full glasses of tea. "We're going to tell the truth. Ida Belle showed up with her shoulder bloody. Gertie patched her up, and they went back to Ida Belle's house while I was on the phone with the sheriff's office."

Fortune sat Deputy Breaux down the minute he arrived and set out a plate of blueberry cheesecake squares and a glass of tea. Before he could ask any questions, a phone rang in another room, and Fortune left to answer it.

Mary-Alice smiled at Deputy Breaux.

"How's your mama and them?"

Deputy Breaux nodded and swallowed his mouthful.

"Mama and them's fine. Thank you for askin', ma'am."

"I certainly hope Ida Belle will be alright," Mary-Alice said brightly. "I couldn't hardly bear to look at her shoulder. She--"

Fortune rushed back into the room.

"Ida Belle is fine, Deputy. Gertie drove her home. I'm so sorry to have bothered you."

Breaux slowly pushed himself to his feet.

"Now, ma'am, I thought you said on the phone she'd been shot by an intruder."

"Oh, I'm sure I didn't say that." Fortune attempted a carefree laugh. "She was *frightened* by an intruder. But she's okay now."

"Well, I think I'd better check up on her. I'm saying, once a report's called in, I have to see it through. I'll just head on over to her place now."

Fortune shot a look at Mary-Alice, panic in her eyes.

"We'll follow you over, then," Fortune said. "Would you like to come along, Mary-Alice?"

Mary-Alice didn't dare say anything as she and Fortune were buckling themselves into Fortune's Jeep. But once they were driving behind Deputy Breaux's car, Mary-Alice asked,

"My goodness, Fortune, whatever happened?"

"Maybe Ida Belle really does need help." Fortune's expression was tense.

"What on earth do you mean?"

"Gertie says there's no body. There's no sign of any shooting victim, alive or dead."

"Oh, my. Do you suppose the man was only wounded, then?"

"There was no blood, Mary-Alice. Ida Belle saw something that wasn't there and shot up her own garage."

Fortune pulled the Jeep over and parked in front of Ida Belle's house.

"Okay, here we are." Fortune turned to Mary-Alice. "Say as little as possible until Breaux leaves. There must be a perfectly reasonable explanation for this. And I hope it's not that Ida Belle's losing her marbles."

CHAPTER 3

Ida Belle's garage was a mess. Car parts, umbrellas, brooms, stacks of old newspaper, and broken glass covered the floor, except for a bare forty inch by forty-eight inch patch on the ground. Where the pallet of Sinful Ladies' Cough Syrup had sat.

"Can't we get a light in here?" Fortune asked. The only illumination came from the narrow shafts of sunlight filtering through tiny holes. From Ida Belle's shotgun, Mary-Alice realized.

"The light bulb was shot out," came Gertie's voice from a dark corner of the garage. As her eyes adjusted, Mary-Alice saw that Gertie was standing with her arm around Ida Belle.

"I swear to y'all, he was right there." Ida Belle pointed to Deputy Breaux's feet. "Right there. I shot Victorin Lowery. I saw him go down."

Breaux paced around the small space, staring at the floor as if the missing corpse might suddenly turn up.

"Ma'am, are you sure it was Victorin Lowery you saw?" Breaux asked.

"Yes, sir, I surely am," Ida Belle retorted. "Unless it was his stunt double."

Breaux scratched his chin.

"You didn't happen to see Leonie Blanchard around at all, did you?"

"Who?" Fortune asked.

"Victorin's girlfriend," Breaux said. "Real pretty, but she likes her drink too. Some folks call her Hollow-Leg Leonie. Her and Victorin got into it at the Swamp Bar yesterday. I had to go down and pull 'em apart."

"I remember Miss Leonie Blanchard," Gertie said. "I had to suspend her several times for smoking in school."

"I thought you taught third grade," Fortune said.

"And so I did. Deputy, what were they fighting about?"

"I couldn't say, Ma'am Dunno. On the way back to the station Leonie was saying something about the Marines. She'd been drinking, though, and wasn't talking too clear."

"Deputy," Ida Belle asked, "are you saying they were both fighting but you only arrested her?"

"She was the one chasing him around the bar, ma'am. He was attempting to flee."

"Sounds like a typical night at the Swamp Bar," Gertie said.

Breaux addressed the two women in the corner of the shot-up garage.

"Miss Gertie, you probably ought to take Miss Ida Belle to the doctor now and get her checked out real thorough-like."

"How *dare* you, Kyle Breaux."

Ida Belle stepped out of the shadows, a pink-poncho-draped vision of wrath. Gertie joined her, looking a little worried. "Don't you go insinuating there's something wrong with me. I am not crazy. I am telling you, there was a body right—OW!"

Gertie quickly removed her foot from Ida Belle's instep and they glared at each other.

"He means for your shoulder, Ida Belle," Gertie said sternly. "The deputy's just trying to help. No need to get yourself all flustered."

"Yes, excellent advice, Deputy," Fortune chimed in. "I'll phone for an appointment as soon as we're done here."

Breaux departed, leaving the women in Ida Belle's shot-up garage.

Ida Belle opened her mouth to speak.

"We believe you, Ida Belle," Gertie said quickly. "And we don't think you're crazy. So if you were about to fuss at us for thinking you were imagining the whole thing, you can just save your breath."

"Oh," Ida Belle rubbed her forehead with her good hand. "Well, I suppose that's alright, then."

"Although I'm not sure you had to tell him you shot someone," Fortune said.

"Well, Fortune, didn't you just tell him exactly that same thing on the phone, not a few minutes ago? I believe that was our plan."

"No. I just said you'd been shot. By an intruder."

Fortune glanced uneasily across the street.

"Don't worry," Gertie said. "Carter's not at home."

"Deputy Carter lives across the street?" Mary-Alice asked.

"He certainly does," Ida Belle said. "That's why I'm always on my very best behavior."

"When you're not brewing moonshine and shooting folks in your garage," Gertie said.

Mary-Alice followed the women into Ida Belle's house. She had completely forgotten about her romantic dilemma. This day was turning out to be more interesting than any mystery novel. Mary-Alice was glad she'd decided to move to Sinful. She marveled at how the tiny town (population 253) had turned out to be a hundred times more exciting than Mudbug.

"I just know Victorin Lowery was in my garage, and I am perfectly sure that I shot him." Ida Belle said as the women took their seats around the kitchen table. Ida Belle pointed to her shoulder, the bandage lumpy under the pink poncho. "And what about this? A hallucination certainly didn't shoot back at me, now did it?"

"Could there have been another shooter?" Fortune asked. "Someone behind him?"

Ida Belle shrugged with her good shoulder.

"I don't know what's going on. There wasn't a drop of blood on the floor when we came back. It's like I was shooting at a ghost."

"You left the garage unattended," Fortune said. "Someone could've come through the side door, dragged the body out, and cleaned up the blood when you came to see us."

"Can't the police tell if there was blood, even after someone tried to clean it up? I've heard that's possible." Mary-Alice didn't say she'd read it in one of her murder mysteries. But she thought she remembered the police detective in the story using something called Luminol.

Gertie brightened.

"Ida Belle," she asked, "where's your LBD kit?"

"LBD?" Mary-Alice asked.

"Latent Blood Detection," Fortune explained.

"I know where it is, but I won't be able to get it down by myself. Gertie, would you please come help me?"

Mary-Alice and Fortune remained at Ida Belle's kitchen table. Mary-Alice tried to think of something to talk about.

"Now, Fortune, I hear you're a school librarian," Mary-Alice said, finally. "It must be lovely, being surrounded by books all day."

"Books? Sure, I'm up to my ears in books." Fortune made a brief attempt at a smile.

"Do you ever get a chance to read any grown-up books at work? Like mysteries and thrillers? Or is it all Peter Rabbit and the Flopsy Bunnies?"

Fortune gave a guilty start.

"Peter Rabbit and the Flopsy Bunnies? Why would you say that?"

Mary-Alice did not know that "Flopsy Bunnies" was the CIA code name for a rogue brigade of the PKK. Nor did she know that Fortune had personally dispatched the Flopsy Bunnies' leader (code name "Peter Rabbit") at a Turkish seaside resort.

It had been one of Fortune's easiest assignments. Now, after a few weeks undercover in Sinful, Fortune doubted she could repeat the performance. She had friends, people she cared about: Deputy Sheriff Carter LeBlanc, Gertie and Ida Belle, even mousy little Mary-Alice with her exasperating optimism. It would be difficult now, to take a human life. Not impossible, of course, but a lot harder than it used to be.

"Do you suppose it would ever be possible for me to get a job like that," Mary-Alice was saying, "at my age?"

"*You?* Oh, you mean being a librarian. No, I don't think a librarian career is for you, Mary-Alice. I think you'd be bored by all the paperwork."

The conversation was cut off by a crash, followed by Gertie's cry of "Found it!"

Gertie and Ida Belle came back into Ida Belle's kitchen, both wearing dark goggles. Gertie carried a box with rubber gloves flopped over the side, and Ida Belle held a lantern with a purple-tinted bulb.

"These are for you." Gertie set the box down and pulled out a handful of gloves and goggles. "We don't have masks, so just try to breathe shallow."

"Come on, you two," Ida Belle said. "We need as many eyes on this as we can get. Gertie forgot her glasses again, and she's as blind as a bat without 'em."

"Ida Belle, darlin'," Gertie made a rude gesture with both hands at Ida Belle's back. "How many fingers would you say I'm holding up?"

Mary-Alice's white capri pants glowed in the blacklight, as

did the lace trim on Fortune's blouse, and Gertie's cottony-white hair. But the garage floor was stubbornly dark. There were no glowing stains to indicate the presence of blood.

"Maybe someone cleaned up the blood with bleach," Mary-Alice suggested.

"If someone cleaned blood stains with chlorine bleach, the LBD kit would still detect something," Fortune said. "And there would be a bleach smell. If they used oxygen bleach, on the other hand, the LBD kit wouldn't catch it, but there still would be visible staining. We have neither."

"Might as well go back inside, then," Ida Belle sighed. "My goodness. Maybe I really did imagine the whole thing."

CHAPTER 4

Mary-Alice appreciated how neat the crew left her kitchen every evening. Things were put away, stacked neatly, and swept clean. Mary-Alice would make sure to compliment Boon on his crew's professionalism the next time she saw him.

Which would be in about an hour, she remembered with a start. She had nearly forgotten about their standing Saturday dinner date. Mary-Alice freshened up quickly and then took out the blank journal she had purchased at Harriet's Books. She picked up her special pen with the big sunflower on the end and sat down at the dining room table. Mary-Alice opened the journal to the first blank page, smoothed it flat, and wrote,

Ida Belle sees Victorin Lowery in her garage. (Is it really him?)

He becomes belligerent, and she shoots him just as he shoots her. (Was it he who shot her, or was it someone else? Did she really shoot him? If not, why does she think she did?)

Ida Belle comes to Fortune Morrow's house for help. When she returns to her house, the body has disappeared. (Ida Belle could have moved it herself before she came over to Fortune's. But why?)

Possible explanations:

Is Ida Belle not telling the truth? Again, why?

Victorin Lowery's body was moved (by whom?)

Mary-Alice was getting tired of writing out Victorin Lowery's name each time. She decided she would shorten it to Vic. This would be easy to remember, as detectives in murder mysteries often referred to the murder victim as the "vic."

Vic was not fatally wounded and left on his own, after cleaning up his blood. (Why would he do that? How did he clean up the blood so completely that he left no trace? And where is he now?)

Ida Belle is misremembering/hallucinating. Perhaps someone has drugged her. (Why? Or accidental drug interaction?)

The body was moved by someone already wrote that (above)

The body was dissolved in something like acid or lime. (Where? Again, who moved it, and how?)

Who shot Ida Belle?

Mary-Alice drummed her peach-colored nails on the dining table and stared at the page.

It was like one of those magic tricks where you can't possibly figure out how they did it.

Mary-Alice's doorbell rang at five minutes after six. Or, rather, it made a strangled sort of "thunk." The doorbell was on the list of things to replace. Along with the fake-candle chandelier and the gold shag carpet. Boon St. Clair and his crew were going to be working on her house for a long time, Mary-Alice realized. Any misunderstanding would have to be straightened out sooner, rather than later.

Boon looked as handsome as ever and seemed as glad to see Mary-Alice as he always did. Mary-Alice relaxed a little. He wasn't going to ask her to marry him, or put him in her will. They were only going to have a nice dinner at Francine's.

"I thought we wouldn't go to Francine's tonight," Boon said.

FRANKIE BOW

"Why ever not?"

"I thought we might could go to my house. I like to cook and I rarely get the opportunity. If that's okay with you, Miss Mary-Alice."

"Why, of course it is, Boon. What a delightful idea."

Boon's place was a single-story brick house with a neat lawn, shaded all around by pecan trees. The exterior did not prepare Mary-Alice for what was inside. The living room had Roman shades of rough linen, travertine tiles, and pumpkin-hued walls. Through a doorway, Mary-Alice saw a hallway with what looked like cork flooring. An open door off the hallway revealed a bathroom done up in black-and-pink tiles.

"My," she said. "The décor is quite something. So eclectic."

"It's a little bit of a hodgepodge," he chuckled. "Sometimes I get materials left over from a job and I hate to see them go to waste. I have to pay for them anyway, so I might as well use them. Would you like me to show you around?"

Mary-Alice feared that Boon, in his enthusiasm about his house, might attempt to show her the bedrooms. Innocent though his intentions might be, that would not do at all.

"Well, as matter of fact, Boon, I'd very much enjoy a tour of the landscaping before it gets too dark. Was it my imagination, or did I spy some lovely white azaleas in the back?"

By the time they went in to dinner, Mary-Alice was feeling more at ease. Boon's motley décor made him seem adventurous and easygoing, and his neat yard indicated a conscientious and trustworthy character. Mary-Alice was also impressed by the simple meal of salad and fried fish. Soon they were chatting happily about remodeling in general, and then Mary-Alice's house in particular. Boon mentioned that he was using apprentices from Mudbug Technical College.

"They have a new apprentice program that's subsidized by the parish," he said. "I've applied for a grant. If it comes through, it could save you a little money. Aren't your people from Mudbug, Miss Mary-Alice?"

"I did live there for many years, although my people are in Arnaudville. I have some fond memories of Mudbug Tech myself. I took a bookkeeping class there, I don't want to tell you how long ago. So those young ladies on your crew, they're from that new program?"

Mary-Alice had noticed a couple of young women on the crew. It had struck her as unusual.

"Times are changing, Miss Mary-Alice, and in this particular instance, I'd say it's for the better. Those young ladies have a work ethic that puts most of my boys to shame."

"People do talk about how times are changing. But I have to tell you, Boon, with all the times I've visited Sinful over the years, it doesn't feel like it's changed at all. The old taxidermist's shop has been there forever, hasn't it? And in all these years, I don't believe I've ever seen a single customer in there."

"That's very true, Miss Mary-Alice. It's a wonder they're still in business. One thing that has changed, unfortunately, is that lately it seems we've been getting more crime."

Mary-Alice was tempted to expand on the topic of crime by telling Boon about Ida Belle's disappearing intruder. But she decided it wouldn't be suitable dinner conversation.

She also considered bringing up the issue of the remodeling bills and decided against that as well. Now that she was enjoying a pleasant dinner with Boon, she wondered why she'd ever been worried in the first place about things moving too fast. Why shouldn't things move fast? Boon was thoughtful, handsome, and judging from the excellent detail work in her kitchen, very good with his hands.

"Why, Miss Mary-Alice," Boon exclaimed, "you're blushing. Is the fish too spicy?"

"Oh, my, no. Not at all." Mary-Alice fanned her face, wishing she had an actual fan to hide behind. "Only I wonder if you might turn on one of those ceiling fans? It's getting quite awfully close in here."

CHAPTER 5

Mary-Alice and Boon met at Mass the next morning. They took their usual seats, side-by-side in the back pew. Mary-Alice fanned herself with the program, while Boone endured the heat with manly stoicism. Mary-Alice's cousin, Mayor Celia Arceneaux, sat up front with her friends. As soon as Mass was over, Celia and her crew jumped to their feet. They were out the door before Father Michael had finished saying "Amen."

"Do you want to catch up, Miss Mary-Alice?" Boon asked.

"I've decided to be a conscientious objector in the Banana Pudding War." Mary-Alice smiled at Boon. "But I wouldn't mind walking down to Francine's for a glass of tea."

The Banana Pudding War was how the locals described the after-church race to Francine's diner. The warring factions were the Catholics and the Baptists (whose church was across the road). The plunder was Francine's limited supply of banana pudding. Celia Arceneaux led the Catholic faction; Fortune, Gertie, and Ida Belle were with the Baptists.

Mary-Alice's divided loyalties made it awkward to choose a side. And as divine as Francine's banana pudding was, Mary-Alice never enjoyed winning if it meant someone else had to lose. (In this way she was the opposite of her cousin Celia, who relished making other people miserable even when doing so made her own life no better.)

"Celia and them are only a little way ahead of us yet," Mary-Alice observed as she and Boon started down the road. After the closeness of the church, even the sluggish breeze felt refreshing. "But I don't see the Baptists anywhere."

"Ever since the Baptists got Marge Boudreaux's niece, they've been unbeatable. I wouldn't be surprised if the Baptists were already down at Francine's Diner, enjoying their banana pudding."

"But Celia's team hasn't given up," Mary-Alice said.

"Nope. And they get madder every time they lose. Peculiar way to spend the Sabbath, if you ask me."

The peaceful morning was pierced by profane yelling. Mary-Alice stopped and placed a hand on Boon's arm.

"Boon, that sounds like Ida Belle."

They turned back to see a knot of people at the front door of the Baptist church. Deputy Breaux was depositing a white-haired woman into the back of a sheriff's car. "It is Miss Ida Belle," Boon said. "Why would Deputy Breaux be arresting her?"

"Well, I cannot imagine. There must be some mistake."

They rushed back to the Baptist church and got there just as the sheriff's car pulled away. Gertie stood at the edge of the road, staring at the departing vehicle.

"Mary-Alice!" Gertie exclaimed. "Did you see what just happened? Deputy Breaux arrested Ida Belle!"

"We saw the whole thing," Mary-Alice gasped, winded from sprinting across the road. "Didn't we, Boon?"

"I surely would not have believed it if I hadn't seen it with my own eyes."

"This is Celia's doing," Gertie fumed.

"Now I know Mayor Celia isn't Miss Ida Belle's biggest fan," Boon said, "but this is still America. You can't be locking people up just because they stole your high school sweetheart and ate your banana pudding."

"Ida Belle stole Celia's high school sweetheart?" Mary-Alice asked.

"Now, Boon, I believe you are confused. He wasn't Celia's high school sweetheart. What happened was Celia…oh, it's not important right now. What's important is that Ida Belle has just been arrested for murder."

"But how?" Mary-Alice asked. "The body was missing!"

"Body?" Boon exclaimed. "What body might that be?"

"No, no, Boon, darlin', she said the body was *missing*," Gertie reassured him. "That means there *wasn't* a body. Now if you don't mind, we'd like to borrow Miss Mary-Alice."

Boon took in the women's worried expressions.

"It appears your friends need you, Miss Mary-Alice."

"I'm ever so sorry, Boon," Mary-Alice said. "Maybe some other time?"

"I understand. I'll be seeing you bright and early tomorrow, in any case. Is there anything that I can do to help y'all in the meantime?"

"Yes, there is," Gertie said. "You head straight down to Francine's and snatch Celia's banana pudding, and then give her a good kick in the shins."

"Sure thing, Miss Gertie." Boon laughed and planted a kiss on Mary-Alice's powdered cheek, and ambled off.

"Are we going to the sheriff's station?" Mary-Alice asked. "It looked like that's where Deputy Breaux was headed with Ida Belle."

Fortune ran up, out of breath.

"Don't tell me you've already run down to the sheriff's station and back," Gertie exclaimed.

Fortune shrugged.

"It's not that far. Anyway, it'll take a while to process Ida

Belle and set bail. In the meantime, we need to figure out how to pay bail. Come on, let's—"

"I can't believe Celia and her henchwomen are down there eating our banana pudding," Gertie grumbled.

"They haven't gotten there yet if that makes it any better," Fortune said. "Gertie, let them have the banana pudding this time. We have more important things to worry about right now."

Gertie's shoulders slumped. "They don't deserve it."

"Gertie, for heaven's sakes," Mary-Alice exclaimed, "would you really enjoy eating that banana pudding knowing Ida Belle was in jail and couldn't have any herself?"

"I suppose not," Gertie admitted. "Fine. See y'all over at Fortune's place."

Mary-Alice pulled up to Fortune's house only to find Deputy Sheriff Carter LeBlanc's gigantic truck parked outside. And it was Carter LeBlanc himself who opened the door when she rang. Mary-Alice felt a surge of anxiety. Had she obstructed the course of justice when she helped Ida Belle tidy up her garage? Would she be the next one to get hauled off to jail?

Fortune joined Carter at the door, shot him a death glare, and then turned to Mary-Alice.

"Mary-Alice, Deputy Sheriff LeBlanc has decided to pay us a call. Please come in and join us. I have sweet tea and shortbread cookies on the kitchen table. It's the purest coincidence, I'm sure, that this is all happening on Sunday, right after Ida Belle's unconstitutional arrest and detainment."

"Why Sunday?" Mary-Alice asked as she followed Fortune and Carter back to the kitchen.

"Deputy LeBlanc has contrived to take advantage of a poor old woman and her harmless foibles," Fortune replied, to Carter rather than to Mary-Alice. "He knows about Gertie's no-lying-on-Sunday rule.

"By the way, Fortune, darling," Mary-Alice whispered, "it's just tea."

"Sorry?"

"We don't call it *sweet* tea. We simply call it tea. Just as you wouldn't call it 'sweet Coke.' It's already sweet."

Carter turned back.

"Are you ladies coming?"

"Right behind you," Fortune said. "So Mary-Alice, what do you ask for when you want unsweetened tea?"

Mary-Alice had no idea how to answer that. Fortune may as well have asked what to say when you want someone to drop scorpions into your tea and then pour it in your lap.

They entered the kitchen to find Gertie seated at the table, her face set in a scowl.

"Gertie, is it true?" Mary-Alice asked. "Do you really have a no-lying-on-Sunday rule?"

Gertie nodded, her eyes fixed on her folded hands.

Mary-Alice did not have any such rule, for she believed lying was always wrong. There were times, of course, when one had to manage the facts to put someone's mind at ease, but that was different. Like when Beulah Monroe got that perm. Or when the police came by asking all those questions right after Joe died.

"Ladies," Carter said. "I just want to get to the bottom of this, as I'm sure you all y'all do."

"The bottom of what?" Fortune asked. "There was no crime committed."

"Well, now, I'm not so sure about that." Carter pulled out a chair and sat down without being invited. Mary-Alice sat down too, but Fortune continued to pace. "Victorin Lowery's mama's reported him missing."

Everyone was quiet for a moment.

Carter wiped his hand across his forehead.

"What I do know is, an intruder shot Ida Belle. Someone

called in and reported it. But by the time Deputy Breaux got to it, somebody'd already messed with the scene. Miss Ida Belle herself told Deputy Breaux that she shot Victorin Lowery."

"Blabbermouth," Gertie muttered.

"If we were trying to cover something up, why would we call it in in the first place?" Fortune demanded.

"A man is missing, Fortune. He's either in danger or he's already dead. Ida Belle won't tell us where he is. That's why she's being held without bail."

"No bail?" Mary-Alice exclaimed. She had already been trying to calculate how much equity she could shake loose from the old Cooper Place.

Fortune burst out with a few words that Mary-Alice would never have guessed were in the vocabulary of a children's librarian.

Celia's behind this, isn't she?" Gertie said, forgetting about her temporary vow of silence.

Carter looked pained.

"The mayor—"

"Who is not supposed to interfere with the activities of law enforcement," Fortune interrupted.

"Who also happens to be my boss's boss," Carter retorted, "is understandably concerned when someone in Sinful confesses to shooting someone dead, and then that someone turns up missing."

"What about the girlfriend?" Fortune asked. "What was her name? Gertie, you were her teacher."

"Leonie Blanchard," Gertie muttered, still trying to say as few words as possible.

"That's right, they were fighting," Mary-Alice said. "That's what Deputy Breaux told us."

"Yes, ma'am," Carter said. "According to witnesses, she threatened his life."

"And?" Fortune prodded.

"Leonie spent that night and a lot of the next day in the drunk tank," Carter said. "She wasn't released until well after you called in the incident. Unless she can turn invisible and walk through walls, she's got a pretty good alibi."

"Mister Lowery was a large man," Mary-Alice said. "I saw him in Francine's Diner yesterday morning. Ida Belle may be in good health, but I don't believe she'd be able to move a body that size."

"You're right, Miss Mary-Alice. Lowery's six and a half foot, and probably closer to three hundred than two hundred pounds." Carter cast an appraising look at Fortune. "It would take at least two people to move him. And at least one of them would have to be pretty strong."

"Hey, I'll admit I'm in good shape," Fortune retorted, "but I'm not a superhero. You think I disposed of a three-hundred-pound corpse and magically got rid of all the bloodstains too?"

"What do you know about bloodstains?" Carter asked.

"I know there weren't any," Fortune replied. "How do you explain that?"

"Now, Fortune," Carter said, "I don't like the situation any more than you do. I'm trying to help here. But Ida Belle won't tell us where Lowery is. If you have any information at all—"

"Oh, well now that you've asked nicely," Fortune said bitterly, "He's right over there, tied up in my pantry. Come on, Carter, don't you think we'd have already told you if we knew anything that could help Ida Belle?"

Carter stood up. "Something's not adding up here, and I want to get to the bottom of it. If you see or hear anything that could possibly be helpful, I expect y'all to let me know. Right away. And—I shouldn't even have to say this—please do not try to investigate this yourselves."

"We hear you loud and clear," Fortune folded her arms. "You know your way out, Deputy."

Carter nodded and left.

As soon as Carter had closed the door behind him, the tension in the room eased.

"Well," Gertie said, no longer on her guard, "I guess there's nothing to do now but stay put and let the authorities handle it."

To Mary-Alice's puzzlement, Gertie and Fortune burst out laughing.

"Now, Mary-Alice, don't go looking so shocked," Gertie said as she wiped her eyes. "You know the Sinful Ladies' Society does more than sell cough syrup at the fair. We work behind the scenes to make sure justice is done in this town. Been doing it for the past fifty years."

Mary-Alice nodded. "And I intend to help."

"Good, we're all on the same page." Fortune picked up a pen and drew a firm line on the pad in front of her. "We can cross off Item One for now. Raise bail money. Replace it with Find Victorin Lowery. Gertie, you think you can get any information out of the girlfriend?"

"Yes, ma'am, I can have a little talk with Miss Leonie."

"But Deputy LeBlanc told us Miss Leonie was in jail all night," Mary-Alice said.

"She still might know a little something," Gertie said. "She might've even ordered a hit from jail. That's how the Mafia guys do it."

"Okay, Gertie," Fortune said, "how about you go down to the Swamp Bar and see whether Leonie has a new boyfriend. If so, he'd be a suspect."

"Certainly," Gertie said. "Now, I might have to have a drink or two. Just so I blend in and get people to trust me and all, you understand. So Fortune, you'll have to be the designated driver."

"Not me. I'm not going to the Swamp Bar."

"I'm sure no one remembers the wet t-shirt contest," Gertie chided.

"Everyone remembers the wet t-shirt contest," Fortune shot back.

"What about me?" Mary-Alice asked. "What shall I do?"

Gertie and Fortune turned to look at her.

"Well, why shouldn't I do something to help? I could come along if Fortune's opposed to going."

"You know," Gertie said, "that's not a bad idea. Fresh meat. What do you think, Fortune?"

"I don't know. Mary-Alice, have you been to the Swamp Bar?"

"Well, not exactly. But I believe I've heard of it."

What Mary-Alice had heard was that "decent women" didn't go there. But Mary-Alice was willing to brave the Swamp Bar to help Ida Belle. And her curiosity egged her on; she had never been anywhere disreputable.

"Sure," Fortune said, finally. "You're just gathering information. How dangerous could it be?"

"We have our plan, then," Gertie said. "Mary-Alice, stop by my house tonight around nine. We'll get dressed and go from there."

Nine? Mary-Alice was usually asleep by nine. But it was too late to back out now.

CHAPTER 6

Mary-Alice felt her heart pounding as she guided her beloved Oldsmobile 88 along the narrow dirt-and-crushed-shell road. She was nervous about the prospect of walking into one of the roughest bars in the bayous. But Mary-Alice's main worry was her car. Gertie's Cadillac wasn't reliable enough to make a quick getaway, so Mary-Alice had volunteered to drive. But as the road narrowed, the bristling blackberry thickets on either side menaced her metallic paint.

To make matters worse, Mary-Alice felt she could barely breathe, thanks to the black vinyl corset that Gertie had laced her into before they left.

"You can't walk into the Swamp Bar looking like you just came from a ladies' prayer breakfast," Gertie had explained. "You have to blend in."

In addition to the corset, Mary-Alice sported fingerless lace gloves, leopard-print leggings, and a spiky platinum wig complete with black roots. At least Mary-Alice's feet were too small for Gertie's shoes. She was able to wear her own comfortable tennis shoes, thank goodness.

Gertie had gone in for Harajuku style. Beneath a frilly pink-

and-white mini-dress, white lace thigh-highs gripped Gertie's bony legs. Tarantula eyelashes and thick liner ringed her eyes. A huge white satin bow teetered atop Gertie's candy-pink wig.

Mary-Alice, who was unfamiliar with Japanese fashion, assumed Gertie was dressed as Bette Davis in *What Ever Happened to Baby Jane?*

Just as Mary-Alice was wondering whether she had gotten them hopelessly lost in the black woods, Gertie cried, "There it is!" Mary-Alice glimpsed light through the trees. The narrow road opened up to a crushed-shell parking lot. Gertie climbed out and led the way into the building, crunching across the cracked white oyster shells in her pink high-heeled boots.

"Gertie," Mary-Alice asked, "are you okay? Those heels seem awfully high."

Gertie was taking tiny, mincing steps, her knees bent and her arms held out for balance.

There's no beauty without pain," Gertie said.

"Wherever did you hear that, Gertie?"

"At a toddler pageant. One of the mothers said it."

At least Mary-Alice's feet were comfortable in her sequined tennis shoes. The rest of her, not so much. The platinum wig made her scalp itch, and the hooks of her mobile-sized earrings tugged on her earlobes like a cheese-cutter.

The Swamp Bar was a one-story building on the edge of the bayou. It had a rust-splotched tin roof, tiny windows, and a general air of hopelessness. Mary-Alice had parked close enough that her car was in the light, but not so close that drunks would bump into her car or be tempted to relieve themselves on her tires on their way out.

It was so dark inside the Swamp Bar that Mary-Alice felt like she was stepping into a cave. A cave that reeked of stale booze, drugstore cologne, and a hint of vomit. For a moment, the only light she could see was from Gertie's glow-in-the-dark heart-shaped earrings.

Mary-Alice gripped Gertie's shoulder and followed her in.

"I can't see a thing," Mary-Alice whispered. "Is the power out?"

"No, it's like this on purpose. So you can't get a good look at the cockroaches. Or the customers."

Mary-Alice's eyes adjusted as she followed Gertie over to the bar. Sunday was a relatively slow night at the Swamp Bar, so Gertie was able to get the bartender's attention. He wore a too-big green t-shirt with "Swamp Bar" printed across the chest in crooked iron-on letters. He wore his sandy hair in a mullet, cut short in front, and long down his back. Tattoos covered his skinny arms, and his nails were crusted with dirt.

"What'll it be, ladies?"

"Bourbon, straight," Gertie cooed coquettishly. "Make it a double. Mary-Alice, what'll you have?"

"I'll just have a Coke, please," Mary-Alice said. "I'm driving."

"Yes, ma'am. Diet or regular?"

"Whatever you have in a can. Thank you so much."

"Don't act too prissy about germs," Gertie whispered when the bartender had moved on to the next customer. "We have to act like normal Swamp Bar customers."

"I know, but did you see his fingernails? He looks like he's been digging up graves with his bare hands."

"You've been reading those vampire mysteries again, haven't you? Oh, there, I believe that's Leonie."

It wasn't hard to spot Leonie Blanchard. She wore a halter top that showed off the lioness tattoo covering her bare back. She coquetted with the men at her table, tossing her auburn hair so it brushed her bare shoulders. When Leonie turned her head to the side, Mary-Alice caught a glimpse of a hardened but still-pretty face, caked with pale makeup that didn't quite match the skin on her neck.

"I'm going in," Gertie said. "Cover me."

Mary-Alice perched on a bar stool and watched Gertie totter

over on her ridiculously high heels, pausing now and then to straighten her pink wig as it listed to one side or the other. Leonie seemed to recognize her former third-grade teacher despite the latter's exotic disguise. She half-stood to give Gertie a hug, one of the men pulled out a chair, and soon Gertie was part of the festive group.

When it was clear Gertie would be a while, Mary-Alice strolled around the perimeter of the bar. Occasionally a man would pop out of the darkness to accost her with a boozy "Evening, darlin'," or "Hey, now, Blondie." She responded each time with a polite "How do you do?" and continued on her way.

Once Mary-Alice had completed her circuit, she decided to check on her car. She pulled the front door open a crack and peered out to the parking lot.

"Go! Go! Go!" Gertie slammed into Mary-Alice's back, and they tumbled out onto the wooden porch.

Gertie was only wearing one high-heeled boot. She yanked it off and flung it tomahawk-style back into the darkness of the Swamp Bar.

"Ow!" cried a woman's voice, followed by a stream of curse words. Gertie pulled Mary-Alice up by the elbow, and the two women sprinted across the lot. Mary-Alice heard a loud crack of splintering wood, followed by the babble of an excited and intoxicated crowd.

"Nice job," Gertie panted. "She slipped on your Coke can and busted the railing."

They jumped into the Oldsmobile, Mary-Alice floored the accelerator, and they peeled out in a spray of oyster shells and dirt.

Neither woman spoke until they were well out of range of the Swamp Bar.

"How are your feet?" Mary-Alice asked, surprised to hear her voice crack. She cleared her throat and tried again. "Are your feet okay, Gertie? Those broken shells are sharp."

"I wore thick socks." Gertie propped one fuzzy, dirty foot on Mary-Alice's dashboard. "I thought I just might have to make a run for it. So I came prepared."

Mary-Alice glanced at the rear-view mirror, but saw only the red glow of her taillights illuminating the blackberry bushes and kudzu that crowded the road. She gripped the steering wheel tighter to keep her hands from shaking.

"Don't worry, no one's behind us," Gertie said. "She just had to make a big production back there. I suppose she did make her point."

"It seemed to me that you were getting on well with Miss Leonie," Mary-Alice said. "Why did she chase you out of the bar?"

"Oh, that wasn't Leonie after me."

"Well, who on earth was it, then?"

"I ran into an old friend, is all," Gertie said primly. "He was happy to see me, and was just giving me an innocent little old hug when his girlfriend walked in. She didn't think it was such an innocent hug, I suppose."

"My goodness, Gertie. You're quite a femme fatale."

"You too, Mary-Alice. You look smoking-hot as a platinum blonde."

Mary-Alice didn't much feel like a femme fatale. Her scalp was itching like crazy, and her corset felt like a particularly vindictive boa constrictor. Most unglamorous of all, she really had to pee.

"What did you find out from Leonie Blanchard?" Mary-Alice asked.

"Oh, I picked up a few things. When we see Fortune tomorrow I'll tell you both everything and then I won't have to repeat myself."

"No," Mary-Alice said firmly. "Whenever someone says, 'I'll tell you tomorrow' or 'I can't talk about it on the phone, I have to tell you in person,' something terrible always happens to them. You just go ahead and tell me right now, Gertie."

"Mary-Alice, that's in mystery novels and on cop shows."

"Better safe than sorry," Mary-Alice insisted, staring at the road ahead. "Did Leonie have any idea where poor Mister Lowery might be?"

"No," Gertie said. "Not that she told me. It didn't seem like she even knew he was missing."

"There must be some misunderstanding, somewhere or other," Mary-Alice said. "I can't believe Cousin Celia would do this to Ida Belle. Especially when there isn't even any proof that a crime's been committed."

"Mary-Alice, with all due respect, that's exactly the kind of thing your cousin Celia would do. She's spiteful and petty and power-hungry. And she never could abide anyone who showed her for inferior, which is one reason she's always hated Ida Belle. And why she's not so very much fond of you these days either."

"Me? Why Gertie, whatever did I do?"

"Didn't you ever wonder why Celia froze you out of the God's Wives? It was on account of you bought the old Cooper place and started fixing it up. All of a sudden everybody's talking about you and how you're here renovating a historic Sinful landmark. And then they got to asking themselves how come you're doing this with your own money while Mayor Celia uses our town's money to hire her idiot relatives, and sits on her derriere while our town's roads get rutted."

"Oh, Gertie, I don't believe I could belong to a group called the 'God's Wives' anyway," Mary-Alice said. "It just seems so irreverent."

They drove in silence for a while. Mary-Alice pondered what Gertie had told her. Gertie's theory certainly fit the facts. But Mary-Alice had trouble believing that Celia--or anyone-- could be so petty.

Finally, she asked, "Did you find out why Leonie was going on about the Marines?"

"I couldn't bring it up directly, of course, but I did manage to guide the conversation around to classmates who'd gone into the military. I told her I thought I recollected Victorin Lowery joining the Marines. She laughed and said he couldn't even get into the NOLA PD, so she doubted very much that the U.S. Marines would ever see fit to have him."

Silence settled over the car again until they reached Sinful. Mary-Alice pulled into her carport.

"So we're really not any further along, now, are we?" Mary-Alice asked.

"I asked everything I could, without being too much of a nosy-Parker." Gertie reached under her pink wig and scratched her scalp. "Maybe Victorin owes a large debt and he's being held for ransom."

"But no one's asked for ransom money yet."

"No," Gertie mused. "Not yet. This is so strange. If I were a suspicious woman, I'd suspect Celia of orchestrating the whole thing."

"But you are a suspicious woman," Mary-Alice said earnestly, "and you have accused Celia already."

"So I have." Gertie reached down and rubbed her foot. "I'm not sure this mission wasn't a complete waste of time, honestly."

"At least we got ourselves some exercise," Mary-Alice said. "They say sprinting keeps you young."

"In that case, a few more nights like this and we'll live forever. Well, it's time for me to turn in and get my beauty rest. Much appreciate you driving, Mary-Alice."

"Don't mention it," Mary-Alice said. "I'm ever so glad I could be of help. I only wish we could have found out more."

CHAPTER 7

Mary-Alice stood at her window and watched Gertie's old Cadillac limp around the first bend of her dark drive. Then she rushed back to her bedroom, pulling off the scratchy blonde wig as she went. She extricated herself from the corset, leggings, gloves, and earrings. Soon she was comfortable and ready for bed in her flowered flannel nightie.

But after the excitement at the Swamp Bar, Mary-Alice was still buzzing with adrenaline. Instead of going to bed, she sat down at her computer and searched for Victorin Lowery.

The man had almost no internet presence. No arrests, at least none flashy enough to make the Picayune metro crime news; no social media; no blogs or newspaper articles. Mary-Alice found exactly one instance of Victorin Lowery's name: on the New Orleans city website. He was among a list of graduates from the New Orleans Police Department Training Academy. But that was it.

Mary-Alice had heard that the parish records were all online now. Maybe there was something to be found there.

But when she logged into the parish records database, she found nothing but a placeholder for the town of Sinful. She entered her credit card information to get premium access. But after all that, there were still no records to be found.

Unfortunately, this was something she'd have to pursue with the mayor.

Mary-Alice reached for her phone as soon as she woke up the next morning. She was an adherent of the "eat the frog" school of time management, which advised getting one's most unpleasant tasks out of the way first. There was one clear candidate for the day's most unpleasant task.

Mary-Alice took a deep breath, leaned back on her pillow, and called Celia.

"Celia, darling," she began, "I know you're busy, and I do hope I'm not calling to early. Did you have a good sleep last night? You must be just simply worn out and probably don't have time for this. But I was wondering if I might ask you about the online parish records…"

"Oh, those folks," Celia sniffed. "If they think my staff has time to run around scanning everything into some stupid computer system, well, they are most sadly mistaken."

"So Sinful's records aren't online?" Mary-Alice thought sadly of the non-refundable access fee.

"No they are most certainly not, I'm thankful to say. That Clerk of Court can huff and puff all he wants but he will have to pry our records out of my cold, dead hands. Anyway," Celia added, with the indignation of the lazy person being called on to do her job, "I don't cotton to having our city records out there where anyone just any old body can get to them. If someone wants to look something up, they can just march themselves on down to City Hall and do it in person. You can't be too careful when it comes to putting things online. After what happened here not too long ago, I prefer to err on the side of caution. I don't think I need to revisit that issue with you again, Mary-Alice, do I, now?"

Sinful's bank accounts had recently fallen prey to online

theft on Celia's watch. Ordinarily, Celia would never bring up such a failure. But because Mary-Alice's grandson had been implicated in the hacking, Celia was happy to rub her nose in it.

"What kind of records would you be needing anyway?" Celia asked.

Mary-Alice froze. She hadn't thought this far ahead. She didn't want to let Celia know she was investigating Victorin Lowery.

"Well, I suppose it's—"

"Oh, it's about the house, isn't it?" Celia crowed. "There's a lien on the Cooper place that you didn't know about, I bet."

"Why Celia," Mary-Alice said, relieved, "you're so perceptive."

"I tried to tell you, Mary-Alice, it would've been better to buy something new and modern. These old houses are absolute money pits."

"Yes, they are. You're so right, Celia."

In fact, Mary-Alice's renovation was going quite smoothly (except for the romantic complications). But Mary-Alice didn't tell Celia that. Good news seemed to make Celia angry and argumentative. Stories of other people's hardships, on the other hand, always cheered her up.

"I've had such terrible luck trying to find what I need online," Mary-Alice said.

"Well, you just come on down to City Hall whenever you like," Celia said warmly. "I'm sure my staff can help you find whatever you need."

"By the way," Mary-Alice said, "There was quite a commotion outside the Baptist church after Mass. It looked as if Deputy Breaux might have gone and arrested Miss Ida Belle. Have you heard any such thing?"

"You're not mistaken, Mary-Alice. Not this time anyway. I probably oughtn't to tell you this on account of it's confidential and very serious." Celia didn't sound serious at all; she sounded positively giddy. "But I can tell you this, Mary-Alice. Under my administration, this town is finally going to punish its evildoers."

"Oh, my, Celia, that sounds serious. Well I thank you ever so much for your help. I will come down and see y'all at City Hall."

Mary-Alice set her phone down slowly. Celia Arceneaux, she was starting to realize, was not a very nice person.

Mary-Alice got dressed and went down to City Hall as Celia had advised. She didn't know what she was looking for, exactly. A criminal record, perhaps. Or evidence of time spent in the Marines?

As she stood in line at the Records and Permits counter, she felt someone walk up behind her. She turned around to see a very familiar face.

"Why, Boon," Mary-Alice exclaimed. "Why aren't you in my kitchen?"

"Just pulling some permits. I'm surely sorry to have startled you, Miss Mary-Alice. If you don't mind my asking, what brings you down here?"

"Oh, I'm just looking into some records. Although I'm not quite sure where to start. Especially when there's no one at the counter to help."

"I think I see someone coming now," Boon said.

"I'm surely not in any rush. Boon, why don't you go first?"

Mary-Alice dashed away, leaving a perplexed Boon standing at the counter.

Mary-Alice had recognized the woman approaching the Records and Permits counter. She was Celia's cousin Dorothy. Unlike Mary-Alice, who was only related to Celia by marriage, Dorothy was a real, blood cousin to Celia, and a member of the God's Wives besides. Mary-Alice knew that anything she did would be immediately reported back to Celia. Celia would surely find out that Mary-Alice was looking into Victorin Lowery's disappearance, and would suspect, correctly, that

Mary-Alice was trying to undermine the case against Ida Belle.

In the hallway, out of Dorothy's sight, Mary-Alice pulled out her phone and frantically texted Gertie.

THANK GOODNESS YOU TEXTED Gertie responded. HANG ON

Mary-Alice paced, watched her phone, and waited an agonizing length of time for Gertie's next message. Finally, it came.

TELL DOROTHY THAT YOU'RE JUST SO FULL OF YOURSELF THAT YOUR COUSIN IS THE MAYOR, YOU'VE DECIDED TO WRITE A HISTORY OF SINFUL.

I'M WRITING A HISTORY OF SINFUL? THAT'S WHY I'M IN THE RECORDS AND PERMITS OFFICE?

DON'T ARGUE NOW, MARY-ALICE, THIS IS A PERFECT PLAN. NOW GET IN THERE!

By the time Mary-Alice returned to the counter, Boon had already left. It was just her and Dorothy.

"Well. Mary-Alice Arceneaux," Dorothy's tone was chilly. "To what do we owe the honor?"

"I'm thinking about writing a history of Sinful," Mary-Alice said. (This was not untrue; she was, indeed, thinking about it.) "There are so many important stories here, and it would be a shame to lose them. Why, Celia's family, and yours too, Dorothy, practically built this town." (Mary-Alice was guessing here, but she had no reason to believe this wasn't true.)

Dorothy's demeanor softened. A history of Sinful, whose founding members included her own ancestors? What a wonderful idea! Dorothy let Mary-Alice into a small room— barely more than a closet—crowded with metal file cabinets and stacks of files.

"If you need to copy anything," Dorothy said, "bring it on out front. I'm supposed to charge you ten cents a page, but I'm not going to be a stickler. Oh, Mary-Alice, let me write down my mother's and my grandmother's maiden names. That'll help you. And make sure you leave everything as you found it. We can't have a mess."

As soon as Dorothy left her, Mary-Alice took a quick mental inventory of the records room. For such a small town, Sinful's level of disorganization was impressive. Stacks of manila folders teetered atop half-empty file cabinets. A single metal desk was buried under piles of yellowing paper, tin document boxes, and half-used legal pads. Next to the submerged desk teetered a stack of old-style waxed cardboard boxes, unlabeled and speckled with mildew. A glass-front bookcase held sheaves of damp, yellowed paper covered with spidery script.

Mary-Alice had worked as a bookkeeper, so she was good with files. But she had never seen such chaos. She heaved a deep sigh, then sat down and started reading.

CHAPTER 8

That evening, Mary-Alice stopped by Francine's Diner to pick up a family dinner of fried chicken and biscuits. Then she headed over to Fortune's house for their scheduled "Council of War." (Only Mary-Alice called it that, and only to herself. She had borrowed the phrase from the Amelia Peabody mysteries.)

Gertie reported first, telling Fortune about the trip out to the Swamp Bar. Most of what Gertie related was familiar to Mary-Alice, of course, as she had been there. But Gertie had held back one detail. She had learned that Leonie had been about to crack Victorin over the head with a perfectly good bottle of Early Times when Deputy Breaux had arrived just in time to stop her. It was unclear whether Gertie's informant had been more concerned about Victorin, or the bottle.

"So we know Leonie was mad enough to hurt him," Fortune said. "Was there anything else?"

"Only that Mary-Alice and I looked spectacular," Gertie said. "Mary-Alice can really rock the leopard leggings."

"You're certainly very kind, Gertie. Now how about when we had to hightail it out of there at the end of our evening?"

Fortune seemed surprisingly...unsurprised by this revelation.

"Do I want to know?" she sighed.

"Sometimes I don't realize the sensual power I hold over men." Gertie patted her hair, and Fortune rolled her eyes.

"Gertie," Fortune said, "you were flirting with Junior Baker again, weren't you? You were supposed to be focused on your mission."

"I was focused on my mission. Where else do you think I came by all this intel? Junior's one of Leonie's drinking buddies, as it happens."

"How could Leonie have hit poor Mister Lowery over the head with a bottle at all?" Mary-Alice asked. "He must be a foot taller than she is, at least."

"Well, it just so happens that Leonie was standing on the bar at the time," Gertie said.

"Mary-Alice," Fortune asked, "did you find out anything in the records office?"

Mary-Alice pushed her plate aside and opened her journal.

"Why, yes, I did. I managed to find some old school records. It turns out that Victorin Lowery is forty-three years old. His mother's name is Eulalie Lowery. His father was...a Bobby Sherman? Although I didn't think that sounded quite right for some reason."

"Who?" Fortune asked.

"Bobby Sherman the singer?" Gertie exclaimed.

"The same name, yes," Mary-Alice said.

"Sounds like she didn't know who the father was and had to put down some name or other," Gertie said. "You find anything else?"

Mary-Alice shook her head. "No, I did not. I thought I might turn up some arrest records, and those would tell me whom he might have tangled with. But there was nothing like that."

"The Sheriff's Office would have those," Fortune said. "And their files are a little harder to get into. Anything else?"

"There is one thing." Mary-Alice glanced at Gertie. "Celia's cousin Dorothy was working at the Records and Permits counter."

"Celia's taking nepotism to a whole new level," Gertie said. "I know for a fact that Dorothy can barely read. So, tell me, did my plan work?"

"What plan?" Fortune asked suspiciously. "There was a plan?"

"I didn't want Dorothy to know why I was really there," Mary-Alice explained "So Gertie suggested I tell her that I was writing a history of Sinful."

"Sounds like it worked," Fortune said.

"You're welcome," Gertie crowed. "I thought that was a genius idea."

"Well, yes, I was able to get access to the records. But Dorothy was so excited about the project that she waylaid me on my way out, and told me she wanted to reserve a copy of my book."

"Guess she'll be waiting a while for that," Gertie scoffed. But Fortune didn't see the humor in the situation.

"Gertie, if Mary-Alice doesn't come up with the book, Dorothy and Celia will wonder what she was doing in the records office."

"Wait, are you suggesting that I actually write a history of Sinful?" Mary-Alice exclaimed.

"Well, that'll be a nice little side project, don't you think?" Gertie said.

"Gertie, I don't know the first thing about writing a book. You do, though. You're a published author."

"That's right, Gertie," Fortune repeated, amused. "You're a published author."

"*Passion's Promise* is not history," Gertie insisted. "It's a fictional work of seniorotica."

"I don't know about that," Fortune mused. "The star-crossed lovers 'William' and 'Ida Mae' do remind me of two people I know."

"Oh, Walter and Ida Belle!" Mary-Alice exclaimed. "It took me until I was almost halfway through *Passion's Promise*, but I figured it out. Fortune, are you saying Gertie can write the history book for me? I must say that sounds like a splendid idea! Thank you ever so much, Gertie. I simply had no idea how I was going to go about doing that."

Before the perplexed Gertie could answer, there was a knock on the door.

Fortune returned to the kitchen with Deputy Sheriff Carter LeBlanc in tow. Mary-Alice could tell he was troubled; he didn't even seem to notice the foil tray that still held a few pieces of Francine's succulent fried chicken.

Fortune sat back down without offering Carter anything to eat or drink.

Mary-Alice was shocked by this. When someone called, it didn't matter whether they had come to tell you they shot your dog, ran off with your husband, or stole your cable. You offered them at least a glass of tea.

But this wasn't Mary-Alice's home; Fortune was the hostess. Besides, Carter was probably used to her strange Yankee ways by now.

So distracted was Mary-Alice by Fortune's lapse in protocol that she missed part of the conversation.

"How did you find him?" Fortune was asking.

"Someone called in a tip. He, uh..." Carter sent Mary-Alice an uneasy glance. "Contact shotgun wound. It took a while to ID him."

"Leonie blew him away with a shotgun, huh?" Gertie took an enthusiastic bite of her chicken. "That girl always was a little wild. Did you hear she was trying to bash his head in with a bottle of Early Times the night before? And screaming that she was gonna kill him?"

So they'd found Victorin Lowery.

"Does the girlfriend own a shotgun?" Fortune asked.

"Yes, ma'am, she does. Just like pretty much everyone else around here."

"Well, that's your case closed, then, son," Gertie said. "It was Leonie. Too bad. She's a nice girl. When are we going to be able to get Ida Belle out?"

Carter shook his head. "No one's getting Miss Ida Belle out."

"Carter LeBlanc, what are you saying?" Gertie demanded. "Why ever not?"

"If you recall, Leonie Blanchard was in custody at TOD."

"Time of death estimates aren't accurate to the second," Fortune said.

"The ME gave me a two-hour window based on body temp, Fortune, and Leonie was in jail for that window of time and beyond."

"Maybe Leonie hired someone," Gertie said. "Did you ever think of that?"

"Miss Gertie, you'll recall that Miss Ida Belle flat out admitted she shot him. And her shotgun had been fired. And she had gunshot residue on her hands. The time that you called in on behalf of Ida Belle was right within the TOD window. The cause of death was a close-range shotgun blast to the head—"

"Okay, okay, I get it," Gertie grumbled. "But can you prove it was Ida Belle's gun that killed him?"

"It's hard to do ballistics analysis with a shotgun wound," Fortune interjected. "Especially when—sorry, Carter, were you going to say something?

Carter sighed.

"I was going to say it's pretty near impossible to trace shotgun pellets, especially if you don't have the cartridge."

"Why, then, a shotgun is a perfect murder weapon!" Mary-Alice blushed as Carter, Fortune, and Gertie stared at her.

"Well, it's an effective murder weapon, anyway," Carter said, finally, as he stood. "Especially at close range. Look, I'm going to keep on looking into this. It's not like there's a whole lot else to keep us busy. If you hear anything, y'all be sure to let me know right away. Please."

Carter shot Fortune a meaningful look. "I didn't have to tell you that we found Lowery. But I thought you'd want to know."

After Carter left, the women sat glumly around the kitchen table, letting the last of the plump chicken pieces sit uneaten.

"I'm just wondering if y'all can think of any way I might could help," Mary-Alice said, finally.

"Invite Celia to lunch," Gertie said, "and slip rat poison into her tea."

"No, I don't think we could do that," Fortune mused, as if going down a checklist of perfectly reasonable alternatives.

"Maybe Celia shot Victorin Lowery," Gertie suggested.

"Now, Gertie, why on earth do you think Celia would want to go and kill Victorin Lowery?" Mary-Alice asked.

"To incriminate Ida Belle, of course, "Gertie said. "And he makes a convenient victim, because he's been such a nuisance for everyone in town. No one is going to miss him all that much."

"His mama missed him enough to report him missing," Mary-Alice said.

"And let's not forget that either he shot Ida Belle, or someone else shot both of them," Fortune said. "Unless there's something Ida Belle isn't telling us. Did either of you see Leonie Blanchard interacting with anyone in particular when you two were at the Swamp Bar? Maybe the girlfriend's side piece saw an opportunity to get rid of the boyfriend while she was in jail?"

Mary-Alice thought she might look up the term "side piece" later, although she was fairly certain she could guess the meaning from the context. Once again, she found herself wondering what sort of children's librarian Fortune was.

"No, Fortune," Gertie said, "I already told you. She was sitting with a tableful of men. But no one stood out as special. Mary-Alice, how about you? Do you have any ideas? Maybe from all those murder mysteries you read?"

"Gertie," Fortune said, "this is real life. Murder mysteries are fiction. No offense, Mary-Alice."

"Fortune, I'm surprised at you," Gertie said. "You're a librarian, remember? Books are your lifeblood, your reason for living. And Mary-Alice's insights have helped us in the past."

"Good point," Fortune conceded. "What do you think, Mary-Alice?"

Mary-Alice scrambled to think of something useful to say.

"Well, now, the one thing that occurs to me is they always say you can solve the crime if you know enough about the victim."

"We know Victorin Lowery was a drunk who fought with his girlfriend," Gertie said.

"And stole cooking sherry from Francine," Mary-Alice added.

Fortune wrinkled her nose. "Cooking sherry. He must've been desperate. That stuff is nasty. Okay. We want to know more about Victorin Lowery. We hit the Swamp Bar already, and we hit City Hall. What else can we try?"

"Ooh, I know," Gertie raised her hand. "Mary-Alice, why don't you arrange a quiet dinner with Boon St. Clair and get him to talking? Between getting people's plumbing up to code and fixing termite damage, I estimate Boon and his crew have been inside most of the houses in Sinful."

Mary-Alice loved being asked to help with the investigation, but she was reluctant to drag Boon into it.

"Well now, I don't know. It may sound old-fashioned to you, Gertie, but I'm not in the habit of asking men out on dates."

Gertie rolled her eyes.

"Mary-Alice, do I have to take away your Southern Lady card?"

"What are you talking about?" Fortune asked.

"Of course she's not going to ask him out directly," Gertie explained. "She will arrange to let him ask her out. And he's going to think the whole thing was his idea. C'mon, Mary-Alice, don't look like that. You've already been out with him. It'll be a piece of cake."

"But Boon and I have only engaged in pleasant small talk. I don't know him well enough to bring up crimes of passion and close-range shotgun wounds over dinner."

"So how do you think you'll get to know him better?" Gertie countered. "I'll tell you. This is how. Do you want your relationship to ever get past the superficial stage? Talk to him about the murder, ask him about Victorin Lowery, and just watch and see what he knows and how he reacts. Anyway, it's for a good cause. Don't forget we're doing all this to help Ida Belle."

Mary-Alice thought about it.

"I suppose you're right. It wouldn't do any harm to mention it to Boon. He saw Ida Belle getting arrested, after all. Gertie, you are very persuasive."

Gertie patted the giant handbag that hung off the back of her chair.

"'Course I'm persuasive. No one's taking *my* Southern Lady card away."

CHAPTER 9

The following evening, Mary-Alice stood before her open closet, trying to decide what to wear for her date with Boon. Her go-to white capris, of course. But should she wear the blue and green flowered blouse, or the red and yellow? Warm colors, she decided. As she pulled the red-and-yellow top over her head, she heard a knock on the door.

It couldn't be Boon, Mary-Alice thought, glancing at her watch. Boon would never show up to a lady's house ten minutes early. He was raised better than that.

Mary-Alice quickly checked herself in the mirror. She patted her hair into place, wiped off an under-eye mascara smear, and answered the door.

There stood Celia Arceneaux, holding a small cardboard box.

Oh dear, Mary-Alice thought. I hope she hasn't found out about our investigation.

"Well, my, Celia! What a lovely surprise. Come in and have a glass of tea."

"I don't have time to stay and chat." Celia said abruptly. She cast a meaningful look around Mary-Alice's house. "I just wanted to let you know how happy I am to see that you're finally doing something worthwhile with your time. Instead of pouring your life savings into this money pit. Now you know that I'm far too busy to help you dig through all the records, but I've told Dorothy to give you all the help you need on your little history book. Oh, and I thought you'd need this."

Celia thrust the box into Mary-Alice's bewildered hands.

"These are some things of Pansy's. Mostly newspaper clippings of her pageant successes. And some things she kept from school. You remember my Pansy, of course."

Mary-Alice recalled a pretty young sociopath who was kicked out of kindergarten for stealing the teacher's lighter and trying to set fire to the school.

"Your precious Pansy. Of course I remember her."

"Now those mementos aren't yours to keep, Mary-Alice. I want them back when you're done. Make sure you handle them carefully, especially the clippings—"

Celia was interrupted by a crunch of shells behind her. Boon St. Clair stepped down from the cab of his battered red truck. He looked dashing in a collared shirt and neat khakis, perfect for a sultry summer evening in bayou country.

Celia grabbed Mary-Alice by the elbow and pulled her into the house.

"Is that Boon St. Clair?" she hissed.

"It is Boon." Was Celia getting as nearsighted as Gertie? It was no secret that Mary-Alice and Boon had been spending time together socially. Why was Celia acting shocked?

"Mary-Alice, I do hope this isn't a social call."

"Yes, Celia. It is a social call. Boon is taking me to dinner."

"I can't believe I have to tell you this, Mary-Alice. Our kind don't mingle with the help."

Mary-Alice recalled overhearing her own mother saying that exact thing to her father, and in much the same tone.

"President Jefferson's regrettable example notwithstanding," Mary-Alice's mother had added drily.

By the time little Mary-Alice woke up the next morning, their pretty young maid had packed and gone.

"He is not the *help*, Celia." Mary-Alice yanked herself back to the present. "Gracious me, Boon is a friend. Thank you ever so kindly for stopping by. It has been just lovely to see you."

Mary-Alice slid her arm out of Celia's grip, set down the box of Pansy's relics on the foyer table, and hurried outside. Boon had seen the whole thing and had been hovering uneasily by his truck. He seemed reluctant to interfere.

"Don't forget about Dorothy helping you with the records," Celia called from Mary-Alice's doorway, as Boon helped her up into the passenger seat. "She'd be glad of something to do. She gets so bored, you know."

Mary-Alice and Boon waved to Celia as Boon drove away. Mary-Alice knew Celia would take the opportunity to snoop through her house, and only hoped that Celia would remember to lock up when she left.

Despite being a work vehicle, Boon's truck was immaculate. A brand-new pine-scented deodorizer swung from the rear-view mirror. Boon's truck was just as dressed up as he was.

"Everything all right, Miss Mary-Alice?" Boon said as he turned onto the main road. "Seems you might have something on your mind."

Mary-Alice had a few things on her mind. She knew that Celia couldn't help her sharp tongue, and one mustn't hold grudges, but there was a limit. The help. Honestly.

"They found Victorin Lowery's body," Mary-Alice blurted. Her hand flew to her mouth. She hadn't planned on bringing up the murder right away.

Boon didn't seem the least bit shocked.

"I heard tell they found a body out in the bayou. You're sayin' they think it's Victorin? Talk is, he was...hard to identify, I guess you might say."

"Deputy LeBlanc came by and told us. He thought we should know because Ida Belle is the only suspect. Celia still won't let the sheriff grant her bail."

"Was that what you and Miss Celia were discussing back there?" Boon asked.

"Well, no, not exactly."

"I don't suppose your conversation had anything to do with me," Boon said evenly.

"Where are we going?" Mary-Alice realized that they were driving out of Sinful.

"Landrieu's Landing. Steaks and seafood. Little bit fancier than Francine's. It's usually hard to get a reservation, but they had a last-minute cancellation."

"Celia doesn't like it that I'm spending time with you," Mary-Alice said.

"I figured as much, from the look she gave me."

"I don't agree with Celia, of course." Mary-Alice glanced at Boon to see his reaction.

Boon nodded thoughtfully.

"You know something, Mary-Alice? There are people in this world like you, who are kind and good."

"That's nice of you to say, Boon."

"And then there are people who, how do I put it? The ones who make you appreciate the people who are kind and good. So how are y'all going planning to get Miss Ida Belle off the hook?"

Mary-Alice stared out the window. The thick woods glowed purple in the dusk.

"How did you know we were trying to get Ida Belle out of jail?"

"I was there when she was arrested, remember? It was pretty clear to me that y'all are not goin' to sit around and let Miss Ida Belle...anyway, here we are."

Mary-Alice wondered how Boon was going to finish that sentence. Not going to let Ida Belle get the gas chamber? Would it come to that?

Boon turned the truck off onto an undistinguished single-lane drive, and soon Landrieu's Landing appeared. With its single-story construction, its crushed-shell parking lot, and its bayou location, it looked like the Swamp Bar's high-end cousin.

The interior of Landrieu's Landing was not at all like the Swamp Bar. It had white tablecloths, pleasant wait staff, and a gleaming parquet floor. Although the restaurant was crowded, Boon had somehow secured a table by the window. Outside, the surface of the water glinted under Landrieu's strategically-placed outdoor lights.

Mary-Alice and Boon ordered dinner and continued to talk about the murder. Mary-Alice was surprised when Boon casually mentioned that Victorin had once worked for him.

"I don't recall you saying anything about that before," Mary-Alice said.

"I'd rather not speak ill of people if it's not necessary. Victorin was a good boy when he was coming up. Didn't give his mama much trouble. But when he came back from New Orleans, he was different. He'd lost ground somehow. I wanted to give him a chance, so I hired him on."

"That was very compassionate of you, Boon."

"It was a big mistake is what it was. He showed up drunk the first day, and I never saw his face again after that. Had let him go."

Boon pulled a plump oyster out of his bowl and ate it with pleasure. Mary-Alice had considered ordering the oyster stew as well, but with Boon sitting right there, ordering oysters seemed like a brazenly suggestive choice. She'd decided on the baked catfish amandine with hot French bread and sweet potato on the side.

"Probably the easiest firing I ever did," Boon continued. "I didn't even have to tell him in person on account of he never showed up again. I just mailed his mama a check for his day's wages. Even though I can't say he earned it."

"His mama's still in town?" Mary-Alice asked.

"Miss Eulalie Cormier? Yes, ma'am, she's still in the same house, still feuding with the neighbors."

"Her last name's Cormier? Not Lowery?"

"Lowery was a few husbands ago. I think that's why she doesn't come to church very often these days. I don't believe she sees eye to eye with them on the question of divorce."

"Well, that's just a shame," Mary-Alice said. "When you're divorced, that's when you'd need your church people the most. You'd be lonesome and hurting. Don't you think?"

"Doesn't seem to me like divorce would be much fun," Boon agreed. "Of course, being widowed is no picnic either."

"No, I suppose not." Widowhood had actually been a great relief for Mary-Alice, but she knew it would not be tactful to say so to Boon.

Mary-Alice didn't attach any particular significance to Boon's remark.

Just as she didn't take much note of the hostess who had greeted them by name and seated them at the best table in the restaurant. Nor the waiter who kept their wine glasses filled and kept asking if there was anything he could get them. And she barely registered Boon's uncharacteristic nervousness.

Mary-Alice was so focused on finding clues to Victorin Lowery's murder that she did not engage her powers of observation. And so she found herself entirely unprepared for what happened over dessert.

CHAPTER 10

Mary-Alice awoke with an uneasy feeling. She wondered whether she had made a mistake the night before. She hadn't precisely turned down Boon's offer of marriage. But she hadn't exactly accepted it, either.

"You and I get along pretty well, Miss Mary-Alice, don't we?" he'd said, as he placed his hand on hers. "I've been thinking that if we're still getting along this well by the time your kitchen's finished, we might consider getting married."

"Married?" Mary-Alice had stammered.

"To each other, I mean," he explained.

He was a lovely man, she'd replied, and she enjoyed his company very much. But she had been a widow for so long, she needed time to think it over.

Now she wondered whether she shouldn't have simply said yes. She enjoyed spending time with Boon, and everything she knew about him told her that he was an honorable and compassionate man. And she was in her eighth decade of life. What, she asked herself, was she waiting for?

Enough dithering, Mary-Alice thought as she sprang out of bed. I'll get dressed, go out there, and tell him…

Tell him what? She sat back down on the bed. The truth was that while she admired Boon and enjoyed his company, becoming engaged to him while he was still in her employ seemed highly improper. And in any event, she simply wasn't ready. She'd endured a good deal of upheaval in her life recently, and she wanted things to settle down before she made any important decisions.

The proper thing would be to act like nothing was wrong. She would sashay on over to Francine's like everything was just as normal as could be. She'd leave off the usual box of baked delights for the working crew and then she'd manage her face to give Mr. Boon St. Clair a gracious and friendly greeting.

But when Mary-Alice came into the kitchen with the pink box from Francine's, Boon wasn't there.

"No, ma'am, Mister St. Clair hasn't come in this morning," one of the young women offered.

Mary-Alice smiled and thanked her.

Well, that tears it, she thought glumly. *I've driven him away.* With a sinking heart, she trudged back to her room and placed a call to Gertie. She hoped that concentrating on Ida Belle's predicament might distract her from thinking about Boon, even if just for a little while.

"Mary-Alice, we were just about to call you," Gertie said. "How soon can you get over to the sheriff's station? They're fixing to let us visit with Ida Belle."

Deputy Breaux met Mary-Alice by the front counter of the sheriff's station and guided her down the hallway to an interview room. Fortune and Gertie were already there, sitting on one side of a battered wooden table. Ida Belle sat on the opposite side. Mary-Alice had expected Ida Belle to be wearing some kind of prison uniform, but she was wearing her usual oxford shirt, and didn't even have on handcuffs. You wouldn't know anything was wrong with her shoulder, except that she only moved her good arm as she talked.

"...I'm not worried about the drunks and the wife-beaters," Ida Belle was saying. "They're more scared of me than I am of them. Remember, I'm a cold-blooded murderess. Hey, Mary-Alice. Come on in. Okay, what'd you all find out? I'm dying to know."

"Lowery spent time New Orleans," Fortune announced. "So I checked into his history there. He was enrolled in the NOLA police academy, but didn't finish."

"So he washed out," Ida Belle said.

"Or they put him undercover," Fortune countered. "Which widens our pool of suspects."

"I surely do wish I could've gotten Leonie to tell me whatever it was that she was hollering about the Marines to Deputy Breaux," Gertie said. "Maybe I should go back to the Swamp Bar and give it another try."

"If you want to get yourself all tarted up and go off to the Swamp Bar just so you can flirt with Junior Baker again, then you just go on ahead," Ida Belle said. "You don't need to use me as an excuse."

Mary-Alice interrupted before Gertie could answer back.

"I was thinking, why don't I call on Victorin's mama, Miss Eulalie? I understand she still lives in Sinful. Now, Gertie can't go, because she's been friends with Ida Belle since they were little children. Fortune is far too young, and she's a Yankee besides. No offense, Fortune, darling."

"None taken," Fortune said.

"I appreciate the thought, Mary-Alice," Ida Belle said. "But just how are you going to introduce yourself? You can't go knock on her door and tell her you're gonna be her new best friend."

"Boon told me that Eulalie attends the Catholic church now and then," Mary-Alice said. "If she's Catholic, I think it might be worthwhile to try meeting up with her on Bingo night."

"When's Bingo night?" Ida Belle asked.

"Wednesdays."

Gertie's eyes widened. "But today's Wednesday! That only leaves me a few hours to pick out my Bingo outfit!"

Ida Belle rolled her eyes, which did not escape Gertie's notice.

"I have to look frumpy so I'll blend in," Gertie continued maliciously. "Ida Belle, you don't mind if I go over to your house and borrow something to wear, do you?"

Fortune raised her hand. "Gertie, do you think it's a good idea for you to show your face at the Catholic church? After all the times we've beaten them in the Banana Pudding War? At least Mary-Alice is a noncombatant."

"That is a good point," Ida Belle said. "Ever since Fortune came to Sinful we've been whuppin' their Catholic butts every Sunday."

Joking about whupping people's butts on Sunday struck Mary-Alice as irreverent, but she knew she shouldn't judge Ida Belle too harshly. Life behind bars changed people, or so she'd read.

"Sorry, Mary-Alice," Gertie said. "I would've liked to go with you, but they're right. You have to do this alone."

"Besides, dressing up like a frumpy Catholic Bingo lady isn't as much fun as getting all dolled up to go out to the Swamp Bar," Ida Belle added.

"There's just one more thing." Mary-Alice glanced at the door of the interview room. Being inside the sheriff's station made her nervous. "I don't know Miss Eulalie by sight."

"Don't worry about that," Ida Belle said. "She'll be the one in pink."

"What if there's more than one woman in pink?"

"Oh, you'll know her," Gertie said. "Trust me. Not just pink. Capital-P- pink."

"Oh, I know who you're talking about, now," Fortune said.

"You can't miss her, Mary-Alice. The woman looks like a Pepto-Bismol bottle."

Deputy Breaux opened the door of the interview room. "Five minutes, ladies." He looked sheepish.

Ida Belle nodded, dismissing him.

"I do appreciate it, Mary-Alice," Ida Belle said when Breaux had withdrawn. "My public defender's an imbecile. If I didn't know better I'd think he was related to Celia."

Then, remembering that Mary-Alice actually was related to Celia, Ida Belle added quickly, "So, any other news before you all have to leave me?"

"Celia called on me," Mary-Alice said.

"Well, that would ruin anyone's day," Gertie said. "What did she get on your case about this time?"

"For one thing, she deemed it her place to let me know she disapproved of Boon. But that aside, she was very excited about the history of Sinful. She brought over a whole box of that pitiful Pansy's things. To help me with my historical research, she said. And she told me she wanted a signed copy of the book when it was finished. If Gertie hadn't agreed to help me out of this situation, I simply don't know what I'd do."

Gertie's hunted look showed that this agreement had entirely slipped her mind.

"Family history?" Ida Belle asked. "What's she talking about?"

Mary-Alice glanced at Gertie. Gertie stared at the scuffed wooden table.

"I had it in mind to look in the city records, to see if I could find anything out about Victorin Lowery," Mary-Alice explained. "And Dorothy, you know she's Celia's cousin by blood and she's in the God's Wives club, she was at the counter. I thought she'd get suspicious and tell Celia everything I was doing in there. So Gertie gave me a wonderful cover story. I told Dorothy I was researching a history of Sinful."

"So Gertie got you into this mess," Ida Belle said, "And now she has to get you out of it. That's a familiar story, let me tell you. Gertie, you know how to research historical records?"

Gertie made a face at her.

"Don't worry about it, Mary-Alice," Fortune said. "You go to Catholic Bingo and talk to Victorin Lowery's mom, and I'll see if I can help Gertie out with this family history business."

Mary-Alice brightened. As did Gertie.

"Of course!" Mary-Alice exclaimed. "Silly me, you're a librarian! Why, thank you so much, Fortune, that is such a relief."

"Yes," Gertie added sincerely. "Quite helpful, Fortune."

"Not as helpful as you're going to be, Mary-Alice," Ida Belle said, as Deputy Breaux opened the door to escort Ida Belle's visitors out. "Mary-Alice, I'm counting on you."

CHAPTER 11

Mary-Alice spent the rest of the afternoon on her shady back porch, reading a murder mystery and sipping iced tea. She did her best to ignore the hammering and whirring sounds coming from her kitchen. The construction noise reminded her that Boon wasn't there.

When it was almost time to leave, Mary-Alice remembered the cardboard box by the entryway. She decided she had better take a look at it in case she ran into Celia at Bingo Night.

Mary-Alice took the box over to the dining table and opened it. Inside she found a quart-sized Ziploc bag filled with newspaper clippings sitting atop a stack of plastic tiaras. She lifted the tiaras out to find a collection of folded satin sashes, yellowed at the edges. At the bottom of the box lay a well-worn writing journal and a small silver cross on a broken chain. It was from Pansy's first catechism. Mary-Alice remembered the little girl yanking off her necklace and throwing it onto the ground, although she didn't remember why.

Mary-Alice took out the brittle newspaper clippings and leafed through them. They were all about the beauty pageants that Pansy had entered, starting at age 4. She replaced them carefully in the plastic bag and took out the journal next. It was scuffed-up and looked as if it had been dropped in the mud.

Mary-Alice opened it to a bookmarked page. She saw neatly-written rows of names and dates, each followed by a number and then some kind of code. Pansy had dotted each "I" with a heart. And all of the names were men's names. Mary-Alice flipped through the pages. They were all like that.

The bookmark slipped out and fell onto Mary-Alice's lap. When she picked it up she saw it was an evidence tag.

Mary-Alice stuck the tag between the pages and placed the journal back into the box. The sheriff's office must have returned the journal to Celia after they'd finished investigating Pansy's murder.

Mary-Alice wondered what she would tell Celia if she asked about the box. She always held that if you can't say anything nice, don't say anything at all.

"Poor Pansy," Mary-Alice could say. "You must miss her so."

That wasn't ideal, but it would have to do.

As it turned out, Celia was not at Bingo Night that evening. Dorothy was absent too, as was the rest of the God's Wives crew. They must be having one of their frequent meetings.

Mary-Alice was relieved. A smaller crowd would make it easier to find Victorin's mother Eulalie. And Mary-Alice wouldn't have to try to think of nice things to say about Celia's dreadful daughter.

The social hall was filled with long picnic-style tables. In the front of the room, next to the kitchen window, two women sat at a low table with a microphone and a bingo ball cage. Mary-Alice was a little disappointed it wasn't one of the fancy machines that blew the balls around, like they had back in Mudbug. Of course, living in a small town like Sinful meant giving up some big-city comforts.

Mary-Alice purchased two bingo cards at the door.

"Is Miss Eulalie here tonight?" Mary-Alice asked.

The woman inclined her head toward the front of the room.

.

"Right up there, sugar."

The woman seemed to be indicating a pink blur near the front of the room. As Mary-Alice approached, the blur resolved into a woman wearing a rose-colored bed-jacket. The jacket's cotton-candy-colored marabou trim matched the woman's pink hair. A dozen bingo cards were spread out on the table in front of her. She was studying them, tapping each in turn with her frosted-flamingo fingernails.

Mary-Alice sat down next to Eulalie Cormier.

"My, twelve Bingo cards," Mary-Alice exclaimed admiringly. "You must be very good at this. Permit me to introduce myself, won't you? I'm Mary-Alice Arceneaux."

Eulalie produced a pink handkerchief and dabbed the corners of her heavily-mascaraed eyes.

"You must be new in town, Mary-Alice."

"I just moved over here from Mudbug. Is there something the matter?"

"I just lost my Vicky. My son. His given name is Victorin, but I always called him Vicky, ever since he was a child."

Eulalie blew her nose energetically into the handkerchief.

"I'm terribly sorry to hear it," Mary-Alice said.

"You ever lose a child?"

Mary-Alice nodded. "Yes. Yes, I did. Years ago. So very much harder than losing a husband, isn't it?"

Eulalie nodded vigorously, dabbed her eyes again, and tucked her handkerchief into her pink handbag. Feather fragments from her marabou trim floated around her like fairy spirits.

"Mind you, Mary-Alice, we had fallen out and didn't care for each other much when he was alive. But kin's kin, and I don't have any other children."

"Do you have grandchildren?" Mary-Alice asked.

"Oh, most likely. That boy had the morals of an alley cat. But he left me well-enough provided for, what with the disability checks. At least I can say that for him."

Eulalie kept chatting with Mary-Alice throughout the bingo calls, keeping her eyes on her dozen bingo cards.

"I thought he might improve once he moved back from New Orleans," Eulalie said. "But then the lawsuits started. That old busybody Gaudet bears some of the blame for all this, believe you me."

Eulalie treated Mary-Alice to a detailed history of her legal woes. The feud had started when Eulalie, exercising her rights as a homeowner, had painted her house shocking pink.

"So cheery," she explained, "and just what that drab old neighborhood needed."

The elderly bachelor who lived across the street promptly sued her for interfering with his pursuit of happiness. Eulalie countersued him, alleging infringement of her constitutional right to Freedom of Expression. Old Beauregard Gaudet fired back with Vexatious Litigation and Intentional Infliction of Emotional Distress.

"It's been such a trial for us," Eulalie continued. "And my poor Vicky, he did feel the strain."

"My goodness," Mary-Alice said. "How awful for you."

"Yes, ma'am, it was. The poor boy was troubled. And Mary-Alice, I am certainly not prejudiced or anything, you understand, I mean, you can ask anyone, but him getting mixed up with that colored girl didn't help him one little bit."

"Colored girl? You can't be referring to Leonie Blanchard?"

Eulalie scoffed. "Hollow-Leg Leonie? No. I'm talking about Marine. Marine Montreuil. Too smart for my Vicky, that was her problem. Made more money than him, too. The marriage didn't stand a chance."

"Victorin was married?" Mary-Alice said.

Eulalie nodded and frowned at her bingo cards.

"And you know what the worst part is? My Vicky'd just got out of rehab. I thought he was finally going to turn things around."

"Bingo!" Someone yelled in the back, and they were on to the next game.

CHAPTER 12

The next morning, Mary-Alice, Gertie, and Fortune sat in a quiet corner of Francine's Diner. They held their conversation until Ally had taken their breakfast order and was out of earshot.

"Before we do anything else," Mary-Alice said, "I think we should report what I found out. To the sheriff."

"I already talked to Carter," Fortune said.

"You mean after I texted you last night?" Mary-Alice asked innocently. "Goodness, it was already quite late. I hope he didn't mind."

"What'd he say?" Gertie asked.

The conversation paused when Ally came back to refill coffee cups and water glasses.

"He said he appreciated the information," Fortune said. "But he didn't think someone of Marine Montreuil's description would be able to sneak into Sinful unnoticed. Much less blow someone's head off with a shotgun and sneak out again."

"But they were divorced," Mary-Alice said. "Doesn't that make her a suspect?"

"I mentioned that. He said there are millions of divorced

people who manage to get through the day without killing each other."

"Well, I just want to say, you did good work, Mary-Alice." Gertie said. "You found out that Victorin was married, which none of us surely did know. And thanks to you we also know what Leonie was going on about to Deputy Breaux. She didn't mean the Marines. She was talking about Victorin's ex-wife Marine. Fortune, are you saying Carter's not even going to go talk to this ex-wife?"

Fortune shook her head. There was another moment of silence when Ally brought the breakfasts. All three had ordered the biscuits and gravy special; it was cheap, delicious, and quick.

"They've halted the investigation," Fortune said. "Sheriff Lee isn't going to stand up to Celia. And as far as Celia is concerned, they have their suspect."

"So if we were to go to New Orleans and just happened to run into a certain Marine Montreuil," Gertie said, "we wouldn't be interfering with any official investigation at all, now would we?"

"We're going to New Orleans?" Mary-Alice asked. "When?"

"Soon as you finish your biscuits and gravy," Gertie said.

Mary-Alice volunteered to drive, but Fortune (disconcertingly) pointed out that "you never know when you might have to go off-road." Gertie climbed into the front passenger seat of Fortune's Jeep. Mary-Alice carefully buckled herself in behind the driver's seat.

"You have the dossier?" Gertie asked.

"In the glovebox," Fortune said. "Can you hand it back to Mary-Alice?"

Mary-Alice found herself holding a manila folder. Inside was information on Marine Montreuil: a small passport-sized photo, a list of current and previous home and work addresses, and an aerial map of the big medical center on Canal Street.

Marine worked there as a nurse, according to the information in the file.

"Why are you giving this to me?" Mary-Alice asked as Fortune pulled out to the main road.

"You're the one who knows Victorin's mother," Fortune said. "That gives you an excuse to talk to her former daughter-in-law."

"You mean just walk right on up to her?"

"I'd say you managed very well with Miss Eulalie last night," Gertie said.

"But I don't want to interrupt a nurse while she's tending to her patients," Mary-Alice pleaded. "That wouldn't be right."

"There's a rest stop up ahead," Gertie said. "Do we have time? I won't be a minute."

Fortune pulled off the road in front of a gas station/bait shop.

"Gertie, did you have to drink that fourth cup of coffee?"

"You want me alert, don't you?" Gertie slowly let herself down from the Jeep and headed into the building.

Fortune turned to Mary-Alice.

"You want to make a pit stop too, Mary-Alice?"

Mary-Alice took in the mildew-eaten siding, ripped screen door, and hand painted sign: *"Fresh" Sandwiches Bait and Gas*

"No thank you," she said. "I believe I'll wait right here."

They reached the Medical Center at around eleven. Fortune pulled into the parking garage and took a ticket, then headed up the ramp to prowl for an empty spot.

Mary-Alice felt a rush of excitement on entering the city. She found New Orleans exhilarating. It was like another planet with its gleaming towers, 24-hour shops, and most wondrous of all, escalators. Mary-Alice had been fascinated with escalators ever since her mother had taken her into New Orleans to shop for her confirmation dress at Krauss, one of the first department stores in the nation to feature "mechanical stairs."

Once they were on the Medical Center grounds, Fortune and Gertie seemed to know exactly where they were going. Mary-Alice followed them into a lobby, down a corridor, outside, and then back inside. Then down a sidewalk under some scaffolding, and around a corner, and through the automatic doors of the hospital cafeteria. (There were no escalators on the way, alas). They bought sandwiches, then went out to the dining room, where Fortune chose a high table by a floor-to-ceiling window.

"We have a good view from here," Fortune explained as she took her seat. Outside, medical personnel in scrubs and civilians hurried past in the punishing heat.

"There she is," Gertie hissed, so suddenly that Mary-Alice nearly choked on her tuna sandwich. "That's her!"

A young woman in pink scrubs, her hair dyed the color of red velvet cake, was walking away from the cash register. Mary-Alice was relieved to see that the woman was alone; she wouldn't have to barge in on anyone's conversation. She grabbed her paper plate and reached the young woman just as she sat down.

"Excuse me," Mary said to the young woman. "Aren't you Marine Montreuil? I feel like I recognize you."

To Mary-Alice's relief, Marine replied,

"Yes I am. Won't you join me, ma'am? Please."

Mary-Alice sat down next to the young nurse. Seconds later, a man approached their table. He was in his late fifties and bald as a plate, with the fiercest eyebrows Mary-Alice had ever seen. Mary-Alice noticed that he wore a gold wedding band.

"I'm real sorry to tell you this, Roger," Marine said with a sweet smile. "I won't be able to join you for lunch today. I have some family business to deal with."

"Family business, huh?"

The man looked from Marine to Mary-Alice and back.

"Fine," he said peevishly, and stalked off.

"I don't believe I know who you are," Marine said quietly, "but thank you so much for showing up when you did. Now I can eat my lunch in peace."

"Was that man bothering you?"

"I don't believe he's dangerous, but he does make me uncomfortable. And I shouldn't hold it against him that he works in the morgue, but it may be that I do. Never mind, now. How can I help you?"

"I'm a friend of Victorin Lowery's mother, Miss Eulalie," Mary-Alice said. "So it really is family business of a sort. My name is Mary-Alice Arceneaux."

"It's a pleasure to meet you, ma'am."

"I'm so sorry about Victorin."

Marine lifted her perfectly-shaped brows.

"How did you know about Vicky? I just got the call from the Sinful Sheriff's Department this morning."

So it seemed that Carter had followed up, if only by telephone.

"I suppose you can't really keep a secret in Sinful," Mary-Alice said.

"That's true as can be. Where is Miss Eulalie? Is she here with you?"

"No, Miss Eulalie's back home. I just happened to be here with friends and when I saw you, I thought you looked familiar."

"How did you recognize—oh, the wedding pictures. Of course. Victorin still has them. *Had* them, I should say."

Mary-Alice had a different answer prepared, but decided to go with Marine's explanation.

"Yes, of course, that's it. Poor Miss Eulalie. She is simply distraught. I must say, she thinks quite highly of you, you know."

Marine smiled slightly.

"Well I must say, that's news to me."

"She let slip that she always thought you were too good for her son."

Marine ripped open a bag of potato chips and shook them onto her paper plate, next to her veggie wrap.

"I wasn't good for him at all, ma'am, sorry to say. I'm a medical professional, and I couldn't help him. I saw it coming, and I couldn't do anything to stop it."

"Stop what?" Mary-Alice asked.

"Vicky ending it all. Now I heard from the sheriff that he got himself shot by some lowlife moonshiner, but I don't believe it. He was much too careful for that to occur. He wouldn't have let that happen unless he wanted it to. Or he simply didn't care anymore."

Mary-Alice wondered how Ida Belle would feel about being called a "lowlife moonshiner." Knowing Ida Belle, she'd probably get a kick out of it.

"Do you believe Victorin was troubled?" Mary-Alice asked.

"Troubled! I should say so. He believed people were monitoring his thoughts. He told me there were cameras behind his eyes, and a big monitor in CIA headquarters showing everything he saw in real time. He thought there were government agents sitting around watching it, taking notes."

"Oh, my, that's quite something," Mary-Alice said.

"When he wanted privacy, he would close his eyes. To make their screen go black, he said. Imagine what it was like...no, don't imagine. You know when I'd finally had enough? It wasn't when he went and got himself fired. No ma'am, I stuck by my man. And it wasn't even when he started going online and spending money we didn't have on body armor and all other sorts of peculiar things. No, now, I put up with all that business until one night Vicky got up and went through our apartment shooting out the smoke alarms. He said they all had listening devices in them, you see. That's when I finally sent him back home to his mama."

"I'm so sorry to hear that."

"I still can't believe he got himself killed. Say what you like about alcoholic paranoia, at least it made him careful. Maybe it hasn't sunk in yet that he's really gone. I don't know. But I just can't bring myself to feel sad today. I already did my grieving. Do you know, I only just talked to him on Friday. He seemed...I want to say he seemed fine. But he wasn't fine. That's for sure."

Marine glanced at her watch.

"Ma'am, it surely was nice talking to you, but I'm afraid I have to leave now. We got a whole bunch of domoic acid poisonings coming in. Listen, I'm not supposed to say anything because they don't want people to panic, but let's put it this way. I'm certainly not going to eat shellfish for a while. Oh, please, ma'am, give Miss Eulalie my love, won't you?"

CHAPTER 13

"Looks like you had a good conversation," Fortune said when Mary-Alice returned. "Ready to go?"

"I need to find a restroom first," Gertie said.

"Yeah, we should all make a pit stop. It's a long drive back. But Gertie, did you have to get a jumbo Coke?"

Mary-Alice kept mum until they were in the car and on their way. As Fortune exited the Medical Center complex and followed the surface streets to the I-10, Mary-Alice recounted her conversation with Marine Montreuil.

"So I think we had a pretty good idea why Leonie was going after Victorin at the Swamp Bar," Fortune said. "I'll bet you she found out Victorin had been talking to his ex-wife."

"Mary-Alice, did Marine really say that he was ordering body armor?" Gertie said. "I just wonder. Do you suppose Victorin could've recovered and walked away after Ida Belle shot him? That would explain us not finding any blood."

"Oh, and maybe that's how Ida Belle was injured?" Mary-Alice added. "Could her shotgun pellet have ricocheted off his body armor?"

"Body armor is supposed to absorb, not to ricochet," Fortune said. "Although I've heard of people putting together these sketchy getups with steel plates. You can get ricochet with those, especially with steel pellets."

"Do you all think we should report what we've found out?" Mary-Alice asked.

"I guess we did promise Carter we wouldn't keep things from him," Fortune said.

"Let's just tell him what we know, but not how we know it," Gertie suggested.

"Sure. Can you get him on speaker? My phone's in my bag. I think you can find his number in my recent calls."

Gertie fetched Fortune's phone and dialed, then clicked on the speaker-phone option. Carter answered after half a ring.

"Hey, beautiful," Carter purred. Mary-Alice saw Fortune's ears turn pink.

"Carter," Fortune said, "you're on speaker."

"Ah. Good afternoon, Miss Gertie. And Miss Mary-Alice?"

"Hello, Deputy," Gertie and Mary-Alice sang out.

"We have some information for you," Fortune said. "Prior to the dissolution of his marriage to Marine Montreuil, Victorin Lowery appeared to be exhibiting signs of alcohol-related psychosis, including paranoia. He purchased body armor, destroyed the smoke detectors in the department, and believed his thoughts were being monitored. However, on the Friday prior to the incident in Ida Belle's garage, Mister Lowery called his ex-wife and appeared to be improved. This is consistent with his mother's claim that he had spent time in rehab. The call to his ex-wife is the likely cause of the fight between the victim and Leonie Blanchard. The fact that Deputy Breaux heard Leonie say the word 'Marine' supports this theory, as Marine is the name of the vic's ex-wife. Carter, are you still there?"

"Yes, ma'am I'm taking notes. How did you happen to discover all of this?"

"Rumor and hearsay," Fortune said. "So what do you think? Does it jibe with what you know?"

"Yes, it does. The vic was found wearing body armor," Carter said.

"You didn't mention that."

"Didn't I, now?"

"Carter, if Lowery was wearing body armor, that means he could've walked away from the confrontation with Ida Belle. Even if she did shoot him, he could have survived."

"Even if that's true," Carter said, "Ida Belle could have tracked him down later."

"Deputy, don't you think a determined murderer might be able to fiddle with the apparent time of death?" Mary-Alice asked.

"That would point to a very carefully planned, premeditated murder," Carter's voice squawked from Fortune's phone. "The killer would have had to be someone with medical knowledge and access to the right equipment. Like that doctor who stored his wife in the morgue to mess up the TOD. But this seems more like a crime of passion. Brutal method, no attempt to hide the body."

"Marine Montreuil, Victorin's ex-wife, has an admirer who works in the morgue," Mary-Alice said, but Carter didn't pick up on it.

"If you want my advice," he said, "I've always thought an insanity defense was a long shot, but if anyone could pull it off, I believe Ida Belle could—"

Gertie mashed the hang-up button and glanced at Fortune.

"Sorry," she said sheepishly. "I couldn't listen to him say those things about Ida Belle."

"He thinks Ida Belle is guilty," Fortune said glumly. "Carter's always been on our side, even if he hasn't always approved of our methods. But not this time. He really believes Ida Belle murdered Victorin Lowery."

The women drove in silence for a long time.

"Can we make a stop?" Gertie asked. "I think this will probably be our last chance for a while."

"Sure." Fortune pulled off the road at Karoline's Kountry Kitchen, an undistinguished single-story building with a dirt parking lot. "You want to get something to eat here? I'm a little hungry. That hospital sandwich wasn't very satisfying and we still have more than an hour to go."

"I'd rather wait and have dinner at Francine's," Gertie said as she climbed down and went inside.

"So how's the remodel going?" Fortune asked Mary-Alice.

"When Boon and I went out to dinner at Landrieu's Landing, he asked me to marry him."

Fortune turned around in her seat.

"He asked you to marry him? Congratulations. Sorry, you're not supposed to congratulate the bride. Best wishes, I guess. But wouldn't getting married disqualify you from membership in the Sinful Ladies Society?"

"I believe it would. Fortune, I like Boon very much, but it's too soon to think about marriage."

"What did you tell him?"

"I said I'd have to think about it."

"Good answer. That's probably what I would say if Carter... if I were in your position. How'd he take it?"

Mary-Alice felt the sting of tears in her eyes.

"Not well. Not very well, at all. He didn't show up to work on my house the next day. I haven't seen him since. Only his crew has been coming. Fortune, I hurt his feelings, and I don't know if I can undo the damage."

Gertie opened the door and climbed back into the passenger seat.

"Mary-Alice, if you hurt anyone's feelings I'll eat my hat. The one that holds the two beer cans."

"That was quick," Fortune said. "Were they closed?"

"No, but that bathroom was too scary for me. And I spent three days sleeping outdoors in the Cambodian jungle. I'm just gonna hold it. Who are we talking about? Whose feelings did Mary-Alice hurt?"

"Boon asked me to marry him," Mary-Alice said. "I didn't say yes right away. And now he's avoiding me. He hasn't shown up to work since then."

"Everybody knows that Boon St. Clair is sweet on you," Gertie said as she buckled in. "And I can certainly believe he was disappointed. But that man would never miss work over a little heartbreak. He must be on another job or something."

"Did you call him?" Fortune asked as they started down the road, leaving Karolyn's Kountry Kitchen behind.

"Well, no, I…"

"Call him!" Fortune and Gertie shouted in unison.

"What would I say?"

"Say you haven't seen him for a while and you hope he's okay," Gertie said.

"I suppose I can do that." Mary-Alice was secretly glad her friends were pressuring her to call Boon. She had considered it, but rejected the idea as too brazen.

Mary-Alice's stomach flipped as she heard the phone ring on the other end. Then the ringing stopped.

"I'm sorry," said a recorded voice. "This voice mailbox is full."

"His voicemail is full," Mary-Alice said.

"Is that his only phone number?" Fortune asked.

"Yes. His work number and his home number are the same."

"Well, then," Gertie said. "Maybe we should just stop by and check on Mr. Boon St. Clair. Just to make sure he's okay."

CHAPTER 14

Mary-Alice rang Boon's doorbell. When there was no answer, she knocked politely.

"His truck's in the carport," Gertie said. "He should be here. Okay, plan B. Both of you turn around."

Mary-Alice and Fortune did as Gertie ordered. They gazed at the houses across the street for a full minute as Gertie made clicking noises behind them.

"You can turn around now." Gertie stood proudly in front of the open door. "Boon got himself some high-end locks, no joke."

Mary-Alice followed Gertie and Fortune into Boon's house. The house looked as she remembered it, but it seemed oddly quiet. The windows were open, but the air was damp and still.

"Well he's not out here," Gertie said. "Let's check the bedroom. Mary-Alice, lead the way."

"Well I'm sure I wouldn't know where the bedroom is," Mary-Alice objected.

"I'm guessing it's down the hallway," Fortune said.

They found Boon in his bed, covers pulled up to his chin despite the afternoon heat.

"Boon?" Mary-Alice whispered.

Boon's eyelids fluttered open. With effort, he turned his head toward them and squinted.

"Miss Gertie?" he said, finally.

Fortune was already on the phone. She had a quick conversation and hung up.

"We have to take him to the ER," she said. "Now. It's quicker than an ambulance."

Fortune pulled up and parked illegally at the ER entrance, and Gertie climbed out. She returned in the company of two burly orderlies pushing a gurney. Mary-Alice was sitting in the back. Boon was lying down with his head on her lap.

The orderlies moved Boon out of the back seat and placed him carefully onto the gurney.

"Someone's gotta come in and do the paperwork," the older of the two men said. "One of you ladies related to him?"

"I'll go," Mary-Alice said.

"You the wife?"

"She's his common-law wife." Gertie gave Mary-Alice an encouraging shove toward the ER entrance. "He needs someone there with him," Gertie whispered.

Mary-Alice smoothed her hair and followed the men through the sliding glass doors.

"Give us a call when you need a ride," Fortune called after her.

Mary-Alice filled out the intake forms as best she could. She couldn't fill in Boon's Social Security number or his birth date, but she knew his street address and his marital status (widowed). His zip code was easy. Everyone in Sinful had the same zip code.

When she had done what she could with the paperwork, she took a seat in the waiting area. She hadn't brought anything to read, but she did have her journal and her sunflower pen.

She would use the time to think about the Victorin Lowery case. Keeping her mind busy would help her ignore the groans and cries that filled the ER waiting room. And would keep her from worrying about Boon.

She opened her journal and read over what she had written so far about the case of Victorin Lowery. Then she turned to a clean page and wrote:

Suspects:

1. Ida Belle. Acquaintance. Motive: Protect supply of cough syrup from theft. Confessed to shooting him?

2. Girlfriend Leonie Blanchard. Motive: Jealous b/c of ex-wife. Had big fight, threatened to kill him.

3. Francine? Motive: Was very angry b/c he broke into her kitchen and may have made her soufflés fall.

Mary-Alice twirled the sunflower pen and ignored the retching sounds behind her.

4. Mother Eulalie Cormier. Motive: Money? Said she was provided for. Legal expenses b/c of pink house.

What was the name of the man who was suing Eulalie? Gaudet.

5. Beauregard Gaudet. Motive: Money? Honor? But why kill Victorin and not Eulalie?

6. Ex-wife Marine. Motive: all the reasons people kill their spouses. Has medical knowledge to change apparent time of death.

7. Ex-wife's acquaintance who works at the morgue and wanted to have lunch with her, only I happened to show up first. Motive: Wants Marine to himself. Also has knowledge to change apparent time of death and access to morgue.

But why would Marine and/or her admirer tamper with the time of death? It was Leonie who needed the alibi.

8. Unless the ex-wife and the girlfriend had plotted together? Like in that song where the wife and the mistress both show up at a man's funeral in matching black Cadillacs, and pretend to be sad.

9. An admirer of Leonie's who wanted Victorin out of the way?

Mary-Alice closed her eyes and imagined her "little grey cells" swinging into action. (Mary-Alice loved Agatha Christie's Hercule Poirot). She tried to ignore the corrosive diaper smell wafting from the baby next to her.

What if this wasn't about Victorin Lowery at all? What if framing Ida Belle was the whole point?

Celia was a strong-willed woman. In fact, Mary-Alice had always admired that about her cousin. But was she ruthless enough to commit cold-blooded murder, just to frame Ida Belle?

10. Celia?

"Mary-Alice Arceneaux?" A woman in Hello Kitty scrubs stood by the door to the patient area, holding a clipboard, and looking around the room.

Mary-Alice put away her journal and her big sunflower pen, closed her eyes, and said a brief prayer for Boon. Then she put on her cheerful face and followed the woman through the double doors.

In the chaos of the emergency room, Mary-Alice was able to stay by Boon's bedside as long as she liked. The patient area was well-secured, but now that she was inside, everyone was too busy to bother kicking her out. A curtain hanging from the ceiling defined Boon's "room." Boon was in a deep sleep, hooked up to various monitors and bags.

A man with a rolling cart full of needles and vials came by to take Boon's blood minutes after another man with a similar cart had done the same thing. There had been a shift change and the first man forgot to mark Boon's chart. As soon as Mary-Alice got that straightened out, she noticed that Boon's saline bag had emptied. When no one came to replace it, Mary-Alice went to find someone to do it.

When she was finished negotiating with emergency room

personnel, Mary-Alice sat and held Boon's hand. One time he opened his eyes, smiled at her, and then drifted off again. Mary-Alice, too, must have dozed off at some point. She awoke to see Dr. Stewart making notes on a clipboard.

"Good morning, Mary-Alice. Were you here all night?"

Mary-Alice stood and straightened her blouse. Her neck was stiff and sore, and she felt grimy. She longed for a toothbrush, a hot, soapy shower, and a clean bed.

"It was no trouble at all, Doctor. How is he doing?"

Boon looked the same as he did the night before. Mary-Alice hoped he was healing as he slept.

"Boon's lucky you found him when you did," Doctor Stewart said. "He was severely dehydrated."

"What's wrong with him?"

"Looks like ASP. Been quite a few cases this summer."

"What is ASP?"

Doctor Stewart pulled a blue paper from his clipboard and handed it to Mary-Alice.

Amnesic shellfish poisoning (ASP) is caused by the consumption of domoic acid, Mary-Alice read, a marine biotoxin found in shellfish. ASP causes gastrointestinal symptoms, disorientation, and loss of short-term memory. There is no known antidote; immediate hospitalization is recommended. Rest and rehydration are the only treatments.

"Loss of short-term memory!" Mary-Alice exclaimed. "Is that why he only recognized Gertie, and not Fortune or me?"

"Quite possibly. Do you know if he's had shellfish?"

"Why, yes. He had oyster stew at Landrieu's Landing. That was the last time I saw him before he fell ill, now that I think of it."

"Well, as I say, it's a good thing you found him when you did. That's one of the drawbacks of living alone. He was lucky."

"I should have thought to call on him earlier," Mary-Alice wrung her slender hands. "He's remodeling my kitchen, you see, and he hadn't been showing up with his crew. They told me he was out. I had no idea it was so serious. I'm sure his workers didn't either."

"Don't blame yourself, Mary-Alice. One thing I've learned is that things aren't always as they seem. The real problem's often hiding behind the obvious diagnosis. A few beds over is a case of acute gastritis that turned out to be a nine-pound baby boy. Why don't you go on home and get some rest?"

Mary-Alice went outside to the waiting benches and called Fortune. Within minutes, Fortune's Jeep pulled up, with Gertie in the passenger seat.

"Well?" Gertie demanded.

Mary-Alice handed Gertie the blue information sheet and then climbed into the back of the Jeep.

"Food poisoning?" Gertie said. "Oh, lord. That's a misery. It certainly is a good thing we came by when we did."

"Is there any news with Ida Belle?" Mary-Alice asked.

"Nothing new," Fortune said. "Gertie and I have been going over all the possible suspects, and there's no one that really stands out."

"I was doing the same thing in the waiting room," Mary-Alice said. "Did you think of Beauregard Gaudet? He and Victorin's mother are suing each other."

"Then why kill Victorin and not Eulalie herself?" Fortune asked.

"Yes, that was exactly my line of thought. What about Celia?"

Fortune and Gertie exchanged a glance.

"Your cousin Celia?" Fortune asked.

"Yes. Gertie, I'm sure you know her better than I do. Do you believe Cousin Celia might kill someone in order to frame Ida Belle?"

"We actually did discuss the possibility," Gertie admitted. "But it seems too clever a plan for Celia, if you'll excuse my saying so."

"And we don't really have any evidence for it," Fortune added.

The women rode in silence for a few minutes.

"Doctor Stewart told me something interesting," Mary-Alice said. "He said the real problem's often hiding behind the obvious diagnosis. Gastritis can turn out to be a nine pound baby."

"Whatever are you saying, Mary-Alice?" Gertie asked. "Someone's having a baby?"

"Well yes, someone in the hospital, but what Doctor Stewart meant to say is that things aren't always as they seem. What's obvious isn't necessarily what's true. So while I was waiting for you I was turning the case over in my mind, trying to consider different possibilities. For example, what if the man they found wasn't Victorin Lowery?"

Mary-Alice braced herself to be laughed at, but that didn't happen.

"It's possible," Fortune said, "If he was working undercover and someone burned him, they could've faked his death and moved him somewhere else."

"Would the government kill someone on purpose like that?" Mary-Alice asked.

"Not usually. Normally they'd find someone who had already died of something else. Then they'd stage a messy death that makes the body hard to identify. Like a fire or a car bomb. Or, in this case, a close-range shotgun blast. Of course, they'd be counting on the fact that no one would bother following through with a DNA identification."

"Victorin was living with his mother," Gertie pointed out. "Undercover agents don't usually live with their mothers."

"Good point," Fortune said.

"Then what if it the victim was Victorin Lowery," Mary-Alice asked, "but he died of something other than the shotgun blast?"

They were just entering Sinful. Fortune pulled off the road and crunched to a stop in the lot of the old taxidermist's shop. Mary-Alice averted her eyes from the glassy, cross-eyed stare of the moth-eaten deer head hanging next to the entry.

"Not bad, Mary-Alice. I wish I'd thought of that." Fortune pulled out her phone and dialed. Gertie turned around and gave Mary-Alice a thumbs-up.

"Carter," Fortune said. "The Lowery case. Did they to a tox screen on the vic? Oh. Yes, hello to you too. Listen. Tox screen? No, I realize it wouldn't be obvious considering... yes, I know about the budget situation. How about blood alcohol? Okay, water in his lungs? Did they check for that?" Fortune leaned her head back on the headrest with exasperation. "Carter, any standard autopsy would have caught water in the lungs—what do you mean they didn't do an autopsy? Are you kidding me—no, I'm not telling you how to do your job."

Yes she is, Gertie mouthed at Mary-Alice.

"Yes, I know that. What did you say? Oh, you haven't begun to see bossy. I'll show you bossy."

Fortune put the phone away.

"What happens now?" Gertie asked.

"We just have to be patient," Fortune said. "Carter told me he'll try again to request an autopsy, but he says even if the coroner will give him the time of day, the chances aren't good. The vic got his head blown off with a shotgun, so they're not going to consider it a top priority to figure out what might have killed him."

"Well, all this brainstorming's made me ravenous," Gertie said. "You ladies up for breakfast at Francine's?"

"Sounds good to me." Fortune started up the Jeep. Shells crunched under the tires as she pulled out to drive the short distance to Francine's Diner.

"Might I trouble you to drop me at my house?" Mary-Alice asked. "I believe I could use a little nap."

CHAPTER 15

A few days later, Fortune called Mary-Alice.

"Carter's here with some news about Ida Belle," she said. "How soon can you get here?"

Fortune met Mary-Alice at the front door and led her into the kitchen. Gertie was already sitting at the table, along with Deputy Sheriff Carter LeBlanc. And someone Mary-Alice hadn't expected to see.

"Ida Belle!" Without thinking Mary-Alice rushed over and smothered Ida Belle in a hug. "Did you get bail?"

"Better than that," Ide Belle said. "I'm free. And I hear you were a big help. So I thank you kindly, Mary-Alice."

Mary-Alice sat down and Fortune placed a steaming mug of coffee in front of her.

"Did the coroner already do the autopsy?" Mary-Alice asked.

Carter nodded. "There was water in Victorin Lowery's lungs. Blood alcohol level of .3 percent. And no obvious indications his body had been moved. It seems Victorin Lowery lost consciousness while intoxicated and drowned in the bayou."

"It's such a shame," Mary-Alice said. "He'd just been through rehab, too."

"Rehab?" Ida Belle exclaimed. "Well, no wonder."

"Why no wonder?" Mary-Alice asked.

"Ida Belle's right," Carter said. "When an alcoholic stops drinking, his tolerance goes down. When he started drinking again, it would've hit him harder than he was used to."

"So someone shot Lowery *after* he was dead?" Fortune asked. "Who? And why?"

"It was Leonie Blanchard," Carter said. "She wasn't cooperative at first. But once we told her Lowery was already dead, she told us everything. When she got out of jail that morning she was still mad, and probably still a little intoxicated. She went home, got her truck, and decided to go for a drive. That's when she saw Lowery lying next to the bayou. Her first thought was, and I'm paraphrasing, look at that lazy cheating SOB sleeping it off, didn't even try to bail me out of jail. Leonie pulled over, got her shotgun from the back of her truck and shot him. She went for the head because she knew about his body armor. I have no doubt she intended to kill him, but she was too late."

"So no murder charges?" Mary-Alice asked.

"No. But it is a crime to mutilate human remains without authority of law. She'll probably have to pay a fine."

"Ida Belle, darling, how is your shoulder?" Mary-Alice asked.

Ida Belle started to unbutton her shirt.

"No, it's okay," Fortune said quickly. "You can just tell us."

"It's not too bad. It was a shallow wound, so it's healing up pretty good. There's just a little scab now. Almost like it never happened."

The next morning, the women celebrated Ida Belle's freedom with breakfast at Francine's. Mary-Alice was a little late, and had just gotten seated when Celia approached their table.

"Just go with it," Gertie whispered to her. Mary-Alice had no idea what Gertie was talking about.

"Why Ida Belle," Celia cooed, her voice as sweet as syrup. "How wonderful to see you've gained your freedom at last. Our Sheriff Lee has become a little overzealous in his old age, I'm sorry to say, but I'm happy to see everything's been straightened out."

"Thank you so much for your good wishes, Celia," Ida Belle simpered back. "I'm certain the letter my attorney sent over to your office this morning had nothing whatsoever to do with your improved attitude."

Celia's eyes flashed daggers at Ida Belle, but her smile remained frozen in place.

"And Cousin Mary-Alice, darling, how is our town history coming along? Dorothy tells me she hasn't seen you down in the records room of late."

"Mary-Alice has been making amazing progress." Fortune plopped a folder stuffed with papers onto the table, and gave Mary-Alice a quick wink. "She was just showing us some of the fascinating family history she's found. Celia, I think you'd be interested in this. You might want to sit down."

Warily, Celia pulled up a fifth chair and sat at the end of the table. She looked at the folder and then at Mary-Alice.

"You found all this?" Celia asked. "May I ask where?"

"Oh, here and there," Mary-Alice stammered.

"There's so much information available on line now." Fortune opened the folder and fanned out the contents. There were land deeds, birth records, newspaper clippings, personal letters, and a number of other documents. "Museum archives, university libraries. It's amazing what you can find."

Fortune might be the most unusual librarian I've ever met, Mary-Alice thought, but my goodness, her research skills are amazing.

"May I have a little peek?" Gertie asked.

Fortune slid the folder over.

"Ooh, look at this." Gertie's eyes were wide. "Why, Celia, were you aware that your daddy was once arrested for bigamy?"

Celia reddened. "That is not true, Gertie."

Gertie shrugged and handed Celia a copy of a newspaper clipping. Celia stared at it and went pale.

"Oh, and just look at this, won't you?" Ida Belle chimed in. "Celia, it says here that your great-grandmamma served time for extortion. She spied on people when they went to confession. It says right here that she 'secreted herself behind the confessional booth and thereby gained knowledge of her fellow parishioners' most intimate secrets.' My, Celia, what a colorful family history you do have!"

Celia snatched the paper from Ida Belle and stared at it with fury.

"I thought a history of Sinful would be boring," Gertie said. "But this looks like best-seller material. And just looky here, Celia, there's more. Your great-great grandfather was a bounty hunter."

"Well, that sounds quite dashing," Ida Belle said.

"He captured escaped slaves and returned them to their owners," Gertie said.

"Goodness," Ida Belle said. "I can just imagine how people would be fascinated to hear that bit of history."

"It's not all scandalous," Fortune said. "When I was looking through it I found a World War I war hero who was related to Ida Belle. And did you know Gertie's great-aunt founded the teacher's college we now know as Mudbug Technical?"

"How delightful for both of you." Celia was stone-faced. "Mary-Alice, do you truly intend to publish this?"

"Me? Oh. I see. Well, in fact, I have been having second thoughts about the project, Celia."

"You have?"

"Yes. I've become rather inclined to allow Sinful to keep her air of mystery. As any proper Southern Lady should."

Celia fairly glowed with relief.

"A wise decision, Mary-Alice. You won't mind if I take these for safekeeping, then."

Celia snatched the folder and hurried toward the exit.

"No bother," Ida Belle called after her. "We have the originals"

"Fortune, however did you find all of this?" Mary-Alice marveled.

Fortune shrugged.

"You should thank Gertie."

"Give me a little time and a little Photoshop, and I can do anything," Gertie preened.

"I'd like to know why you were so late arriving here, this morning, Mary-Alice," Ida Belle demanded. "I mean, fortunately you caught on, but I was afraid you were going to mess up the whole thing."

"Oh, there were some details I had to attend to with the remodel," Mary-Alice said vaguely.

CHAPTER 16

Mary-Alice had been late to breakfast because Boon St. Clair showed up to work that morning. Mary-Alice was so used to his not being there that when she saw him in her kitchen, she shrieked with surprise. Everyone laughed at this, including Boon. He looked a little thin, but otherwise healthy.

"Why Boon," Mary-Alice exclaimed. "It's wonderful to see you back."

"Right?" chimed in one of the apprentices, a young woman with skinny, tattooed arms and a bandanna tied over her hair. "You didn't even tell us you were sick, Boss."

"No sir," said one of the men, "you don't mess with food poisoning."

"No, I certainly do not recommend it. I'll be right back."

Boon moved out to the dining room to talk to Mary-Alice in private.

"Sounds like I owe you a mighty big favor, Miss Mary-Alice," he said. "Doctor Stewart tells me you might have saved my life."

"Oh, it wasn't just me. Fortune and Gertie were there too. I, we hadn't heard from you in a while so we thought we'd stop by and see how you were doing."

Boon looked down at his feet, and back up at Mary-Alice.

"I'm not quite a hundred percent," he said. "It's gonna take a while for me to build back up. Anyway, I was hoping to ask you something."

Mary-Alice was aware of her heart thumping. Was he going to bring up the marriage thing again? If he pressed her for an answer now, what would she say? She knew she didn't want to lose him.

But she hadn't even known him for a month. Could she ask him to slow things down without hurting his feelings? Especially now, after his brush with death?

"Miss Mary-Alice," Boon said finally, "I realize this may not be entirely proper, given the circumstances of our acquaintance, and for that I apologize in advance, but...may I take you to lunch some time?"

"Lunch?"

"Not now, of course. But once the kitchen is finished."

Mary-Alice blinked.

"You don't have to give me an answer right now," Boon said.

"Boon, I'd love to have lunch with you."

Boon smiled, and then hurried back into the kitchen to resume working.

Short term memory loss, Mary-Alice thought. He forgot he already asked me to marry him.

Two weeks later, Mary-Alice's kitchen passed its final inspection. The finished product was even prettier than she'd imagined. White appliances gleamed against bright sunflower-patterned wall tiles. The morning sun streamed through newly-enlarged windows and a skylight. A ductless air conditioner system kept everything cool, and because it was powered by roof-mounted solar panels, it wouldn't add much to her utility bill.

The next day, when Mary-Alice went out to collect the mail, she found an envelope with the return address St. Clair

Contracting, Boon's company. As she opened it, Mary-Alice felt sad and relieved, in equal measure. Boon was billing her for the job after all, so there would be no question about being in his debt. She hoped it wouldn't be too expensive. Mary-Alice was by no means wealthy, and this remodel would definitely stretch her finances.

But then she saw that it wasn't a bill. It was a letter.

Boon St. Clair was happy to inform her that the parish retraining grant had come through. Because of the unique and historic nature of the old Cooper Place, Mary-Alice's kitchen qualified as an approved training site, and several apprentice certificates would come out of her remodeling project. The grant would pay Boon for his time and materials. Mary-Alice would have the satisfaction of knowing that opening her house to him and his Mudbug Technical College apprentices helped a number of young people. In return, the parish would reserve the right to post photographs of her kitchen on their workforce development website.

The following Sunday, Mary-Alice and Boon St. Clair arrived at Mass at the same time, and sat together in the back pew. Celia sat in the front with her friends, ready to dash off to Francine's as soon as Father Michael said Amen. Across the street, Fortune, Gertie, and Ida Belle were warming up for their part in the weekly Banana Pudding War.

Mary-Alice glanced at Boon, and he smiled back at her. After Mass, if he suggested taking her to lunch, she would say yes. And someday soon, she might invite him back for a glass of iced tea in her bright new kitchen.

ALOHA, Y'ALL

CHAPTER 1

The woman known as Sandy-Sue "Fortune" Morrow pressed her phone to her ear and paced. Now and then she cast an anxious glance over the bayou that ran across the back of her lawn.

"So Ahmad's men are back in New Orleans?" she asked.

"And that's not all. We're picking up on some chatter indicating one or possibly two of them might be headed to Sinful."

"I can handle two. When can I expect them?"

"Don't even think about it. We need to get you out of there."

"But Harrison—"

"Don't worry, it's not a permanent relocation. We'll just send you on vacation for a few days until we get a better handle on this."

"Great. What forsaken backwater are you going to drop me into to this time?"

"Morrow wants to send you to Hawaii."

"Hawaii? I'm listening."

"We have a safe house, and someone there who can help you get settled in. You're flying out of Lake Charles Regional Airport tomorrow morning."

"Geez, Harrison, thanks for the advance notice. Tomorrow? What am I going to tell everyone?"

"Who do you have to tell? You're not answerable to anyone."

"Look, I'm doing my best to blend in. But that means I've become part of the community and I can't just disappear."

In fact, Fortune had done better than just blend in. After several weeks in Sinful, Louisiana, she was starting to feel she fit in. It was getting harder to maintain her emotional detachment. Maybe a few days away would be just what she needed to regain it.

"How about this?" Harrison suggested. "Tell whoever needs to know that your family wants you to take a look at some property out west for them. Don't give any more details than that, and do not tell anyone you're going to Hawaii. Keep it vague. Oh, and there's something else. Ahmad's guys will be looking for a young woman traveling alone, so you need to find someone to go with you."

"Oh, that won't be a problem—"

"Uh-uh. The Director will have an aneurism if you even think about getting those two geriatric loose cannons involved."

"Are you saying I can't bring Gertie and Ida Belle? They're the only ones I don't have to maintain cover with."

"You should be keeping cover anyway. You have a ten-million-dollar bounty on your head, remember? Look, don't you know any sweet, non-trigger-happy old ladies with nice manners?"

Fortune paused for a moment. She saw a ripple on the surface of the bayou that might have been an alligator. Or it could have been nothing more than a floating stick. It was hard to tell in the early-morning light.

"Actually, I might know one."

"Great. One is all you need. Think you could talk her into coming to Hawaii with you tomorrow?"

"It's not as easy as you're making it sound. The locals aren't exactly jet-setters. I've met people here who've lived their whole lives without leaving the parish. But look, I'll try. I'll ask her."

"And you might want to think about changing your appearance a little. In case Ahmad's men saw you in New Orleans."

"Hey, does that mean I can get rid of these stupid hair extensions?"

"Knock yourself out. As long as you're on that plane tomorrow morning."

CHAPTER 2

Mary-Alice Arceneaux had always held that if you can't say anything nice, don't say anything at all. Mary-Alice was sitting across from Sandy-Sue Morrow at Francine's Diner, trying very hard to think of something nice to say about the young lady's new hairdo. Mary-Alice felt it was particularly incumbent upon her to be gracious on the occasion of her birthday breakfast.

Sandy-Sue, or "Fortune," as everyone called her, was the niece of the late Marge Boudreaux, come to Sinful for the summer to wrap up Miss Marge's affairs. Word was, Fortune worked as a children's librarian, and before that she had been a teenage pageant queen.

But to Mary-Alice's eyes, young Fortune looked more like a drill sergeant than a beauty queen. Her long, golden hair was gone, and in its place was a dirty-blonde buzz cut. Mary-Alice hoped Ida Belle or Gertie would say something first, and then Mary-Alice could follow their lead.

"I love your hair," Ida Belle said to Fortune. "You look just like Charlize Theron in *Mad Max: Fury Road.*"

"That's exactly what I was thinking!" Gertie exclaimed. "I couldn't think of where I'd seen the look."

Fortune ran a hand over her fuzzy head. "I like it too. It's so cool in the humidity."

"It's quite striking," Mary-Alice agreed.

"Do you have the present?" Ida Belle asked Gertie. Gertie pulled out a small package.

Mary-Alice couldn't help but smile. The gift looked about the size of a small book, and Mary-Alice loved books, especially mysteries. She reminded herself that making it to one's 70th birthday in good health was a blessing.

"Well this is lovely," Mary-Alice said, taking the package. "I believe I made the right choice moving from Mudbug to Sinful. I'm feeling quite thankful today."

"No, we're the ones who are thankful," Ida Belle said. "You've been a thorn in Celia's side ever since you got here, and we're loving it."

Fortune suppressed a smile, and quietly sipped her coffee.

Mary-Alice's face fell. "Why, I never meant to be a thorn in anyone's side."

"What she means," Gertie explained, "is that Ida Belle and I have this friendly rivalry with your cousin going way back to, well, forever. And since she was elected mayor she's been—"

"Unbearable," Ida Belle interrupted. "Mary-Alice, your cousin's been spitting nails ever since you finished your kitchen remodel. Trying to tell everyone your décor isn't in keeping with Sinful's stately traditions. She's one to talk, with her avocado shag carpet and her macramé owls hanging on the wall."

"Open your present!" Gertie said. "It's from the three of us."

Mary-Alice undid the pale blue ribbon and flowered wrapping. But when she opened it, it wasn't a book. It was a small, flat box.

"It's an e-reader," Fortune said. "It can hold hundreds of books."

"And when your vision starts to go," Ida Belle added, "like

Gertie here, but you don't want to wear the glasses you so obviously need, you can make the font as big as you want, and no one will be the wiser."

Gertie didn't respond to Ida Belle's jab. She simply rested her chin in her hand and gazed at Ida Belle while scratching her cheek with her middle finger.

"My goodness," Mary-Alice exclaimed. "This is lovely. Thank you all."

Mary-Alice's eyes shone, and one fat tear ran down the side of her nose, cutting a channel in her face powder. "I'm sorry. I suppose I'm simply overwhelmed. I've had so much going on lately, what with the move and the remodel and all, and now here I am turning seventy."

"Seventy!" Gertie exclaimed. "Why, Mary-Alice, you're a mere child. But I agree, birthdays do have a way of making you take stock of your life."

"Well, I talked Francine into making a special batch of banana pudding just for the occasion," Ida Belle said. "Shall we tell Ally to bring it out now?"

When they'd finished the banana pudding, Ida Belle and Gertie excused themselves to check on their batch of home-brewed cough syrup. Sinful Ladies' Cough Syrup had a higher alcohol content than Wild Turkey 101, and was a popular cold remedy in the dry town. So popular that it sold out every year at the church bazaar.

Mary-Alice was about to leave as well but noticed that Fortune was still sitting at the table. She settled back in, as it would have been rude to leave Fortune by herself.

"Do you know, I've been thinking of getting one of these e-readers," Mary-Alice said, by way of making conversation. "Thanks again to all of you. I can't wait to get started using it."

"We knew you liked murder mysteries so we pre-loaded the reader with a few," Fortune said.

"It was terribly thoughtful of you. I must say I'm fortunate to have an honest-to-goodness librarian pick out my reading for me."

"I'd like to take the credit, but Gertie's the one who chose the books. You should thank her."

Ally came by with a coffee pot and a tea pitcher and refilled Fortune's and Mary-Alice's drinks, respectively.

"Thanks Ally," Fortune said. "Your coffee's awesome, as always."

"And the banana pudding was absolutely lovely, darling," Mary-Alice added. "What a treat!"

The young waitress smiled.

"And there's a box of blueberry cheesecake squares up front for you, Aunt Mary-Alice. For when your dessert stomach has room again. Happy birthday."

"Well now, wasn't that thoughtful," Mary-Alice said when Ally left.

Fortune pushed her coffee aside and leaned forward.

"Mary-Alice. Think you can handle one more birthday present?"

"My goodness, I should say not. All of these lovely gifts are making me feel quite spoiled."

"What would you say to a trip to Hawaii?"

Mary-Alice lit up. "Oh, Fortune, you didn't. The hibiscus-print stationery that Harriet's just brought in? I have been rather coveting it, such a darling design. Goodness, y'all really are spoiling me today."

Fortune became serious.

"Sorry. I did not buy you those Hawaiian print note cards. Although now I know what to get you for Christmas. What I'm saying is I'm actually going to Hawaii and I'd like you to come with me."

Mary-Alice brought her hand to her throat, touching imaginary pearls.

"But Fortune, darlin', I couldn't possibly..."

"It's not as generous an offer as it sounds. Here's the deal. My family wants me to go check out some property for them, and they're worried about me traveling alone. They told me to bring a respectable traveling companion to make sure I behave myself, and they insist on paying for everything."

"Fortune, I'm so honored. But surely Gertie or Ida Belle would like to—"

"Yeah, no, they were pretty specific about the 'respectable' part. Besides, Mary-Alice, I think you'd be a great travel partner. You'd be a calming influence when I'm about to blow my top going through security."

Mary-Alice looked puzzled.

"Security?"

"You know, when you're holding your high heels in one hand, you have your boarding pass under your arm and your driver's license between your teeth, and you're trying to kick your stupid pink luggage along fast enough so the person behind you doesn't start grumbling, and meanwhile your hair extensions are falling into your face and sticking in your lip gloss?"

Mary-Alice smiled at Fortune.

"I suppose you won't need to be concerned with the hair extensions on this trip."

Fortune ran her hand over her fuzzy head and grinned.

"Dam— I mean darn straight. So will you come? Honestly, you'd be doing me a huge favor."

"Do you know, I've never flown in an airplane before?"

"Well then, what a perfect way to celebrate a milestone birthday. Can I take that as a yes?"

Mary-Alice's fine features creased with concern.

"Will I need a passport?"

Fortune laughed, and then stopped herself.

"Hawaii became a state in 1959. You just need your driver's license."

"Oh dear, you're right, of course. My goodness, where is my head today? When are we leaving?"

"Tomorrow morning. We're flying out of Lake Charles Airport."

"Tomorrow?" Mary-Alice faltered.

"That gives you a whole day to pack."

Fortune stood up and gave Mary-Alice a chummy pat on the shoulder. "I'll pick you up at three."

"Three in the morning?"

"You okay with that, Mary-Alice?"

"Why yes, of course I am, darling. It's just that I'm feeling so very overwhelmed by your generosity!"

"Great. See you then. Oh, one more thing. Please don't mention Hawaii to anyone else. I don't want any hurt feelings or jealousy. If anyone asks, just tell them we're going out west."

Mary-Alice watched Fortune stride out of Francine's Diner. People glanced up as she passed. They were mildly curious at the sight of her buzz-cut hair, but not surprised. Everyone in Sinful knew Marge's Yankee niece was a little odd.

Hawaii. Mary-Alice could scarcely believe it. After all these years.

CHAPTER 3

After breakfast, Mary-Alice rushed home to research Hawaii, where she'd be heading to in less than twenty-four hours. She opened her computer and began to search. Maybe she should re-watch the musical South Pacific, which she hadn't seen in years.

But Mary-Alice quickly discovered to her surprise was that Hawaii was not in the south Pacific. Instead, it was located north of the equator, although not by much. The entire state lay well south of Sinful, Louisiana. In fact, Hawaii was around the same latitude as Mexico City.

The second surprise was that it wasn't clear where Hawaii was, precisely. Although there is a Hawaii Island, the state of Hawaii is a series of islands, of which Hawaii Island is just one. And the capital, Honolulu, is not on Hawaii Island (also known as the Big Island because it is, in fact, the biggest of the islands) but on another, smaller island, called Oahu.

This was turning out to be much more complicated than Mary-Alice had expected. As she continued her online research, she found the images of Hawaii drew her in. Blazing ocean sunsets, luaus illuminated by tiki torches, and the palm-lined

Waikiki Beach Walk beckoned. Everything looked clean and vividly colorful. Unlike Sinful, which always seemed to be smothered under a greenish haze, Hawaii was sparkling-clean.

Mary-Alice picked up the phone and called her best friend from Mudbug, Beulah Monroe.

"Can we move up my birthday lunch to today?" Mary-Alice asked, although she was so full from breakfast she couldn't imagine eating for a week. "I know we planned for tomorrow but something's come up, and it would be ever so nice to see you."

Mary-Alice hopped into her Oldsmobile and made the hour drive out to Mudbug to see Beulah. Mary-Alice had had many friends in Mudbug, or so she'd thought. But Beulah Monroe was the only one who'd stood by Mary-Alice after Mary-Alice's grandson had gone to prison for arson. Mary-Alice came back to Mudbug now and then to attend Crafting Circle, but found she was surrounded by acquaintances there now, not friends. Except for Beulah.

They met at the café on Mudbug's main street. Beulah ordered the fried oyster platter with boudin balls. Mary-Alice, still full from breakfast, got bread pudding with bourbon sauce.

Beulah caught Mary-Alice up on the latest gossip from the Office of Motor Vehicles, whose internal politics appeared to rival those of eleventh-century Byzantium.

"Why Beulah," Mary-Alice exclaimed, "I thought you were fixin' to retire."

"Well, I did retire, sugar, you know I can't stay on my feet all day. But I came back part-time. I didn't care for sitting at home all day, and I do enjoy meeting folks. And how are you getting on in Sinful? Last I heard you were fixing up that old house."

"Sinful is a lovely place," Mary-Alice said. "Although I find I do miss Mudbug now and then."

"How many folks you got living in Sinful?" Beulah asked.

"I believe the official population is 253."

"Well there you go, Mary-Alice. Mudbug has nearly twice that. Five hundred and two, at last count. You're just not accustomed to living in a small town, is all."

"As a matter of fact, Beulah, I have been considering expanding my horizons a bit. It's occurred to me that I might consider traveling to Hawaii."

"Hawaii! Mary-Alice, you're not serious."

"Well, why ever not? I'm seventy years old today, and I don't believe I've ever been outside the state of Louisiana."

"Well my goodness, Mary-Alice," Beulah exclaimed. "Aren't you adventurous. So are you going to be getting yourself a passport?"

"No, it seems they don't require a passport to travel to Hawaii," Mary-Alice said, feeling a little worldly. "Just a driver's license. Hawaii is a state, you see."

"Well now, I suppose I should have known that." Beulah laughed good-naturedly.

"Beulah, I've been doing a little of my own research, and I've learned ever so much. For example, did you know where Hawaii is located?"

"Well I believe I do," Beulah said. "It's right off the coast of California."

"Well now, that's just what I used to think, Beulah, right up until quite recently."

"Now Mary-Alice, I certainly don't want to contradict you, but I'm telling you, I'm as sure of that as I could be. We got a big map of the United States back in the break room at the OMV."

"It's nowhere near that close. The folks who draw the maps just put it there to save space. It's actually right in the middle of the ocean, just as far away as it could be. As a matter of fact, come to find the distance from here to California is less than the distance from California to Hawaii."

"You're not seriously considering going that far." Beulah

gasped and placed a hand on her ample chest. "This isn't all on account of that old postcard, is it?"

"Well, now that you mention it, Beulah, I'll admit to it maybe being on my mind of late."

"You just be careful now, Mary-Alice. Oh, of course you will. I mean, it's not like you're leaving for Hawaii tomorrow."

"No, nothing like that," Mary-Alice agreed.

After lunch with Beulah, Mary-Alice didn't drive straight back to Sinful. Instead, she made a detour to Grand Coteau. She hadn't been to the church for a good long while, but it was exactly as she remembered it, white and stately on a velvety carpet of lawn. Its chunky bell tower looked like a miniature townhouse stuck onto one end, with windows on each of its five floors. The top of the bell tower looked like a gazebo, with its graceful arches and hipped roof. Inside was the three thousand pound bell that one Mrs. Eleanor Millard had donated in honor of her late husband.

Had the hulking edifice with its gargantuan bell been anything but a Catholic church, Mary-Alice's mother might have denounced it as tacky. But it was a Catholic church, and a well-established one at that. Mary-Alice's mother had always attended faithfully, along with Mary-Alice. Mary-Alice's father would come along now and then, usually on Christmas or Easter.

Mary-Alice made her way around the building back to the cemetery. There was a large flat-screen display at the entrance; this was new.

Welcome from the Catholic Cemeteries of the Archdiocese of St. Louis. No pets allowed. No firearms.

Mary-Alice's mother certainly would have found this tacky, Catholic church or not. Mary-Alice made her way back to the Laval family plot. She found the one particular headstone she was seeking, and kneeled down in the grass in front of it. She paid no mind to her white capris. If the dirt and grass stains didn't wash out, she could always purchase another pair.

"Well, I've reached my three score and ten today, Mama." Mary-Alice said to the headstone. There was no one else in the cemetery on this bright afternoon, so Mary-Alice reckoned she could speak her mind. "It's quite a milestone, I must say. It's caused me to take stock of my life. Especially seeing as…well, I suppose I don't have to explain it to you, mama."

The date of death on Thelma Rose Laval's tombstone marked her 70th birthday.

"Mama, I do hope you can forgive me for not visiting more often. But Lord forgive me, as much as I miss you, Mama, I must confess I can't say the same for him."

Mary-Alice glared at the adjacent headstone, the one with her father's name on it.

"Ninety-two years old, mind you, and the day he had you declared dead, that very day, he had the everlasting gall to propose marriage to his personal attendant. I never told you this before, and far be it from me to spread gossip, but I mean to say, honestly. Young girl, she was, maybe thirty years old at most. Well, you'll be pleased to know she turned him down, Mama, and you know what? He passed away on the spot. There were some who made light of it, said he died doing what he loved. Mind you, Mama, I thought it was terribly tacky of him. Anyway, I came by to let you know I'm fixin' to travel to Hawaii. There's this young lady Sandy-Sue Morrow, goes by the name of Fortune, invited me. She's a Yankee, but she's got a good heart, I'll swear to that. And I must confess, I'm kind of excited about it. You know I've never gone in an airplane before. I'd like to think that you'd be proud of me for being so brave. Imagine, tomorrow I'll be flying over the ocean! Okay, Mama, I have to go home and pack now. But I'll come again soon. And I'll tell you all about my trip, I promise you."

CHAPTER 4

Mary-Alice was in sitting in the aisle seat of a luxurious jumbo jet. She had been sitting a long time and supposed she might get up to walk around. Except when she stepped into the aisle, the floor was gone. She awoke with a start right before she splashed down into the Pacific Ocean, and was immensely relieved to find herself safe in her own bed.

The clock on her night table read one-thirty. There was no point in trying to go back to sleep; her alarm was going to ring in another half hour. Mary-Alice got up and got dressed, and then checked and double-checked the contents of her little travel bag. At exactly 2:59 am Mary-Alice heard a knock. She slipped her new e-reader into her purse and wheeled her bag to the front door.

"Miss Gertie!" Mary-Alice exclaimed. "My goodness, what are you doing here at such an hour?"

"I'm driving you to the airport," Gertie said. "Fortune's already in the car. Is that all you have?"

"Yes. I read online that there are two kinds of luggage, carry-on and lost. If I find I'm missing anything, I imagine I can purchase whatever I need right there." Pinterest-fueled visions of Waikiki shopping were dancing in Mary-Alice's head. "And of course my new e-reader has enough books on it to last me the whole trip. I must say, Miss Gertie, you do have excellent taste in literature. I thank you for the wonderful selection of murder mysteries."

"It was fun to pick them out. Who doesn't love a good murder?"

"Only the fictional kind, of course, Miss Gertie," Mary-Alice laughed as she locked her door.

On the drive to Lake Charles Regional Airport, Fortune briefed Mary-Alice on airport security procedures. Mary-Alice listened carefully to every word. As soon as Gertie pulled up to the curb, Mary-Alice took out her driver's license so she wouldn't be caught fumbling for it when someone asked to see it. When they reached the stairs to the terminal level, Fortune grabbed Mary-Alice's rolling bag and bounded up the steps two at a time.

Mary-Alice didn't follow Fortune up the stairs. Instead, she stepped onto the adjacent escalator. Why take ordinary stairs when there are mechanical stairs right there? Fortune reached the top before Mary-Alice and waited for her there.

"I'm terribly sorry, darling," Mary-Alice said. "I didn't mean for you to have to wait for me. It's a habit of mine never to miss a chance to take an escalator."

"No problem," Fortune said, as she scanned the terminal. "Funny, I never noticed until you mentioned it, but I guess there aren't any escalators in Sinful, are there? We have some time. Let's go wait in the Business Lounge. It's right down there."

The business lounge at St. Charles Regional Airport looked to Mary-Alice like the lobby of a cozy hotel.

"Let's grab those two chairs," Fortune said. "The ones against the wall. You go get comfortable, and I'll go get us some coffee."

Mary-Alice settled her tiny frame into one of the overstuffed armchairs.

"Fortune, I do thank you for taking me along on your travels," Mary-Alice said when Fortune returned with two brimming china cups. "This is ever so lovely. I'm starting to believe that traveling suits me."

Fortune sat in the armchair next to Mary-Alice's. She used her long legs to scoot the chair back until it was braced against the wall. Then she turned around and knocked on the wall, and seemed to be reassured by its solidness.

"Yeah, this is pretty nice," Fortune's eyes darted around the half-empty lounge. "I like small airports. Easier to keep an eye on things."

"You mean so we don't miss our flight?" Mary-Alice asked.

"So we don't miss our flight. Exactly."

Fortune kept looking around the lounge as she sipped her coffee. Mary-Alice assumed Fortune must be an experienced traveler; hadn't she spent her youth on the pageant circuit? Maybe Fortune was one of those people who never shook their fear of flying. Come to think of it, how would Mary-Alice herself feel once she was in the air?

I should never have read those flying phobia message boards late last night, she thought. Would she find herself seized by panic when she realized she was stuck in a metal tube thirty thousand feet off the ground, hurtling through the stratosphere at five hundred miles per hour? Mary-Alice certainly hoped not. She didn't want to ruin Fortune's trip. She decided that if she got too scared, she'd simply close her eyes and imagine she was back home in bed.

Fortune was clearly in no mood to chat. She got up several times to refill her coffee, and even when she was sitting, she kept leaning over to look out the window onto the tarmac. Rather than try to force conversation, Mary-Alice took the opportunity to set up her new e-reader. Soon she was absorbed in one of her new mysteries. It starred a lawyer-turned-restaurateur-turned-amateur sleuth, included a number of tempting Italian recipes, and had nothing to do with flying.

When Mary-Alice stepped onto the plane, she found it looked quite familiar; she had seen the interiors of airplanes so often on movies. What she hadn't expected was the narrowness of the aisle and the crush of early-morning commuters on their way to Houston.

Fortune offered Mary-Alice the window seat. Mary-Alice felt some trepidation, but did not wish to turn down a kind offer. If the view got too scary she would simply squeeze her eyes shut and look away. She watched attentively as the flight attendant demonstrated how to buckle the seatbelt, even though she had already figured it out on her own. Finally the plane started to move, accelerated so quickly that Mary-Alice felt herself pressed back into her seat, and then lifted off the ground. Mary-Alice watched in wonder as the ground dropped away.

Now that they were airborne, Mary-Alice felt her worries drop away as well. They hadn't missed their flight, lost their luggage, or shown up with the wrong tickets. And in less than 24 hours, they'd be landing in Hawaii! The ground beneath turned into a green patchwork as they gained altitude. As they flew westward, Mary-Alice watched the green fade to brown, wondering all the while what kinds of human dramas were taking place in the towns and truck stops below.

"Mary-Alice?" Fortune was saying.

"I'm sorry?"

A flight attendant stood, hand on a rolling stainless-steel cart, looking expectantly at Mary-Alice.

"Would you care for something to drink, ma'am?" the flight attendant asked.

"Certainly, darlin'. Might I trouble you for a Sazerac Cocktail?"

As soon as the words were out, Mary-Alice's hand flew to her mouth. *Sazerac Cocktail? Where did that come from?*

CHAPTER 5

"I'm terribly sorry, ma'am," The flight attendant told Mary-Alice. "We have coffee, water, or Coke."

"A Coke would be lovely," Mary-Alice said, thoroughly embarrassed.

"That sounds good," Fortune said. "I'll have one too. Can I get a Diet?"

"Just regular for me," Mary-Alice said. "Thank you ever so much."

Fortune turned to Mary-Alice when the flight attendant had moved on.

"What was that you asked her for?"

"A Sazerac cocktail."

"What's in it?"

"Do you know, I'm not quite certain. But I do recall my mama was awfully fond of her Sazerac cocktails. I suppose I've been thinking of her. Especially after riding the escalator."

"The escalator reminds you of your mother?" Fortune asked.

"You see, the first time I rode an escalator was at the old Krauss Department Store in New Orleans. Well it's long gone now, but my, what a treat it was to go out there. My mother had taken me into town to buy my confirmation dress, and they had what they called back then the 'mechanical stairs.' They were quite a sensation at the time. Well, I wanted to try them out, but when I got to them, there they were, coming out of the ground so fast, I thought I might never sum up the courage to go on. So mama took me by the hand and pulled me onto the stairs with her, and it went as smooth as you please. Well, she held my hand all the way up, and then when we were finished shopping for my outfit, she rode back down with me. Then we went next door and had our lunch at the St. Charles Hotel, which was terribly grand, and after that we stopped by Fuerst & Kraemer for chocolates and pralines to bring home for the neighbors and the help. Every time I set foot on an escalator, it brings me back."

Fortune nodded. She was staring out the window at the pale sky.

"Fortune, I do hope you'll excuse me for rambling on like a foolish old woman."

"Nothing foolish about missing your mother." Fortune took a sip from her little plastic cup. "I totally understand."

The rest of the trip was a shiny, sleepless blur. After the short flight came a three-hour layover in Houston. Mary-Alice eagerly perused the shops. There was even a real bookstore, but as tempted as she was, Mary-Alice didn't buy any books from them. She had dozens of books on her e-reader already, and besides, she didn't want to be disloyal to Harriet's Books back in Sinful.

The next airplane was much larger than the previous one, but even more crowded, if that were possible. This took them on a flight so long that Mary-Alice was able to finish two murder mysteries and start on a third. She stared in amazement as the plane began its descent toward Honolulu Airport. With its crashing surf, golden beaches, and stately hotels, it looked just like the opening credits of Hawaii 5-0!

"Fortune," Mary-Alice said, "I'm not saying we need to stop there overnight or anything, but do you suppose we'll have a chance to have a peek at that grand pink hotel?"

"That's not a hotel, Mary-Alice. It's Tripler Army Medical Center. Anyway, we're not stopping here. We still have one more short flight to go."

Fortune ignored the signs to the Wiki Wiki Shuttle.

"We don't want to stand around on a crowded shuttle bus," she explained to Mary-Alice. "It'll be nice to walk after the long flight."

Fortune strode down the broad, open-air walkway, and Mary-Alice hurried to keep up with her. They passed through sliding glass doors, and came to a convergence of covered walkways. At the center was a pretty tropical garden. But was no time to dilly-dally in Honolulu Airport as they had in Houston. Fortune led them on to a short moving walkway, then off the moving walkway, through another sliding doors to an indoor terminal. The cold indoor air was a shock after the soft heat outside. They passed gift shops, a food court, and a display of invasive plants and animals that were presumably intercepted as they tried to enter the state.

PROTECT HAWAII! The sign read. DON'T PACK A PEST! Mary-Alice was hurrying to keep up with Fortune, so she couldn't make out what all the items were, but one of the objects was clearly a yellow snake, coiled up and floating in a jar.

"Is it true they've kept all the snakes out of Hawaii?" Mary-Alice panted, her short legs making two steps for every one of Fortune's.

"That's right," Fortune called back to Mary-Alice without breaking her stride. "No rabies, no snakes. Not bad, huh?"

They reached the end of the terminal building, and Mary-Alice was certain they must be done walking.

"Is this our gate?" she asked hopefully.

"Not yet."

Fortune blew past Gate 61 and disappeared down a stairway. Mary-Alice followed her into a makeshift tunnel constructed of plywood and opaque plastic sheeting. The tunnel led to a grim concrete waiting room, and Mary-Alice wondered whether they had made a wrong turn. But there were a few other people standing around with roller bags, which was reassuring. Fortune stood with her back pressed to the wall, giving each of the other passengers the up-and-down as if she were assessing them.

Mary-Alice sidled up to her.

"What are we waiting for?" she asked.

"Shuttle bus. It's the only way out to the commuter terminal. If we'd chosen another airline we could've connected from the main interisland terminal but it looks like my family went for the discount airline."

The shuttle bus arrived, and the passengers filed on glumly. After a short ride, they were dropped off in front of low building that looked to be from the airport's earlier days. They disembarked from the shuttle and followed the walkway across the tarmac into a sort of Terminal of the Damned.

It was packed with families. Every seat was taken, and people were sitting on the floor. The gum-stained carpet looked as if it had spent a few seasons in a discount movie theater. Mary-Alice was relieved when it was time to board their final flight. Once again, she savored the exhilarating feeling of watching the ground fall away as they soared skyward, admiring the lapis-blue water frosted with whitecaps.

She noticed a dark shape, and was about to ask Fortune whether she'd spotted a whale. But just in time, she realized the whale seemed to be keeping pace with the plane. Either she had discovered a species of whale capable of traveling hundreds of miles per hour, or she had been watching their shadow.

As excited as she was, Mary-Alice was also tired after a full day of traveling. She dozed off, and awoke to the sensation of pressure in her ears.

"Here we are," Fortune said. "Mary-Alice, welcome to Hawaii Island."

Mary-Alice looked down to see a carpet of green jungle, studded by the occasional corrugated tin roof. The ocean foamed against a rim of black rocks. There wasn't a golden beach in sight.

CHAPTER 6

The plane bumped gently down on the runway of Hilo Airport. Mary-Alice followed Fortune up the Jetway and out to a raised walkway open to the outdoors. Mary-Alice could see rain sweeping across the tarmac, but the air was warm and dense. Just past the security exit was an escalator down to ground level. This time, Fortune joined Mary-Alice on the escalator.

Fortune stepped aside at the bottom of the escalator, reached into her backpack, and pulled out a gray hoodie. She slipped it on, put on sunglasses, and then pulled up the hood. Mary-Alice thought it was too warm for a jacket, and wondered why Fortune needed sunglasses when it was so overcast and drizzly.

"Oh dear me," Mary-Alice apologized. "I forgot to pack an umbrella. I suppose I expected Hawaii to be sunny. It surely was, in all of the photographs I saw."

"I brought one." Fortune pulled out a compact travel umbrella about the size of a corn cob, held it aloft, and pressed a button. It bloomed to the size of a golf umbrella, big enough to shelter both of them from the rain. Mary-Alice noticed as they hurried down to the taxi stand that she and Fortune were the only ones with an umbrella. Passengers stood around waiting to be picked up at the curb, and no one else seemed to care that they were getting rained on.

The taxi driver was a friendly middle-aged woman whose car smelled like old cigarettes. She started chatting as soon as she pulled away from the curb. She asked Mary-Alice and Fortune where they were from, and confessed she'd never been to Louisiana. She did go to Vegas a few times a year, though, she told them, and she'd flown to Nebraska when her niece graduated from Creighton University.

"My, Nebraska's awfully far," Mary-Alice said. "Why did she choose to go all that way, if you don't mind my asking?"

"Lotta Hawaii kids like go Creighton. Never discriminate against the Japanese after Pearl Harbor, that's why. Kept their doors open to everyone."

"Are you Japanese?" Mary-Alice asked.

"Japanese, Hawaiian, Chinese, Podagee, Filipino, Scottish, German, an' Irish."

The rain thinned out as they drove out of town and up the coast. Fortune sat quietly in her hoodie and sunglasses while Mary-Alice marveled at the ocean view.

"It's so unspoiled," Mary-Alice exclaimed.

"Used to be all sugar plantations," the driver said. "My parents both worked for C. Brewer. Back then, everyone worked the plantations. Get up at four, work by five. Lotta the old timers still talk about plantation days."

"They used to have plantations too, where I'm from," Mary-Alice offered. "Although I don't believe folks recall them all that fondly."

Mary-Alice had assumed that she and Fortune would be staying at a seaside resort. Her online research hadn't turned up any other kind of accommodation. But the driver turned off the main highway and instead of heading down to the water's edge, went inland and up a narrow, overgrown road. Mary-Alice almost felt like she was right back in the bayous. Kudzu climbed up fences and tree trunks. The only difference she could see was that the road was paved with blackish-gray dirt instead of crushed white oyster shells.

Fortune instructed the driver to drop them about a hundred yards past a cluster of cube-shaped, tin-roofed houses. She then handed the driver a fat stack of bills and stayed put until the taxi had disappeared back down the hill.

Mary-Alice thought the little houses looked nice and welcoming, with their broad front porches. She wondered which one they'd be staying in, and also why Fortune didn't have them dropped off closer.

It turned out they wouldn't be staying in any of them.

"Through here." Fortune snatched Mary-Alice's rolling bag and disappeared into the trees. Mary-Alice followed her onto a narrow hiking trail.

"My goodness," Mary-Alice panted as she tried to keep up. "This is quite off the beaten path."

Mary-Alice and Fortune emerged from the forest onto a road remarkably like the one they had left behind, with another cluster of little tin-roofed houses that looked slightly shabbier than the ones they'd left behind.

"Well now," Mary-Alice exclaimed. "It certainly seems like we took the long way around. I do wonder why our taxi couldn't have brought us directly here. If we need her again, I'm afraid she might not be able to find us."

Fortune pulled her hood down, revealing her cropped hair, and pulled off her sunglasses.

"My family likes giving complicated directions," she said matter-of-factly, as if picking through an overgrown jungle path were a perfectly normal part of traveling. She pulled out her phone and made a call, watching the houses.

"Will we be staying in one of these?" Mary-Alice asked.

"We'll find out."

The door of the dark-green house opened, and a vision in pale blue stepped out.

"Fortune?" the vision called from the porch.

"Nadia?" Fortune called back.

The woman made her way slowly down the front stairs. Her impossibly-glossy platinum hair hung like a curtain from under her powder-blue cowboy hat. She wore a matching blue western shirt, and bolo tie, skirt, and boots.

She looks to be in her mid-eighties, Mary-Alice thought. If my mother were still alive she'd be about that very same age.

But Nadia's features did not look at all familiar, and when she spoke, it was with the clipped cadence of a Yankee.

"I'm Nadia Nygaard," she said when she reached the bottom of the stairs. "You're in the white house with the green roof. I'll show you around. Make sure to take your shoes off before you go inside."

The house looked small from the outside, but felt surprisingly roomy inside, thanks to the high ceilings and large windows. Nadia explained how the old plantation camp, as she called it, had been retrofitted with solar power and catchment water. Their community was "off the grid," which was apparently a good thing. Mary-Alice was glad that Fortune seemed to understand what Nadia was telling them about maintaining the batteries and filtering the catchment water, and hoped they would never have to do those things.

Then Nadia led them over to the window, which had a view of a flourishing garden. In the corner was a white, wooden beehive, with a few honeybees circling nearby.

"Why, this looks lovely," Mary-Alice exclaimed. "It's like a victory garden."

"We're very proud of what we've done here, but it's not a bed of roses, if you'll pardon the pun. See that papaya tree over there?"

Nadia indicated a tree with a skinny trunk and bulbous green and yellow fruit clustered under a crown of leaves.

"I've never seen a papaya tree before," Mary-Alice said.

"It's a volunteer. Sprouted from our compost. Problem is, it's a commercial engineered papaya, which means that the seeds probably came from one that someone bought at the supermarket. This has turned out to be quite a source of controversy. Some of our residents like 'em just fine, others won't so much as touch them. You ladies eat papaya?"

"I've never tried it," Mary-Alice said.

"Tomorrow morning you can go out and help yourself," Nadia said. Half of papaya with a squeeze of lime juice, it's a nice way to start the day. And if you don't have any plans for supper, we're having a little neighborhood luau tonight. Come on out and join us when you're up to it."

A luau! Now that was more like it.

CHAPTER 7

Mary-Alice had picked the smaller of the two bedrooms in an effort to be polite, but it was certainly large enough, and completely charming. The house had single-wall construction, so the walls were vertical white planks with a single horizontal belly band that gave the effect of wainscoting. The floor was a reddish-brown hardwood that Mary-Alice later learned was eucalyptus. She had packed light, just three pairs of white capris and five flowered t-shirts to hang in the wardrobe. Mary-Alice panicked for a moment when she couldn't find her tennis shoes, and then recalled she had removed them on the front porch.

The smell of brewing coffee lured her back to the kitchen. It was by then nearly nightfall, but the long flight had gotten Mary-Alice's internal clock all out of whack, and the coffee smelled tempting. The kitchen, like the bedroom, was neat and simple, with white walls and cabinets and pale yellow linoleum floors.

"Well, this is quite an adventure," Mary-Alice said as she entered the kitchen. "And we're going to have a luau! Do you suppose they'll have those men who twirl the fire around? I imagine Gertie would enjoy that. Miss Nadia seems quite nice. What sort of name do you suppose Nygaard is?"

Fortune perched on the counter and took a thoughtful sip from her mug. It seemed to Mary-Alice that she was still tense.

"Nygaard means new homestead or new farm. The name's a little on-the-nose, if you ask me. Hey, good news, though. The kitchen's stocked, so we don't have to go grocery shopping."

Fortune took down a mug from the cabinet, filled it with coffee, and handed it to Mary-Alice.

"You don't think Nadia Nygaard is...Nadia Nygaard's real name?" Mary-Alice asked.

"I don't think it's the name on her birth certificate, if that's what you're asking. Have you ever had real Kona coffee before? Try it. Kind of mild for my taste, but not bad. You even have an authentic cup there."

Mary-Alice examined the white mug. *46th Annual Kona Coffee Cultural Festival,* read the blue printing. *Hawaii's Oldest Food Festival.* Mary-Alice was more of an iced tea person, but the coffee smelled enticing, and the taste was pleasant.

"I think you can expect a lot of that here," Fortune continued. "This is exactly the kind of place people come to re-invent themselves. They leave their old selves behind, and take on names like Phoenix or DesertSpring."

"Why ever do they do that?"

Fortune shrugged.

"Looking for a fresh start. And if you're gonna start over, you might as well do it where the weather's nice. You see the same thing in some parts of California too. Or you used to, before real estate got so expensive."

"Well, that's just awful." Mary-Alice set her mug down on the kitchen table. "Imagine being so at odds with your family that you feel the need to change who you are and pick an entirely new name."

"Yeah." Fortune drained her mug and then emptied the rest

of the coffee into it. "If I had to pick a name for myself, it sure as hel--, uh, heck wouldn't be Sandy-Sue. You hungry?"

"Now Fortune, you've been working as hard as you possibly could be, getting us through all those checkpoints and all. You just sit yourself down and I'll fix us a little something to eat, to tide us over until the luau. Oh my, are those tropical birds I hear?"

A shrill whistling noise sounded outside. Peep-PEEP! Peep-PEEP!

"I think that's the infamous coqui frog," Fortune said. "The whistling noises are coming from the males looking for mates. It's going to get louder as night falls. They're little frogs, about the size of a quarter, but they can make a big noise."

"My goodness, Fortune, you surely have done your homework."

"Well, when you're looking at buying land, you want to do your due diligence. Sellers have to disclose the presence of coquis. That's how much of a pest they are. Hang on a sec, I've gotta call my family and let them know we arrived."

Fortune left the kitchen—the young lady did value her privacy, Mary-Alice thought—and Mary-Alice opened the refrigerator. She was relieved to find it full of familiar-looking food, although she couldn't say what she had expected. She assembled eggs, butter, a yellow onion, and a nice andouille sausage (which was labeled "Portuguese Sausage" for some reason). She cut a lump of butter into the pan and set it to warming up, found a knife and a cutting board, and started chopping the onion.

"Is everything okay with your family?" Mary-Alice asked when Fortune returned to the kitchen.

"Uh huh." Fortune seemed more relaxed now. "Wow, what-ever you're cooking smells great, Mary-Alice. It seems like everyone I've met in Sinful knows how to cook. I'm almost inspired to learn myself. Oh, yeah, see what I mean about the frogs?"

Mary-Alice realized that while the sausage and onions had been sizzling in the pan, the individual peeps of the Coqui frogs had swelled to a clamor.

"Well now, isn't that something. All those little gentleman frogs peeping their hearts out for a chance at love. Fortune, I thank you for bringing me along on your travels. I suppose it's always been in the back of my mind to visit Hawaii one day, and now here we are. I can scarcely believe it."

"Hey, no problem," Fortune said from inside the refrigerator. "Thank you for keeping me company. I wonder if they left us any beer. They did. This day's looking better and better. Big Swell IPA. Mary-Alice, you want a beer?"

"No thank you, I'm just fine."

Fortune emerged from the fridge, closed the door, and popped the cap off the beer bottle.

"So is it what you expected?"

"Well now, I'm not sure I knew what to expect. But so far it's lovely, and the folks we've met seem very kind. It's a lovely birthday present, and I thank you."

"Glad to hear it," Fortune said. "I know birthdays can be kind of a downer."

"The last memory I have of my mother was at her 70th birthday dinner." Mary-Alice kept stirring the pan and didn't turn around.

"What happened?" Fortune asked gently.

"Well, the men had already left the table. My husband, Joe Arceneaux, you know, Celia's husband's cousin, he'd had more than enough to drink and I believe he was taking a little nap under the oleander hedge. My father had taken his walker and gone off to pester one of the young ladies who was doing the catering. My mama, Miss Thelma Rose, called for a toast. She declared that she was grateful to have been given her three score and ten, thanked everyone for coming to celebrate with her, excused herself, and walked out. None of us ever saw her again."

Mary-Alice cracked the eggs in to the pan, one at a time.

"It was thought that she had died by her own hand."

"Oh, Mary-Alice. I'm so sorry."

"But do you know, about a month after that, I got a postcard from Hawaii in the mail. No return address. And it's the funniest thing, I don't know anyone in Hawaii. I suppose it could've just been a mistake. But I believe I recognized my mama's handwriting."

"Did you keep the postcard?"

Mary-Alice turned off the stove, slid the eggs and sausage onto two paper plates, and brought the plates over to the kitchen table and set them down. Then she went back into her bedroom, and returned with the postcard.

It was a photo postcard, showing a mound of black lava rock with a jet of orange-red lava spurting from the top and running down the sides.

Kilauea Volcano was printed across the front. And on the back was written, *Having a marvelous time.*

"Kilauea Volcano is on this island," Fortune said.

Mary-Alice nodded. "I know. It's quite a coincidence, isn't it? It was most likely a mistake that it ended up in my mailbox. But it always gave me hope. That instead of passing away in despair, my mama might've gotten away somehow and spent her last days in Hawaii. Oh, Fortune, I see there's some activity outside. They must be setting up the luau already. Want to go have a look-see?"

Mary-Alice whisked away Fortune's plate and placed it in the sink with her own.

"Well I'm not hungry anymore, thanks to that delicious eggs and sausage, but sure. Why not? Might as well mix a little pleasure with business."

CHAPTER 8

The evening's luau seemed to be nothing more than a small potluck for the residents of the little plantation camp. Someone had set up a grill in the unpaved common area at the center of the cluster of houses, and people had brought out their own lawn chairs and blankets. Two large coolers held drinks and doubled as seating for people who didn't have lawn chairs. Fortune and Mary-Alice were offered plates of grilled spam, rice, and potato-macaroni salad, but besides that no one spoke to them much. They sat side-by-side on one of the coolers (Fortune made sure to get a beer out first before they sat down on the lid).

"Fortune," Mary-Alice whispered. "These folks all seem perfectly nice, but not a soul has come to introduce themselves or ask us our business."

"I think this is just one of those places where people respect each other's privacy," Fortune answered. "I'm fine with it, to be honest. I barely have enough energy left to sit here without falling over, much less have friendly conversations with strangers."

"Well it's certainly a world of difference from Sinful," Mary-

Alice said. "Oh, it looks like we're going to have music. How nice!"

A few of the older folks had brought out guitars or ukuleles, and someone had a sort of triangular thing that Fortune said was a "balalaika," from Russia. How handy to have a librarian as a traveling companion! Mary-Alice didn't know any of the songs except for "Over the Rainbow," but she enjoyed the music all the same. Even when Mary-Alice didn't understand the words. Next time she had to sit on a cooler, she thought, she'd bring a pillow. But despite the uncomfortable seating, she listened gratefully as the sweet harmonies blended with the chirping of the lovelorn coqui frogs.

Mary-Alice noticed a man sitting in a lawn chair on the other side of the dancer. She nudged Fortune.

"Do you see that man across the way?" she asked. "Wouldn't you say he looks a little like your deputy sheriff Carter LeBlanc?"

"I don't know. Maybe. I'm going to avoid men on this trip, though. Don't forget what Ida Belle always says."

"Being around men makes you muddle-headed. Well, I suppose I see your point. You want to be alert and clear headed if you're going make a good choice about buying that property for your family."

"Exactly." Fortune glanced over at the man and took a swig from her beer bottle. Fortune and Mary-Alice listened to a few more songs, and all at once Mary-Alice felt her fatigue hit her.

"Fortune," she said, "I believe all that traveling's finally catching up with me."

"Yeah, I'm pretty wrecked too. I'll come back with you."

But on the way back, they heard raised voices coming from behind their house. Fortune tiptoed around the back to see what the commotion was, and Mary-Alice followed her. Next to the papaya tree, a man with long gray hair and a rainbow headband was shouting. The handsome man that Mary-Alice had pointed out to Fortune stood with his arms folded.

"Looks like they just had too much to drink," Fortune whispered to Mary-Alice.

"Your rights end where my plot begins," the gray-haired man was yelling at the younger one. "That pollen's airborne."

"Come on, Mary-Alice," Fortune whispered. "It's none of our business,"

Then the older man lunged at the younger one. It seemed to Mary-Alice that she blinked, and there was Fortune, holding the older man in a hammerlock while the younger man was dusting himself off, looking utterly baffled.

"How are you doing this evening, sir?" Fortune said as she released the old hippie. He jerked himself away, glared at her, and stalked off into the night.

"Is everything okay here?" Fortune asked.

"I'm fine. Listen, I appreciate your rescuing me, but old Blaze is harmless. He's just been on my case about this stupid tree. We can't cut it down without putting it to a vote, and I've just discovered I like papayas. So I'm not voting to cut it down. If he doesn't like it, tough."

Mary-Alice smiled and offered her hand.

"I'm Mary-Alice," said the always-polite Mary-Alice. "It's a pleasure to make your acquaintance. And this is—"

"Fortune," the man interrupted with a mischievous grin. "Pleasure to meet you, Mary-Alice. And it's nice to see you again, Fortune."

Fortune squinted at him.

"Jeffrey?" she exclaimed. "Is that you?"

"Call me Jodie. Jodie Gordon. Like the upgrade?" He gestured to his face.

"It's very...nice," Fortune said.

"I told 'em I wanted cheekbones. You don't think they overdid it?"

"Well it was nice to see you, Jodie—" Fortune began.

"Hey, you ladies smoke?"

He pressed his thumb and forefinger together and put them to his lips.

"Listen, we just got in today, and it was a really long flight," Fortune said. "I think I'm going to call it a night."

"I believe I'll be turning in as well," Mary-Alice said. "It was ever so nice to meet you, Mister Gordon."

"What a coincidence," Mary-Alice said to Fortune when they were inside the house. "Why, you were just telling me how people move here, change their names, and start over. And here you've run into an old friend who's done just that."

"I'd say he's more of an acquaintance than a friend," Fortune said. "And he's not doing a very good job at making a fresh start. Who gets into a fight over a papaya tree?"

"Well, this has already been about the most thrilling vacation I've ever had," Mary-Alice. "I'm not certain I could take any more excitement."

CHAPTER 9

The next morning, Mary-Alice was awakened by a scream from the direction of the garden. She looked out her back window to see Fortune, in sweats and a tank top, bounding through the garden in the direction of the scream. Mary-Alice knew that the safest course of action would be to stay indoors, but she was worried about Fortune. What was that girl thinking, running out there like that?

Mary-Alice dressed and headed out in the direction she'd seen Fortune going. She found Fortune standing with Nadia and a few of the neighbors she recognized from the previous night's luau. They were back behind the garden, at the edge of the jungle.

On the ground lay the handsome Jodie Gordon. A woman was kneeling next to him.

"Oh my goodness, is he okay?" Mary-Alice asked, and then felt silly. If he were okay, he wouldn't be lying there, perfectly still, surrounded by his confused-looking neighbors.

"I can't find a pulse," The woman kneeling by him said.

"I already called 9-1-1," Nadia said. "Although I don't believe it'll do him much good now, poor man."

FRANKIE BOW

No one wanted to be the first to leave the dead man's side, so the neighbors stood around awkwardly until they heard the whoop of a siren and a crunch of gravel.

"Let's go inside," Fortune was next to Mary-Alice. "Let the professionals handle it. We don't need to mix in."

"What happened?" Mary-Alice asked as she followed Fortune into the house. "He didn't look injured at all."

"I don't know," Fortune said. "It's strange, isn't it?"

Fortune disappeared into her room and shut the door behind her.

Poor thing, Mary-Alice thought. *She's probably never seen a dead body before.*

Mary-Alice repaired to her own room to get some reading done. She was absorbed in the doings of Inspector Ian Rutledge when a sharp rap on the door broke the spell.

"Come in," Mary-Alice called out.

Fortune opened the door.

"Jodie Gordon was dead on arrival." Fortune pulled the chair over from the window and sat down on it backwards.

"Oh dear. How did the poor man die?"

"They don't know yet. But my family's worried, and they want me—us—to move down to town. They're afraid this place might not be safe."

"So we need to pack up again?"

"Yeah. Sorry about that. The good news is, there's an apartment right in Hilo town that's ready for us to move in. Nadia's driving down to the farmers' market tomorrow morning, so she can give us a ride."

284

CHAPTER 10

The drive down to town was much less comfortable than the cab ride up had been. Nadia Nygaard reserved the front seat of her truck for her delicate potted seedlings. Which meant that Fortune and Mary-Alice had to ride in the back with boxes of cabbage and lettuce and basil, and the grouchy man who had tangled with Jodie Gordon the night before he died.

Mary-Alice gazed out at the gray light over the Pacific Ocean as they wound down the narrow, cliffside road. She tried to banish the mental image of the truck's wheel hitting a bump and bouncing her out of the truck bed to tumble hundreds of feet down to the water. She turned to the gray-haired man.

"Permit me to introduce myself," Mary-Alice shouted over the wind and road noise. "I'm Mary-Alice Arceneaux."

The man nodded.

"I'm Blaze Ocean."

"Hey there, Blaze," Fortune said. "I'm Fortune."

The man glared at her, obviously still holding a grudge about Fortune tackling him.

"How early does the farmers' market open?" Mary-Alice asked the man.

"Six," the man said. "But we wanna get there early so we can get the place by the sidewalk before Madam Jasmine does."

"Who is Madam Jasmine?" Mary-Alice asked.

The man shrugged, as if Madam Jasmine wasn't worth wasting any more breath on.

When the truck pulled up to the farmers' market, only a few tables were already in place, but Madam Jasmine had already grabbed the coveted sidewalk spot by the time they arrived.

Her purple tablecloth was spangled with golden astrology symbols, crescent moons, and stars. On the table sat tarot cards, a row of little bottles, and a real crystal ball. Madame Jasmine herself wore a purple robe, and her face and hair were swathed in colorful veils. Mary-Alice noticed that her nails were painted purple with gold stars to match the tablecloth. Mary-Alice examined her own pale-peach manicure and wondered if it wasn't time to try something a little more adventurous. Perhaps she'd ask Madame Jasmine where she got her nails done.

"Let's get out of here," Fortune whispered to Mary-Alice. She hoisted her backpack over her shoulder, grabbed Mary-Alice's rolling bag, and hopped out of the truck. Then she helped Mary-Alice down, waved to the gray-haired man and to Nadia, and led Mary-Alice down the quiet street.

Mary-Alice loved their new apartment. It was on the second floor, over a row of shops, right on the bay front road. The view of the swaying palm trees and waves crashing on the rocks was more like what Mary-Alice had been expecting.

"Let's call Gertie and Ida Belle," Fortune said. "What do you think?"

Fortune pulled out a laptop and set it up on the kitchen table, and invited Mary-Alice to pull up a chair.

"Don't worry," Fortune said as she brought up the video chat software. "It's secure."

After a few tries, the image of Gertie and Ida Belle, side by side, came onto the screen. Mary-Alice noticed that the background looked like Fortune's kitchen.

"Hey girls," Gertie cried. "How's Hawaii? Don't worry, we won't tell anyone where you are."

"Well, that didn't take you long," Fortune said. "How'd you know?"

"It looks like it's early morning," Gertie said, "which gives us some idea of the time zone you're in. And I can see palm trees outside your window."

"Not to mention we can see your kitchen shelves behind you," Ida Belle added. "Someone stocked them with doomsday-prepper amounts of Spam."

"Well, please don't tell anyone where we are," Fortune said. "You know how secretive my family is. How are things in Sinful?"

"Deputy Sheriff Carter LeBlanc's a little mopey without you around," Gertie said.

"He'll be fine," Ida Belle said. "And we're keeping an eye on your house."

"So you two are okay out there?" Ida Belle asked. "No murders so far?"

Fortune became serious.

"Probably not, but we did have an incident. The original place we were staying was a little way up the coast, and yesterday morning one of the neighbors collapsed and died. You know how my family worries about me, so they moved us down to town."

"Fortune, didn't you know the man?" Mary-Alice blurted out. "I thought you called him Jeffrey."

"Fortune!" Gertie and Ida Belle exclaimed at once.

"Someone you knew was killed?" Ida Belle demanded. "Right after you got there?"

"No wonder your family is worried!" Gertie added.

"Yeah," Fortune mused. "It was weird."

"How did he die?"

"They don't know."

They were interrupted by Fortune's phone ringing.

"There's my family now," Fortune said. "I better get this."

"It was ever so lovely to talk to you," Mary-Alice called out to Ida Belle and Gertie as Fortune clicked off. Honestly, that young Yankee had a good heart, but her manners could use some work.

CHAPTER 11

Fortune pulled the bedroom door shut behind her and sat on the bed. Her buzz-cut reflection in the dressing-table mirror caught her by surprise. She was still used to the hair extensions.

She pressed the phone to her cheek so she could speak quietly.

"Harrison. Any news about Jeff? Or I guess I should say Jodie? What killed him?"

"They still don't know. We're looking at anaphylaxis."

"An allergy? Do they think it was an accident?"

"If it was an accident, it was an awfully lucky one. For you."

"For me? What are you talking about?"

"Remember that flyer Ahmad's guys were circulating around New Orleans?"

"Black and white photocopied picture of me, Arabic and English writing, announcing a reward for my capture. If I recall correctly, I was described as a ringworm-infested daughter of a shoe, may she burn in sixty thousand hells."

"Daughter of a shoe?"

"It's a serious insult. I guess it loses something in the translation."

"We had one of our people go through Jodie Gordon's things. He had a copy of that flyer, Fortune. It was an encrypted photo on his phone."

Fortune's shoulders slumped.

"I'm losing my edge, Harrison. Jeff—Jodie—was an annoying jerk, but I didn't think for a minute he posed any danger. Seriously, he was going to hand me over to Ahmad?"

"Listen, I feel responsible. Morrow and I both thought you'd be safe there. But I guess a ten million dollar bounty can make people rethink their priorities."

"Yeah, the phrase out of the frying pan and into the fire springs to mind. Maybe I should just come back to Sinful."

"No, no, no. Let's give it another couple days. Things haven't quite settled down here. Anyway, it looks like your guardian angel was looking out for you this time."

"Harrison, was Jodie Gordon working with anyone?"

"No indication of that so far, but we're still looking into it But in the meantime, be careful."

"Be careful? That's real helpful, Harrison. It wouldn't have occurred to me otherwise."

"You're being sarcastic, aren't you?"

"You think?"

Fortune emerged from her bedroom, went over to the sink, filled a glass of water, and gulped it down. The empathetic Mary-Alice perceived that Fortune's nerves seemed to be back.

"Well, we have the whole day in front of us. What are we going to do?" Mary-Alice asked cheerfully.

"Actually, Mary-Alice, I'm feeling a little sick to my stomach. I think I'm going to lie down. Don't let me spoil your vacation for you. Why don't you go explore the town?"

Fortune retreated to her bedroom, looking positively greenish.

"I'll see if I can find you some chamomile and ginger tea," Mary-Alice called as she slung her purse over her shoulder. "It does absolute wonders for a tummy ache."

Mary-Alice made her way back to the farmers' market. She was curious about the nefarious Miss Jasmine, but her table had so many people crowding around, waiting to get their fortunes told, that Mary-Alice couldn't get close. Instead she went over to where Nadia and Blaze had their booth. Although it was punishingly hot under the canopy, Nadia hadn't removed her pink cowboy hat, nor rolled up the sleeves of her Western shirt.

Mary-Alice bought tomatoes, lettuce, and a bunch of skinny Japanese eggplants, figuring she could fry it up, no matter the shape. She dropped the groceries off at the apartment, careful not to disturb Fortune, whose bedroom door was closed. Then she went back downstairs and strolled up to the public library, where she passed a few hours in the lovely outdoor reading area. When it started to get dark she thought of calling Fortune, but decided not to, in case she was asleep. Cooking might disturb her too, if she was a light sleeper. Bringing dinner home would be the best option in this case.

When Mary-Alice returned to the apartment she found Fortune sitting at the kitchen table staring at her open laptop. Fortune snapped her laptop shut and gave Mary-Alice a rather forced-looking smile.

"Mary-Alice, is that a pizza box?"

"Yes it is. Oh, Fortune, I was afraid that the only sort of pizza available would be the 'Hawaiian' kind. You know, with the pineapple and ham?" Mary-Alice set the box on the table. "I mean to say, I suppose pineapple and ham would do in a pinch, but it's certainly not my favorite. Imagine how relieved I was to see all the ordinary kinds of pizza toppings they had available. I don't believe pineapple was even an option, can you imagine? Anyway, I got half pepperoni and half plain cheese."

Mary-Alice and Fortune settled in to enjoy their pizza. Mary-Alice noticed Fortune kept glancing at the front door. She was every bit as on edge as she'd been in the business lounge at Lake Charles Airport.

And then a knock on the door caused Fortune's pizza to stop halfway to her mouth.

"We're not interested," she called out.

Whoever it was knocked again, and suddenly Fortune was standing, both hands on a large pistol, aiming at the door.

"Fortune!" Mary-Alice whispered.

Fortune stood for a few moments and then stuck the firearm

into the back of her waistband (where had she been keeping it? Mary-Alice wondered). She went to the door and peered out the peephole.

Then she rolled her eyes and opened the door.

"Good evening, officer," Fortune said evenly.

"Sandy-Sue Redding?" the police officer asked.

"Unfortunately."

"Do you know a man named Jodie Gordon?"

The officer sat at the kitchen table. Mary-Alice offered him pizza and he declined, so she resigned herself to not eating any pizza until he left. Fortune, on the other hand, casually munched a slice as the officer asked questions.

Neither Mary-Alice nor Fortune could enlighten the officer as to Jodie Gordon's recent activities and whereabouts, but they did tell him about the fight over the papaya tree. The officer was not surprised to hear it. Judging from his suppressed eye roll, such conflicts were not unusual.

"What a terrible thing to have happen," Mary-Alice said when the police officer had left.

"No big loss. Jodie Gordon was a jerk." Fortune sat back down at the kitchen table and happily helped herself to a slice of pizza. Mary-Alice stared, shocked by Fortune's lack of sentiment. "Hey, you do anything interesting today?"

Mary-Alice collected herself. Fortune was clearly not a very good traveler. Every time they moved, Fortune seemed to get rattled. She most likely couldn't help it, and it wouldn't do to condemn her for it. Perhaps if she told Fortune about her day, it might be enough of a distraction to calm Fortune's nerves.

"I went back and visited the farmers' market first thing," Mary-Alice said. "I made sure to buy some vegetables from Nadia and that man Blaze. She had these Japanese eggplants that she said were very sweet and tender, and don't need to be salted before cooking, so I thought I'd try fixing us some eggplant fritters."

Talking of food made Mary-Alice realize she was hungry. She helped herself to a slice of pizza. "And they didn't only have food, which was a surprise to me. One of the booths had all sorts of lovely things carved out of koa wood. I'd never heard of it before, but it's lovely. I bought this letter opener. Isn't it the most gorgeous thing? So simple, but the grain's just beautiful."

Mary-Alice pulled the letter opener out of her purse to show Fortune.

Fortune laughed.

"They'll never let you take it on the plane, Mary-Alice. You'll have to mail it back if you don't want it confiscated. It is very nice, though."

"Confiscated? My goodness. Thank you ever so much for warning me, Fortune, I believe I will send it back. Oh, I also happened to find a real estate office downtown. It was at the end of the row of shops along the shore, just before the road turns into the bridge that crosses the river. It was a lovely pink building. Now Fortune, you might find this interesting. They had several nice looking lots for sale."

"Are you looking to buy land?"

Mary-Alice was confused.

"Me? Buy land? Well no, darlin', I was under the impression that you were fixing to purchase a parcel on behalf of your family."

Fortune coughed and swallowed.

"Of course. That's the whole reason we're here in Hawaii, right? Sure, let's go have a look tomorrow. You have the locations?"

Mary-Alice pulled a couple of brochures out of her purse and handed them to Fortune.

"Volcano, huh? Like your mysterious postcard. Sure, let's do it. When do you want to go?"

"Well, the young lady who gave me these brochures informed me that they have a farmers' market in Volcano on

Sunday mornings. You missed the one today, and they had ever so many interesting vegetables and things that you don't ever see back in Sinful."

"Okay. We'll go first thing tomorrow. I have the feeling we'll be going home soon, so we might as well catch the sights while we can."

CHAPTER 13

The Volcano farmers' market was smaller than its Hilo counterpart. It was also much, much colder. Mary-Alice noticed many of the same vendors that she had seen the previous day. Nadia was there in a mint-green cowboy hat. Blaze hovered around the table, putting things in bags for customers or refilling the display trays with eggplants or lettuces. On the opposite side of the market was Madame Jasmine's fortune-telling booth.

Mary-Alice wondered whether Blaze Ocean was one of those invented names that Fortune had been telling her about. Mary-Alice's crafting circle back in Mudbug had a Candy Barr and a Mary Christmas, and you might think those were made up, but in fact they were their honest-to-goodness names.

"We should go over there and say hello to Miss Nadia when the crowd goes down a little," Mary-Alice said.

"I hope it's okay if we don't buy anything," Fortune said. "I have just enough cash for the cab back to town. I didn't realize how far it was."

Mary-Alice rubbed her arms to fight off the chill.

"What did you think of the lots we saw?"

Fortune shrugged.

"I don't know. All I saw both times was an overgrown lot with a real estate sign. Hard to tell what you're getting."

"Fortune, do you suppose it's possible that my mother was here in this town?"

"Oh, Mary-Alice. Anything's possible. Hey, you could ask Madame Jasmine. She sees all and knows all."

"Oh my goodness, a fortuneteller? I mean, I suppose I'd be curious to know what she has to say, but I do wonder what Father Michael would say. He seems to take a rather unfavorable view of divination and sorcery and the like."

"How about this: I'll be your fortune teller. Fortune Morrow, Fortune Teller."

Fortune closed her eyes and pressed her fingertips to her temples.

"Your mother loved you very much. So do your friends. We all want you to be happy. And Boon St. Clair totally likes you."

Fortune opened her eyes and grinned.

"How was that?"

"I'm sure Mister Boon St. Clair would be utterly mortified," Mary-Alice tittered. "Fortune, I've seen most of these booths already, and I could do with some breakfast. What do you say? My treat."

Mary-Alice and Fortune walked over to the local diner, a pink clapboard building with a green corrugated metal roof. When the waitress came over to take their order, Mary-Alice ordered sweet bread French toast and then asked whether she had heard of a lady from the South who might have lived in the area.

"She would have been from Arnaudville, Louisiana," Mary-Alice explained. "But her final resting place would be Grand Coteau. St. Landry Parish."

"Sorry, Aunty," the young woman said. "Never met her. I can get your order, Miss?"

Fortune ordered the loco moco, a local specialty. It was a

heap of rice with a burger patty on top, smothered with brown gravy and topped with a fried egg. Mary-Alice was glad to see Fortune's appetite was back.

As they were finishing their breakfast, Fortune's phone rang.

"I'm sorry, Mary-Alice," Fortune said. "It's Ida Belle."

"You go on and answer Ida Belle's call," Mary-Alice urged. "I'll meet you outside."

When she had finished paying (the price was surprisingly reasonable, only a little more expensive than Francine's Diner), Mary-Alice found Fortune video-chatting on her phone with Ida Belle and Gertie.

"Oh, hey there, Mary-Alice," Ida Belle said.

"You will not believe what happened," Gertie added, breathlessly. "Is anyone there to hear us?"

"Only me," Mary-Alice said.

Fortune started walking into the woods, and Mary-Alice tagged behind her.

"I think we'll have some privacy here," Fortune said to her phone screen. "So you were saying?"

"This doesn't look like Hawaii," Ida Belle exclaimed. "There's kudzu everywhere! Did you even leave the parish?"

Mary-Alice looked around and saw a coating of the familiar trifoliate leaves covering the ground and trees. Goodness, that pesky vine was everywhere.

"Where are you really?" Gertie asked.

"Volcano," Fortune said. "We came for the farmers' market and had a nice breakfast."

"Volcano?" Ida Belle challenged. "Where's the lava?"

"It's off the main road, kind of a hike. So what's the big news?"

"Well, you know how Ida Belle and I are staying at your house while you're gone to keep an eye on it?" Gertie asked.

"Sure," Fortune said.

"You had intruders," Ida Belle said. "Don't worry. We shot 'em."

Fortune went a little pale.

"Intruders? How many?"

"Just two," Ida Belle said, as if having to shoot only two intruders were no big deal. "Young guys, maybe late twenties, early thirties."

"And wearing leather jackets," Gertie exclaimed. "Can you imagine, in this heat?"

"What were they after?" Mary-Alice asked, genuinely curious. "I mean to say, Fortune, you do have a lovely house, but it doesn't seem like the sort of place that would attract the attention of young miscreants in leather jackets."

"Well, we could ask them," Gertie said.

"Except they're dead!" Ida Belle cried, and to Mary-Alice's horror, Ida Belle and Gertie high-fived.

"Probably stalkers from Fortune's beauty pageant days," Ida Belle added, in a serious tone.

"Yes," Fortune said. "Those beauty pageant stalkers can be persistent."

"If you can find a copy of the Times-Picayune you'll see the story," Ida Belle said. "Oh, wait, we can show her."

Fortune's little phone screen was filled with a blurry newspaper page.

"I can't read it," Fortune said. "Oh, wait. Local woman defends home from burglars. Gertie, that's you in the photo!"

"That's right," Gertie said. "So if any more beauty pageant stalkers are out there looking for you, they'll see this story of mistaken identity and conclude you're not in Sinful."

"Good thinking," Fortune said. "Thank you."

"Now how about this Jodie fellow who died?" Gertie asked. "You two gonna look into that? Oh, wait, does Mary-Alice know?"

Fortune glanced at Mary-Alice.

"There's some indication that the man who died meant me harm," Fortune said.

"Oh my, how simply awful. And he seemed like such a nice man! Was he a beauty pageant stalker too?"

"Yes, something like that."

"Why Fortune, you didn't say!" Mary-Alice exclaimed. "If I had known, I daresay I would have been much less polite to him."

A rustle in the bushes made Fortune turn her head, as alert as a pointer.

CHAPTER 14

"You have company?" Ida Belle asked as Fortune turned to the rustling in the underbrush.

Fortune laughed and pointed her phone down. A black snout and the outline of two flaring ears poked out of the leaves.

"A wild pig?" Gertie exclaimed. "Fortune, I've changed my mind since yesterday. I don't believe you're in Hawaii at all."

"Me neither," Ida Belle added. "I believe you and Mary-Alice are camping out on Number Two Island and you're just pulling our leg."

Fortune and Mary-Alice headed back to the farmers' market, which was wrapping up. Nadia Nygaard was packing up her truck. She looked up and waved, and Mary-Alice and Fortune headed over.

A few parking spaces down, Mary-Alice noticed Madame Jasmine loading her things into her own car—a powder-blue 1955 Cadillac with a spacious trunk. The woman had removed her veils for this quotidian task. From the back Mary-Alice saw shimmering blue-black hair. Although elderly, the woman moved with languid elegance. Mary-Alice watched admiringly, and wondered how she would look if she traded her own trademark red hair for blue-black. After all, her mother—who had been on her mind a lot lately—wasn't there to scold her for making unsuitable fashion choices.

No, black hair would probably clash with her freckles, she thought sadly. Or I could go platinum, like Nadia. Of course that's a wig, which makes it easier to switch.

"You two have a way back down to town?" Nadia asked as they approached.

"We were going to get a cab," Fortune said.

"I saw a bus stop in front of the diner," Mary-Alice said. "Would you recommend the bus?"

"Bus doesn't run on Sunday. Why not ride with us? Sorry I can't invite you to sit up front, but the seedlings are delicate and can't ride in the back."

Mary-Alice peered into the truck and saw the seats were covered with newspaper, on top of which sat cardboard trays full of seedlings in little green plastic pots.

Blaze Ocean was already sitting in the truck bed, glowering when Nadia opened the gate to let Mary-Alice and Fortune climb in. Mary-Alice smiled and said, "Good morning."

The old hippie nodded and gazed into the distance. The truck jolted to a start and Blaze took hold of the closest object, a half-empty cardboard box of lettuce heads.

Nadia drove slowly down the highway, creeping along in the right lane as cars and trucks whizzed by on the left. The scenery was beautiful but monotonous; towering trees embedded in a thick carpet of greenery.

"Invasive species, all of 'em," Blaze said, glaring at the verdure.

"Invasive species?" Fortune asked.

"Albizia trees. Strawberry guava. Kudzu."

Mary-Alice rubbed her bare arms, wishing she had brought a sweater. Sitting in the metal bed of a moving truck made the damp cold even worse. Mary-Alice wouldn't have imagined that traveling to Hawaii in the middle of the summer would involve her freezing her bottom off.

"Would you say we human beings are an invasive species?" Mary-Alice asked, hoping conversation would take her mind off being so cold.

For the first time, the man cracked a grin.

"You can call me Blaze. And yes, I believe we're one of the worst. As far as Mother Earth is concerned, we're a skin infection. A parasite."

For the rest of the drive down, Blaze Ocean expounded on this topic in off-putting detail.

Finally, they reached Hilo, and Nadia pulled the truck up in front of the apartment building. As Nadia and Blaze helped Mary-Alice down from the back of the truck, Nadia said, "Why don't you two come up for dinner tonight? We feel so terrible that our tragic accident scared you away. I'll be using the produce that didn't sell today, so we can look forward to some lovely salad."

"I hate to impose," Fortune said. "We'll probably just have a quiet evening here in town."

"Oh, nonsense," Nadia said. "What are you going to eat? All of the restaurants are closed Sunday night."

"Oh. Sunday," Fortune said.

"We have friends driving up from town," Nadia said. "They can pick you up and bring you back."

CHAPTER 15

Nadia's friends, two friendly, gray-haired men in their seventies who looked alike enough to be brothers, stopped by as promised to drive Mary-Alice and Fortune to dinner. Their names were Fred and Frank. One was a real-estate agent and the other was a contractor, so the drive passed quickly with conversation about the merits of various subdivisions on the island, the fine points of fee simple versus leasehold property, and the new downtown building code that was so stringent that it had effectively brought new construction to a halt.

Nadia Nygaard had set a table for six: Herself and Blaze, Fortune and Mary-Alice, and Fred and Frank. When she had seated her guests, Nadia brought out a large, bristling bowl of salad, which Mary-Alice assumed would be the first course for the entire table. But she set the bowl in front of Fortune, and then went back into the kitchen and brought out an equally large salad bowl for Mary-Alice. This continued until everyone had a huge bowl of greens in front of them. This, it seemed, would be the entire meal. To Mary-Alice, this was by no means a proper supper. But the polite thing was to eat what was put in front of you, even if it was spiny greens with shredded beetroot and what appeared to be raw black-eyed peas.

Just as Mary-Alice took her first bite, the front door burst open.

There stood an elderly woman with blue-black hair, long purple nails, and impeccable posture.

"Madame Jasmine." Nadia snarled. She braced herself on the table, and stood up slowly.

Mary-Alice stared at the woman in the doorway.

Two police officers, one man and one woman, stepped into the house from behind the fortuneteller.

As the female officer cuffed Nadia and Blaze, the male officer snapped on gloves and went around the table, dumping each serving of salad into a separate evidence bag. When he got to Mary-Alice's salad, he peered closely at the bag.

"Has anyone consumed any of this salad?" he asked. Fortune, Fred, and Frank shook their heads.

"Oh dear," Mary-Alice said. "I did take a few bites of mine. I didn't want to be impolite, you see. Did I do something wrong?"

CHAPTER 16

Mary-Alice woke up in a bright room. Something was clamped on her finger, and a machine was beeping in the background. The woman with the blue-black hair was sitting by her bedside, watching her. The light slanted in from the window to highlight the woman's elegant cheekbones and remarkably smooth skin.

Mary-Alice blinked at the fortuneteller. For a few minutes, she just stared.

"Mama?" Mary-Alice said, finally.

"Right here, darling," said the woman.

"Mama, you're not dead."

"No, darling. Not in the least."

The woman reached over and brushed a stray bit of red hair off Mary-Alice's face.

"Mama, what's going on? Why am I in the hospital?"

"It was that Nadia Nygaard. She put rosary peas in your salad. If I hadn't alerted the police, you'd surely be dead by now."

"Dead?" Mary-Alice exclaimed. "Gracious! How did you come to find all this out?"

"When I saw you were fixin' to come to Hawaii after all these years, well, one thing I was sure of, and that was I was going to keep an eye out for my baby girl. So when I saw you getting mixed up with that Nadia Nygaard, I kept a close watch. This isn't the first time I've seen that woman do something nefarious. Lord, someone should have put her away years ago."

"But what on earth would Miss Nadia have against me?"

"I swear to you, I have racked my brains trying to find rhyme or reason in that woman's actions. I'm just happy she's finally come to justice."

Mary-Alice squeezed her eyes shut and tried to get her bearings.

"How'd you know I was fixin' to come to Hawaii, mama?"

"Darlin', I'm a fortune-teller. And that's just a fancy term for private detective."

"You're a private detective?"

"Yes indeed. Your mama has what I believe is called a day job. Imagine! It's a mercy your father isn't here to see it."

"So you've been keeping an eye on me all these years?"

"That I have. I've been following everything you've been up to, sweetheart. I know you lost your home in Mudbug to a fire, and moved out to Sinful to be closer to Joe's cousin's Celia. And of course I recall the news about Joe Arceneaux. Never met a man who deserved getting eaten by a gator more than him."

Thelma Rose smiled, and Mary-Alice squinted at her.

"Mama, whatever you've been doing here in Hawaii, it certainly agrees with you. I hope you don't mind my saying, I believe you look younger than when I saw you last."

Thelma Rose touched her flawless cheek.

"Well now, I do go in for a little touch-up now and then. That's something else your father would never have permitted."

"Mama, I've missed you." Mary-Alice said. "Did you miss me at all?"

Mary-Alice's mother touched the imaginary pearls at her throat and blinked, and Mary-Alice felt embarrassed that the moment had taken such an emotional turn.

Thelma Rose Laval reached over and gently squeezed her daughter's hand.

"I've missed you every day, darling. Every day I've said a prayer for you."

"Then why did you leave, Mama?"

Thelma-Rose sighed. "Seventy years of being a perfect lady was all I could manage. I simply couldn't do it another day. And I suppose I wanted to leave you with that perfect memory. Of the lady I was. Not the woman I am now."

"Mama, you saved my life. There's absolutely nothing wrong with the woman you are now. Nothing could make me think less of you."

Mary-Alice's mother smiled sadly.

"Mary-Alice, I dress up in outrageous costumes and tell bogus fortunes for the entertainment of tourists."

"Oh Mama, that's just harmless fun."

"I'm living in sin with a Chinaman young enough to be my son. Mind you, he's still pretty old."

"Oh. Well, Mama, you deserve to be happy. Although I don't believe they're called Chinamen nowadays. Anyway, you're still going to confession, so that fixes it."

Thelma Rose gently pulled her hand back and placed it on her lap.

"As a matter of fact, I've joined the Baptist church. I've not been to confession for twenty years."

Mary-Alice was quiet for a few moments. The only sound was the speeded-up beeping of her heart monitor.

"So those prayers you were saying for me, Mama. Those were Baptist prayers?"

"Yes, Mary-Alice. Baptist prayers."

Mary-Alice took a deep breath. The beeping slowed back down.

"Well you know something, Mama? When the fire started in my house, Celia and I were inside. It went up real fast, and it looked like we weren't going to get out of the house in time. And you know who broke into the house and risked their own lives to save us? Fortune, Ida Belle, and Gertie. And every one of them attends the Baptist church. So if you've gone and decided to be a Baptist, I believe the Almighty will understand."

They were quiet for a moment.

"Will you be able stay and visit for a while before you go back home?" Mary-Alice's mother asked. "Your friend is welcome as well. We have two guest rooms. One looks out on the mountain, so you can see the snow at the top, and the other has a lovely view of the bay. We'd be honored to have you."

"I believe I'd like that, Mama."

CHAPTER 17

Fortune and Mary-Alice stayed on another week. They enjoyed
the company of Thelma Rose Laval and her husband Anson Lee,
a wiry, intense man who taught political science and Hawaiian
history at the community college. (Thelma Rose and Anson
were "living in sin" in the sense that they had been married in
the Baptist church.) Mary-Alice briefly wondered whether
Anson Lee's surname indicated he was related to Sheriff Lee
back in Sinful, but decided he probably was not.

Mary-Alice enjoyed all of the attractions of Hawaii Island,
but she loved the planetarium most of all. She enjoyed lying
back and gazing up at the stars. Only it was better than really
gazing at the stars, because a professional astronomer was
explaining all about the constellations, and she wasn't getting
bitten by mosquitos.

On the last day of their visit, Mary-Alice was sitting with her
mother in the kitchen, enjoying a cold glass of iced tea and the
view of the ocean.

"Mama," Mary-Alice said, "I have to ask you something. Was
this postcard from you? I'd been keeping it in my glove box, and

it's a good thing, too, because I lost everything inside my house when it went up...anyway, I still have it."

Thelma Rose took the yellowed postcard from Mary-Alice, and turned it over.

"Well, if that doesn't...Anson, darlin'!"

Anson came shuffling into the kitchen.

"You remember this, sugar?" She held it up. He shook his head.

"Anson and I were just settling in, weren't we darling, and I was so happy here, I wanted to let you know. I sat down to write you a postcard. But after I began, I changed my mind. I figured hearing from me would upset you, and I didn't want your father to find out and ruin everything. So I got up and went about my business and when I came back I didn't see the card again and I assumed it got thrown away."

Anson was staring at the card, frowning, and then the light came on.

"I mailed it, Thelma. I thought you'd just forgotten. I put a stamp on it and put it into the mailbox with the bills."

CHAPTER 18

Fortune Morrow excused herself from the festive group gathered at Francine's Diner. She didn't answer her phone until she was sure she was alone, standing in the brutal bayou heat in Francine's parking lot.

"Hey, Harrison. So whaddaya know. It looks like Gertie and Ida Belle cleaned up our mess for us."

"Yeah, I have to admit it worked out pretty well. I don't think Ahmad's bounty hunters are gonna be visiting Sinful again any time soon. Word's out that there's nothing there but some ornery old ladies with shotguns."

Fortune climbed into her Jeep and turned on the ignition. She had privacy here, and also air conditioning.

"Hey, just out of curiosity," she asked, "what exactly happened in Hawaii? Because I seem to remember that our safe-house contact tried to poison us, and then some nice old fortune-teller with a Southern accent saved our lives and invited us to stay with her and her husband for a few days. Care to catch me up?"

"Look, we thought Nadia Nygaard was reliable. She's been

managing our safe house for decades. But a ten-million-dollar bounty can make people do strange things."

"How did she know about the bounty?"

"By now everyone with any connection to intelligence knows about it. Ahmad's doing whatever he can to get the word out. You killed his brother, Fortune. He's not gonna let that go."

"So Nadia Nygaard and Jodie Gordon were both planning to turn me over to Ahmad?"

"Nadia cooperated with Jodie long enough to get the contact info for Ahmad, and then she got rid of him."

"Whoa. Ruthless. Poison salad?"

"No. Jodie Gordon was highly allergic to bee stings. All she had to do was stir up the hive and let nature take its course. So aside from the attempt on your life, how'd you like Hawaii?"

"It was nice. I'd actually like to go back some day. For a plain old vacation, though, not while I'm fleeing for my life. Listen, I've gotta get back inside. I had to duck out in the middle of breakfast. Everyone's come out to hear about our real-estate-buying trip."

"What are you going to tell them?"

"I'll tell them I saw some interesting properties, but I'm not going to buy anything. We're content with our current situation. No, better than content. I'd say we're happy."

Fortune slipped her phone into her pocket, and went back inside to join her friends.

RECIPES

BLUEBERRY CHEESECAKE SQUARES

1 (8 ounce) package cream cheese (softened)
 1/2 cup white sugar
 1 dash vanilla extract
 1 dash lemon extract
 1 cup heavy cream
 1 ½ cups blueberry preserves or 1 can blueberry pie filling
For the crust:
 1 ½ cups finely crushed graham crackers (24 squares)
 1/3 cup butter, melted
 3 tablespoons sugar

Heat oven to 350°F. In a medium bowl, stir the crushed crackers, melted butter, and 3 tablespoons of sugar until well mixed. Press the crust into a jelly roll pan or deep baking sheet. Bake for 10 minutes, remove from the oven, and let cool.

In a large bowl, combine the cream cheese, sugar, lemon and vanilla extracts. Mix well.

In a medium bowl, whip cream until stiff peaks form.

Fold 3/4 of the whipped cream into cream cheese mixture.

Spread onto the crust.

Dot with preserves or pie filling, and smooth with spatula to cover.

Chill in refrigerator at least 2 hours.

Garnish with remaining cream.

BREAD PUDDING

1 loaf stale bread
    2 tablespoons vanilla
    1 quart milk
    3 tablespoons melted butter or oleo (margarine)
    3 eggs
    1 cup raisins
    2 cups sugar

Soak bread in milk; crush with hands till well mixed. Then add eggs, sugar, vanilla and raisins and stir well. Pour oleo in bottom of thick pan and bake at 350 degrees for 1 hour.

Let cool; then cube pudding and put in individual dessert dish. Serve with bourbon sauce.

BOURBON SAUCE

1 stick butter or oleo, room temperature
    1 cup sugar
    1 egg
    Bourbon to taste

Mix the butter and sugar until creamy. Cook sugar and butter in double boiler till very hot and well dissolved. Then add well-beaten egg and whip real fast so egg doesn't curdle. Let cool and add bourbon to taste.

SAZERAC COCKTAIL

1 cube sugar
    1½ ounces (35ml) Sazerac Rye Whiskey
    ¼ ounce Herbsaint or Absinthe

3 dashes Peychaud's Bitters

Lemon peel

Pack an Old-Fashioned glass with ice

In a second Old-Fashioned glass place the sugar cube and add the Peychaud's Bitters to it, then crush the sugar cube

Add the Sazerac Rye Whiskey to the second glass containing the Peychaud's Bitters and sugar

Empty the ice from the first glass and coat the glass with the Herbsaint, then discard the remaining Herbsaint

Empty the whiskey/bitters/sugar mixture from the second glass into the first glass and garnish with lemon peel

ST. CHARLES HOTEL CHICKEN GUMBO (ORIGINAL 1920 RECIPE)

For five gallons of Creole Gumbo use: Three gallons of chicken broth; two pounds of chicken giblets; two pounds knuckle of ham. Cut both in one inch pieces and fry them brown in some good lard. Add to them four or six large crabs, cut up; two dozen of lake shrimps, two dozen of Bayou Cook oysters. Cut ten dozen of fresh okra pods, half-dozen of Spanish onions, two dozen of green peppers, cut up in dices. Add one gallon of peeled tomatoes, one tablespoonful Creole file, salt and pepper to taste. Let simmer on slow fire for about one and one-half hours. Serve with Louisiana steamed rice.

CAJUN SCRAMBLED EGGS

2 teaspoons oil, bacon fat, or butter

1/2 teaspoon garlic - minced

2 Tablespoons onion - chopped

1/4 cup green pepper - chopped

1/4 cup tomatoes - chopped

1/4 teaspoon Cajun seasoning blend

1/4 pound Andouille sausage - cooked and diced
4 large eggs beaten with 2 teaspoons milk
1/4 cup grated Cheddar cheese - optional
Note: You can replace the Andouille sausage with Portuguese sausage or smoky breakfast sausage links.

In large, heavy skillet over medium-high heat, sauté the garlic, onions and green pepper in oil or butter. Stirring often, cook until the green peppers are softened and the onion starts to become translucent. Toss in the tomatoes and sausage and reduce heat to medium. Season with Cajun seasoning.

Add the beaten eggs. As soon as the eggs begin to set, start stirring (scrambling) all ingredients. Continue until eggs are completely set. Turn off heat.

If desired, sprinkle with grated cheddar cheese. Wait one minute for the cheese to start melting.

Serve and enjoy with hot sauce if desired.

HAWAII STYLE POTATO MAC SALAD

½ lb. macaroni
    8 hard-boiled eggs
    3 red potatoes, cooked and cubed
    1 Tbsp. salt
    1 Tbsp. vinegar
    2 cups mayonnaise
    ½ tsp. ground allspice
    ½ tsp. pepper
    1 package frozen peas, thawed and drained (10 oz.)

Cook macaroni according to package directions; drain. Separate egg yolks from egg whites. In a small bowl, mash yolks and chill. Chop egg whites; put into a large bowl with macaroni and potatoes. Stir in salt and vinegar; chill overnight.

Add egg yolks and remaining ingredients; gently mix into macaroni mixture. Chill.

SPAM FRIED RICE

2 tablespoons vegetable oil, divided
   2 large eggs, beaten
   2 cloves garlic, minced
   6 ounces Spam, diced
   1/2 cup frozen corn
   1/2 cup frozen peas
   1/2 cup frozen diced carrots
   3 cups cooked rice
   1 1/2 tablespoons soy sauce
   1/2 tablespoon fish sauce
   1/4 teaspoon sesame oil
   1/4 teaspoon white pepper
   2 green onions, sliced

Heat 1 tablespoon vegetable oil in a large skillet over low heat. Add eggs and cook until cooked through, about 2-3 minutes per side, flipping only once. Let cool before dicing into small pieces.

Heat remaining 1 tablespoon vegetable oil in the skillet over medium high heat. Add garlic and Spam, and cook, stirring often, until light golden brown, about 3-4 minutes.

Add corn, peas and carrots. Cook, stirring constantly, until vegetables are tender, about 1-2 minutes.

Add rice and gently toss to combine.

Add soy sauce, fish sauce, sesame oil and white pepper. Cook, stirring constantly, until heated through, about 1-2 minutes.

Stir in green onions and eggs.

EGGPLANT FRITTERS

Aubergines en Beignets ou au Natural (From The Picayune's Creole Cook Book, published 1910)

2 Young Eggplants. 1/2 Pint of Milk.
   Salt and Pepper. Flour.

Slice the eggplants nicely and thin. Roll them in milk in which you have put salt and pepper to taste. Pass the eggplant in flour, dusting lightly, and fry in boiling lard. The eggplant must float in the lard. Drain on brown paper in the mouth of the oven and serve hot.

LOCO MOCO

Per serving:
   4 ounces ground beef
   Salt and pepper to taste
   1/2 Cup brown gravy
   1 large egg
   2 cup steamed Calrose rice or your favorite fried rice

Press the ground beef into a patty, season with salt and pepper. Grill or fry to desired doneness.
   Place rice in a bowl. Place the burger on the rice and keep warm.
   Fry the egg sunny side up. Just before the egg is done, pour the warm gravy over the burger so it glazes both the burger and the rice.
   Slide the sunny side up egg over the burger. Serve immediately.

FROM THE AUTHOR

Thank you for taking the time to read this book. If you enjoyed it, please consider telling your friends or posting a short review. Word of mouth is an author's best friend and much appreciated.

If you like the *Miss Fortune stories*, pick up *Trust Fall*, a free short story in *The Professor Molly Mysteries*. I wouldn't say the Professor Molly Mysteries are autobiographical, but they are close to my heart. Like Professor Molly, I work at a university in rural Hawaii. Unlike my protagonist, I am blessed with delightful students, sane colleagues, and a perfectly nice office chair.

Want to be the first to learn about events, promotions, give-aways, and new releases? Go to **subscribepage.com/MissFortune** to sign up for my newsletter.

Frankie

facebook.com/frankie.bow.1
twitter.com/Frankie_Bow
instagram.com/frankie_bow

THE TWO-BODY PROBLEM

THE MARY-ALICE FILES BOOK 5

Retired part-time bookkeeper Mary-Alice Arceneaux, recently-arrived resident of the town of Sinful, Louisiana (population 253), was having breakfast at Francine's Diner. Sinful is a small bayou town, and Francine's is the only restaurant in Sinful. But it would be a mistake to write off the tiny municipality as a place where nothing ever happens.

Mary-Alice was finding Sinful to be quite interesting indeed. She had purchased the old Cooper Place, right in town on the edge of the bayou, and the restoration of the historic building had been keeping her agreeably occupied. Mary-Alice's cousin-by-marriage, Celia Arceneaux, had recently been elected mayor, having won an impressive number of votes from the deceased (a recount was underway.) Mary-Alice had made a few new friends in Sinful, and together with them had fallen quite by accident into investigating a local murder or two.

And when Mary-Alice tired of real-life intrigue, there was Harriet's Books, just a short walk from her house, to supply the murder mysteries she loved.

But Sinful had hidden depths of which even Mary-Alice was unaware.

The young woman sitting across from her, former pageant queen and current children's librarian Sandy-Sue "Fortune" Morrow, was, in fact, an undercover CIA operative in hiding. Fortune had annoyed an arms dealer by killing his brother, and the agency had parked her in Sinful, which was the most out-of-the-way hiding place they could find. Fortune kept her mind active and her skills sharp by helping to solve local crimes.

Mary-Alice did not know Fortune's secret. She thought that Fortune, with her detailed knowledge of weapons, warfare, and spycraft, was a very peculiar children's librarian indeed. But then Fortune was a Yankee, and Yankees were a bit odd.

So when a stranger paused in Francine's doorway, glanced around the crowded dining room, caught sight of Fortune, then sped over to their table, Mary-Alice was fascinated, but not surprised. The stranger wasn't from around Sinful, of that Mary-Alice was certain. The woman's hair was short, and its texture was natural. Behind enormous black-framed glasses was a round, pleasant face devoid of makeup. She wore an oversized black t-shirt with a picture of a spaceship on the front (the U.S.S. Enterprise from *Star Trek*, Mary-Alice found out later), dark gray leggings, and black high-top sneakers, a most un-summery color scheme.

"Professor Jackson!" Fortune exclaimed, and half rose out of her seat.

"They told me I'd find you here." As soon as the woman spoke it was obvious she was from up north. "I tried to call ahead, but I only had your address, not a working phone number. Please, call me Gwendolyn. I'm sorry to intrude. I know it seems strange, my dropping in on you like this. But I was hoping...oh, hello."

The stranger had just noticed Mary-Alice.

Despite her bright red hair, colorful flowered t-shirts, and the bejeweled reading glasses that hung from her neck, people tended not to notice Mary-Alice Arceneaux. Mary-Alice was not offended by this. To be inconspicuous was to be ladylike. It was a sign of good upbringing.

And it had turned out to be quite an advantage during Mary-Alice's recent forays into sleuthing. Mary-Alice had come to think of her near-invisibility as her very own superpower. Naturally, she kept this observation to herself.

Fortune moved a syrup bottle holder from the empty place setting next to her and Professor Gwendolyn Jackson sat down.

"Professor Jackson—I mean Gwendolyn, this is Mary-Alice Arceneaux. Mary-Alice, Dr. Gwendolyn Jackson. Gwendolyn taught that computer class I was taking out at Mudbug Tech."

"I'm still teaching it," Gwendolyn said, with a smile. "Too bad you had to drop."

"I did enjoy the class, but things got kind of crazy."

"I know," Gwendolyn's smile faded. "That's why I'm here. I heard you saved a woman's life out in Mudbug. Is that right?"

"Why that's absolutely correct," Mary-Alice said cheerfully. "And I can tell you that for certain because I was that woman. This young lady and her friends happened to be passing by at the time. I must say, I'm as thankful as I can be. Things might have gone quite badly for Celia and me."

"I driving home from your class," Fortune explained. "We saw an orange glow in the sky, figured out what it was, and drove over to help. We called the fire department on the way."

"Well it's an awfully good thing you pulled us out when you did," Mary-Alice said. "By the time the firemen got there, bless their hearts, my entire house was a pile of ashes, and I dare say we would've been, too."

"That's amazing," Gwendolyn said. "So you live here in Sinful now, Ms. Arceneaux?"

"Well, when life hands you lemons, you make lemonade, don't you? I took the insurance money and bought the old Cooper Place. It's right out there past the trees. It needed a little

TLC when I moved in, but it's a delightful place, right on the bayou. And I owe it all to Fortune, Gertie, and Ida Belle."

Fortune shrugged.

"We were in the right place at the right time. Just lucky, I guess."

"I'm hoping you're still on your lucky streak," Gwendolyn said. "I need your help."

Francine, the proprietor of Francine's Diner, lured from the kitchen by the sight of a stranger, came over with a pot of coffee in one hand and a pitcher of iced tea in the other.

"Good morning, ladies," she said as she refilled cups. Then to Gwendolyn, "What can I get you, honey?"

"Coffee, please."

"Ready to order? Or do you need a little time to decide?"

"I'll just have coffee for now. Thank you."

Francine looked expectantly from Gwendolyn to Fortune to Mary-Alice but didn't get any more information. Finally, she said,

"Well, you let me know if you need anything."

She walked back to the kitchen, glancing behind her several times.

"So how can I help?" Fortune asked.

"My husband just passed away."

"Oh my goodness," Mary-Alice exclaimed. "I'm so terribly sorry for your loss."

"Were the circumstances of his death suspicious?" Fortune asked.

"He was fifty, he smoked, I mean I sure wasn't expecting it. But the thing is…I'm sorry, let me start from the beginning. If you don't mind. Do you have a few minutes?"

Fortune shrugged. "We pretty much have all day. Go for it."

"Yes, please do," Mary-Alice said eagerly.

"Mike, my husband, owns a novelty shop. Owned, I should say. Jape & Jest. It's in the French Quarter."

Gwendolyn paused to take a sip of coffee, and her eyebrows raised.

"My goodness, this coffee isn't bad. Wow. Anyway, he had a business meeting with a vendor or supplier or something out near Beaumont a couple of weeks ago, nothing out of the ordinary. I didn't really hear from him when he was gone, but that's normal for him. He's not great at keeping in touch when he's traveling. I finally got a voicemail from him on the morning of July 29. He told me he'd see me the next day. So I went out and did some grocery shopping. I came back, got the mail, and this was in it."

She handed Fortune a sealed plastic sandwich bag with a newspaper clipping inside.

"Make sure to look at the date," Gwendolyn said.

"July 29," Fortune read. "*ORANGE, TX - A 50-year-old Louisiana man was discovered dead in his hotel room Friday morning. The man's body was found by motel staff ... died sometime during the previous night... cause of death appeared to be from natural causes, no sign of foul play. The man's name is being withheld pending notification of family.* So this man passed away the day before your husband called you."

"Fortune, this man *is* my husband."

RECIPES

RECIPES

BLUEBERRY CHEESECAKE SQUARES

1 (8 ounce) package cream cheese (softened)
  1/2 cup white sugar
  1 dash vanilla extract
  1 dash lemon extract
  1 cup heavy cream
  1 ½ cups blueberry preserves or 1 can blueberry pie filling
  For the crust:
  1 ½ cups finely crushed graham crackers (24 squares)
  1/3 cup butter, melted
  3 tablespoons sugar

Heat oven to 350°F. In a medium bowl, stir the crushed crackers, melted butter, and 3 tablespoons of sugar until well mixed. Press the crust into a jelly roll pan or deep baking sheet. Bake for 10 minutes, remove from the oven, and let cool.

In a large bowl, combine the cream cheese, sugar, lemon and vanilla extracts. Mix well.

In a medium bowl, whip cream until stiff peaks form.

Fold 3/4 of the whipped cream into cream cheese mixture.

Spread onto the crust.

Dot with preserves or pie filling, and smooth with spatula to cover.

Chill in refrigerator at least 2 hours.

Garnish with remaining cream.

BREAD PUDDING

1 loaf stale bread
  2 tablespoons vanilla
  1 quart milk
  3 tablespoons melted butter or oleo (margarine)
  3 eggs
  1 cup raisins
  2 cups sugar

Soak bread in milk; crush with hands till well mixed. Then add eggs, sugar, vanilla and raisins and stir well. Pour oleo in bottom of thick pan and bake at 350 degrees for 1 hour.

Let cool; then cube pudding and put in individual dessert dish. Serve with bourbon sauce.

BOURBON SAUCE

1 stick butter or oleo, room temperature
  1 cup sugar
  1 egg
  Bourbon to taste

Mix the butter and sugar until creamy. Cook sugar and butter in double boiler till very hot and well dissolved. Then add well-beaten egg and whip real fast so egg doesn't curdle. Let cool and add bourbon to taste.

SAZERAC COCKTAIL

1 cube sugar
  1½ ounces (35ml) Sazerac Rye Whiskey
  ¼ ounce Herbsaint or Absinthe

3 dashes Peychaud's Bitters

Lemon peel

Pack an Old-Fashioned glass with ice

In a second Old-Fashioned glass place the sugar cube and add the Peychaud's Bitters to it, then crush the sugar cube

Add the Sazerac Rye Whiskey to the second glass containing the Peychaud's Bitters and sugar

Empty the ice from the first glass and coat the glass with the Herbsaint, then discard the remaining Herbsaint

Empty the whiskey/bitters/sugar mixture from the second glass into the first glass and garnish with lemon peel

ST. CHARLES HOTEL CHICKEN GUMBO (ORIGINAL 1920 RECIPE)

For five gallons of Creole Gumbo use: Three gallons of chicken broth; two pounds of chicken giblets; two pounds knuckle of ham. Cut both in one inch pieces and fry them brown in some good lard. Add to them four or six large crabs, cut up; two dozen of lake shrimps, two dozen of Bayou Cook oysters. Cut ten dozen of fresh okra pods, half-dozen of Spanish onions, two dozen of green peppers, cut up in dices. Add one gallon of peeled tomatoes, one tablespoonful Creole file, salt and pepper to taste. Let simmer on slow fire for about one and one-half hours. Serve with Louisiana steamed rice.

CAJUN SCRAMBLED EGGS

2 teaspoons oil, bacon fat, or butter

1/2 teaspoon garlic - minced

2 Tablespoons onion - chopped

1/4 cup green pepper - chopped

1/4 cup tomatoes - chopped

1/4 teaspoon Cajun seasoning blend

1/4 pound Andouille sausage - cooked and diced
4 large eggs beaten with 2 teaspoons milk
1/4 cup grated Cheddar cheese - optional
Note: You can replace the Andouille sausage with Portuguese sausage or smoky breakfast sausage links.

In large, heavy skillet over medium-high heat, sauté the garlic, onions and green pepper in oil or butter. Stirring often, cook until the green peppers are softened and the onion starts to become translucent. Toss in the tomatoes and sausage and reduce heat to medium. Season with Cajun seasoning.

Add the beaten eggs. As soon as the eggs begin to set, start stirring (scrambling) all ingredients. Continue until eggs are completely set. Turn off heat.

If desired, sprinkle with grated cheddar cheese. Wait one minute for the cheese to start melting.

Serve and enjoy with hot sauce if desired.

HAWAII STYLE POTATO MAC SALAD

½ lb. macaroni
8 hard-boiled eggs
3 red potatoes, cooked and cubed
1 Tbsp. salt
1 Tbsp. vinegar
2 cups mayonnaise
½ tsp. ground allspice
½ tsp. pepper
1 package frozen peas, thawed and drained (10 oz.)

Cook macaroni according to package directions; drain. Separate egg yolks from egg whites. In a small bowl, mash yolks and chill. Chop egg whites; put into a large bowl with macaroni and potatoes. Stir in salt and vinegar; chill overnight.

Add egg yolks and remaining ingredients; gently mix into macaroni mixture. Chill.

SPAM FRIED RICE

2 tablespoons vegetable oil, divided
    2 large eggs, beaten
    2 cloves garlic, minced
    6 ounces Spam, diced
    1/2 cup frozen corn
    1/2 cup frozen peas
    1/2 cup frozen diced carrots
    3 cups cooked rice
    1 1/2 tablespoons soy sauce
    1/2 tablespoon fish sauce
    1/4 teaspoon sesame oil
    1/4 teaspoon white pepper
    2 green onions, sliced

Heat 1 tablespoon vegetable oil in a large skillet over low heat. Add eggs and cook until cooked through, about 2-3 minutes per side, flipping only once. Let cool before dicing into small pieces.

Heat remaining 1 tablespoon vegetable oil in the skillet over medium high heat. Add garlic and Spam, and cook, stirring often, until light golden brown, about 3-4 minutes.

Add corn, peas and carrots. Cook, stirring constantly, until vegetables are tender, about 1-2 minutes.

Add rice and gently toss to combine.

Add soy sauce, fish sauce, sesame oil and white pepper. Cook, stirring constantly, until heated through, about 1-2 minutes.

Stir in green onions and eggs.

EGGPLANT FRITTERS

Aubergines en Beignets ou au Natural (From The Picayune's
Creole Cook Book, published 1910)

2 Young Eggplants. 1/2 Pint of Milk.
    Salt and Pepper. Flour.

Slice the eggplants nicely and thin. Roll them in milk in which
you have put salt and pepper to taste. Pass the eggplant in flour,
dusting lightly, and fry in boiling lard. The eggplant must float
in the lard. Drain on brown paper in the mouth of the oven and
serve hot.

LOCO MOCO

Per serving:
    4 ounces ground beef
    Salt and pepper to taste
    1/2 Cup brown gravy
    1 large egg
    2 cup steamed Calrose rice or your favorite fried rice

Press the ground beef into a patty, season with salt and pepper.
Grill or fry to desired doneness.

Place rice in a bowl. Place the burger on the rice and keep
warm.

Fry the egg sunny side up. Just before the egg is done, pour
the warm gravy over the burger so it glazes both the burger and
the rice.

Slide the sunny side up egg over the burger. Serve immediately.

FROM THE AUTHOR

Thank you for taking the time to read this book. If you enjoyed it, please consider telling your friends or posting a short review. Word of mouth is an author's best friend and much appreciated.

If you like the *Miss Fortune stories*, pick up *Trust Fall*, a free short story in *The Professor Molly Mysteries*. I wouldn't say the Professor Molly Mysteries are autobiographical, but they are close to my heart. Like Professor Molly, I work at a university in rural Hawaii. Unlike my protagonist, I am blessed with delightful students, sane colleagues, and a perfectly nice office chair.

Want to be the first to learn about events, promotions, give-aways, and new releases? Go to **subscribepage.com/MissFortune** to sign up for my newsletter.

Frankie

facebook.com/frankie.bow.1
twitter.com/Frankie_Bow
instagram.com/frankie_bow

THE TWO-BODY PROBLEM

THE MARY-ALICE FILES BOOK 5

Retired part-time bookkeeper Mary-Alice Arceneaux, recently-arrived resident of the town of Sinful, Louisiana (population 253), was having breakfast at Francine's Diner. Sinful is a small bayou town, and Francine's is the only restaurant in Sinful. But it would be a mistake to write off the tiny municipality as a place where nothing ever happens.

Mary-Alice was finding Sinful to be quite interesting indeed. She had purchased the old Cooper Place, right in town on the edge of the bayou, and the restoration of the historic building had been keeping her agreeably occupied. Mary-Alice's cousin-by-marriage, Celia Arceneaux, had recently been elected mayor, having won an impressive number of votes from the deceased (a recount was underway.) Mary-Alice had made a few new friends in Sinful, and together with them had fallen quite by accident into investigating a local murder or two.

And when Mary-Alice tired of real-life intrigue, there was Harriet's Books, just a short walk from her house, to supply the murder mysteries she loved.

But Sinful had hidden depths of which even Mary-Alice was unaware.

The young woman sitting across from her, former pageant queen and current children's librarian Sandy-Sue "Fortune" Morrow, was, in fact, an undercover CIA operative in hiding. Fortune had annoyed an arms dealer by killing his brother, and the agency had parked her in Sinful, which was the most out-of-the-way hiding place they could find. Fortune kept her mind active and her skills sharp by helping to solve local crimes.

Mary-Alice did not know Fortune's secret. She thought that Fortune, with her detailed knowledge of weapons, warfare, and spycraft, was a very peculiar children's librarian indeed. But then Fortune was a Yankee, and Yankees were a bit odd.

So when a stranger paused in Francine's doorway, glanced around the crowded dining room, caught sight of Fortune, then sped over to their table, Mary-Alice was fascinated, but not surprised. The stranger wasn't from around Sinful, of that Mary-Alice was certain. The woman's hair was short, and its texture was natural. Behind enormous black-framed glasses was a round, pleasant face devoid of makeup. She wore an oversized black t-shirt with a picture of a spaceship on the front (the U.S.S. Enterprise from *Star Trek*, Mary-Alice found out later), dark gray leggings, and black high-top sneakers, a most un-summery color scheme.

"Professor Jackson!" Fortune exclaimed, and half rose out of her seat.

"They told me I'd find you here." As soon as the woman spoke it was obvious she was from up north. "I tried to call ahead, but I only had your address, not a working phone number. Please, call me Gwendolyn. I'm sorry to intrude. I know it seems strange, my dropping in on you like this. But I was hoping…oh, hello."

The stranger had just noticed Mary-Alice.

Despite her bright red hair, colorful flowered t-shirts, and the bejeweled reading glasses that hung from her neck, people tended not to notice Mary-Alice Arceneaux. Mary-Alice was not offended by this. To be inconspicuous was to be ladylike. It was a sign of good upbringing.

And it had turned out to be quite an advantage during Mary-Alice's recent forays into sleuthing. Mary-Alice had come to think of her near-invisibility as her very own superpower. Naturally, she kept this observation to herself.

Fortune moved a syrup bottle holder from the empty place setting next to her and Professor Gwendolyn Jackson sat down.

"Professor Jackson—I mean Gwendolyn, this is Mary-Alice Arceneaux. Mary-Alice, Dr. Gwendolyn Jackson. Gwendolyn taught that computer class I was taking out at Mudbug Tech."

"I'm still teaching it," Gwendolyn said, with a smile. "Too bad you had to drop."

"I did enjoy the class, but things got kind of crazy."

"I know," Gwendolyn's smile faded. "That's why I'm here. I heard you saved a woman's life out in Mudbug. Is that right?"

"Why that's absolutely correct," Mary-Alice said cheerfully. "And I can tell you that for certain because I was that woman. This young lady and her friends happened to be passing by at the time. I must say, I'm as thankful as I can be. Things might have gone quite badly for Celia and me."

"I driving home from your class," Fortune explained. "We saw an orange glow in the sky, figured out what it was, and drove over to help. We called the fire department on the way."

"Well it's an awfully good thing you pulled us out when you did," Mary-Alice said. "By the time the firemen got there, bless their hearts, my entire house was a pile of ashes, and I dare say we would've been, too."

"That's amazing," Gwendolyn said. "So you live here in Sinful now, Ms. Arceneaux?"

"Well, when life hands you lemons, you make lemonade, don't you? I took the insurance money and bought the old Cooper Place. It's right out there past the trees. It needed a little

TLC when I moved in, but it's a delightful place, right on the bayou. And I owe it all to Fortune, Gertie, and Ida Belle."

Fortune shrugged.

"We were in the right place at the right time. Just lucky, I guess."

"I'm hoping you're still on your lucky streak," Gwendolyn said. "I need your help."

Francine, the proprietor of Francine's Diner, lured from the kitchen by the sight of a stranger, came over with a pot of coffee in one hand and a pitcher of iced tea in the other.

"Good morning, ladies," she said as she refilled cups. Then to Gwendolyn, "What can I get you, honey?"

"Coffee, please."

"Ready to order? Or do you need a little time to decide?"

"I'll just have coffee for now. Thank you."

Francine looked expectantly from Gwendolyn to Fortune to Mary-Alice but didn't get any more information. Finally, she said,

"Well, you let me know if you need anything."

She walked back to the kitchen, glancing behind her several times.

"So how can I help?" Fortune asked.

"My husband just passed away."

"Oh my goodness," Mary-Alice exclaimed. "I'm so terribly sorry for your loss."

"Were the circumstances of his death suspicious?" Fortune asked.

"He was fifty, he smoked, I mean I sure wasn't expecting it. But the thing is...I'm sorry, let me start from the beginning. If you don't mind. Do you have a few minutes?"

Fortune shrugged. "We pretty much have all day. Go for it."

"Yes, please do," Mary-Alice said eagerly.

"Mike, my husband, owns a novelty shop. Owned, I should say. Jape & Jest. It's in the French Quarter."

Gwendolyn paused to take a sip of coffee, and her eyebrows raised.

"My goodness, this coffee isn't bad. Wow. Anyway, he had a business meeting with a vendor or supplier or something out near Beaumont a couple of weeks ago, nothing out of the ordinary. I didn't really hear from him when he was gone, but that's normal for him. He's not great at keeping in touch when he's traveling. I finally got a voicemail from him on the morning of July 29. He told me he'd see me the next day. So I went out and did some grocery shopping. I came back, got the mail, and this was in it."

She handed Fortune a sealed plastic sandwich bag with a newspaper clipping inside.

"Make sure to look at the date," Gwendolyn said.

"July 29," Fortune read. "*ORANGE, TX - A 50-year-old Louisiana man was discovered dead in his hotel room Friday morning. The man's body was found by motel staff ... died sometime during the previous night... cause of death appeared to be from natural causes, no sign of foul play. The man's name is being withheld pending notification of family.* So this man passed away the day before your husband called you."

"Fortune, this man *is* my husband."

Printed in the USA
CPSIA information can be obtained
at www.ICGtesting.com
LVHW020954130424
777331LV00033B/354

9 781393 855392